DONN TAYLOR

MURDER MEZZO FORTE

MURDER MEZZO FORTE BY DONN TAYLOR
Published by Lamplighter Fiction
an imprint of Lighthouse Publishing of the Carolinas
2333 Barton Oaks Dr., Raleigh, NC, 27614

ISBN: 978-1-938499-09-8
Copyright © 2016 by Donn Taylor
Cover design by Elaina Lee
Interior design by AtriTeX Technologies P Ltd
Interior graphic by Susan F. Craft

Available in print from your local bookstore, online, or from the publisher at:
www.lighthousepublishingofthecarolinas.com

For more information on this book and the author visit: http://www.donntaylor.com/

All rights reserved. Non-commercial interests may reproduce portions of this book without the express written permission of Lighthouse Publishing of the Carolinas, provided the text does not exceed 500 words. When reproducing text from this book, include the following credit line: "*Murder Mezzo Forte* by Donn Taylor published by Lamplighter Fiction. Used by permission."

Commercial interests: No part of this publication may be reproduced in any form, stored in a retrieval system, or transmitted in any form by any means—electronic, photocopy, recording, or otherwise—without prior written permission of the publisher, except as provided by the United States of America copyright law.

This is a work of fiction. Names, characters, and incidents are all products of the author's imagination or are used for fictional purposes. Any mentioned brand names, places, and trademarks remain the property of their respective owners, bear no association with the author or the publisher, and are used for fictional purposes only.

Scripture quotations from The Authorized (King James) Version. Rights in the Authorized Version in the United Kingdom are vested in the Crown. Reproduced by permission of the Crown's patentee, Cambridge University Press.

Scripture quotations taken from the New American Standard Bible®, Copyright © 1960, 1962, 1963, 1968, 1971, 1972, 1973, 1975, 1977, 1995 by The Lockman Foundation (www.Lockman.org). Used by permission.

Brought to you by the creative team at Lighthouse Publishing of the Carolinas:
Eddie Jones, Ann Tatlock, Marsha Hubler, Shonda Savage, Brian Cross, Paige Boggs

Library of Congress Cataloging-in-Publication Data
Taylor, Donn.
Murder Mezzo Forte / Donn Taylor 1st ed.

Printed in the United States of America

PRAISE FOR *MURDER MEZZO FORTE*

Bravissimo! Music, mayhem, and murder. Donn Taylor delivers another delightful mystery full of surprises, sarcasm, puns, and edge-of-your-seat plot twists – a winner for sure!
~ Sadie & Sophie Cuffe
Authors of *The Maine White Pine Cone Conspiracy*

Author Donn Taylor brings to life Professor Preston Barclay in *Murder Mezzo Forte*. Soon, you'll find yourself trying to help the professor escape the mortal coils of this intricate plot.
~ James R. Callan
Author of *Over My Dead Body* (A Father Frank Mystery)

In his distinctive voice, Donn Taylor delivers a murder mystery set to music--even if the musical accompaniment is only in Professor Barclay's head. Loved it!
~ Mary Hamilton
Author of *Hear No Evil* (Rustic Bible Camp Series)

If Donn Taylor has as much fun writing mysteries as his fans have in reading them, he and his writings will remain forever ageless. Professor Preston Barclay's "musical hallucinations" give him a special quirkiness, and his stubborn independence has charm that reminds me slightly of Tim Downs' "Bug Man" character. Who but a retired college professor could poke fun so humorously at the current state of higher education? Whether or not you're already a Donn Taylor fan—I've been one for years—the first sentence will make you want to keep reading.
~ Roger E. Bruner
Author of *The Devil and Pastor Gus*, *Found in Translation*, and *Lost in Dreams*

PRAISE FOR *RHAPSODY IN RED* BY DONN TAYLOR

Richly embellished with literary and musical references and peopled with academia's most intriguing eccentrics and snobs.
> **~ CBA Retailers and Resources Magazine**

The descriptive wording is a delightful change from the clichés of most novels.
> **~ Christian Review of Books**

This book is dedicated in gratitude

to

the **National Association of Scholars** (www.nas.org),
"Reasoned scholarship in
a free society," for its efforts to restore intellectual integrity
in higher education,

and to

the **Foundation for Individual Rights in Education**
(http://thefire.org) for its efforts
"to protect the unprotected" by defending the constitutional
rights of students and faculty.

ACKNOWLEDGMENTS

Overton University (formerly Overton Grace College), its faculty, and its students exist only in fiction, but they share many denominational colleges' conflicts of academic standards vs. commercialism, education vs. indoctrination, and Christian heritage vs. secularism. Overton City and the geography of the novel are also fictional, as is the Council for Individual Rights on Campus (CIRCA).

I am indebted to my friend Don Roose for briefing me on corporate finance, and to Veronica Farley and Dr. Richard L. Mabry, M.D., for information on antibiotics and potential allergic reactions. My daughter Karen Taylor Saunders provided essential information on mobile phones to her troglodyte father.

Special thanks to my agent, Terry Burns, for leading me to Lighthouse Publishing of the Carolinas, and to my editor, Marsha Hubler, who greatly improved the novel through her editorial skills.

I would also like to express appreciation to Ivory Doakes, housekeeper extraordinaire, whose excellent work and many kindnesses assisted Mildred and me through difficult times.

Most of all, I am deeply indebted to my wife, Mildred Taylor, who blessed my life with love, understanding, encouragement, and sound judgment throughout the sixty-one years, seven months, and four days of our marriage until her promotion to the mansions of the Lord.

...imagination is the star of man and the rudder of this our ship, which reason should steer, but overborne by phantasy [Imagination] *cannot manage, and so suffers itself and this whole vessel of ours to be over-ruled and often overturned.*
—Robert Burton, *The Anatomy of Melancholy*

A man's heart deviseth his way; but the Lord directeth his steps.
—*Proverbs 16:9 (KJV)*

CHAPTER 1

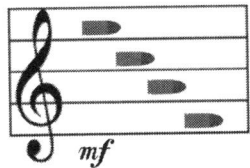

In that first week of February, we didn't know that Overton University was about to exceed its annual quota of murders. We had no inkling of it that Thursday evening when the college administration held a reception for trustees and faculty. I didn't know then that Professor Mitra Fortier would make trouble or that I would have to defend myself against scandal and worse. We would learn all of that later.

The administration called it a reception, but it had no receiving line. Everyone just showed up at the gymnasium, now called "The Fitness Center" because the new president who joined us after The Crisis renamed everything either a Center or a Service. Faculty straggled in half frozen by the Midwestern winter and joined whatever groups they could find. The event had been billed as a mixer, but it didn't mix. Trustees talked to trustees, the president and dean talked to trustees, and faculty cliques talked to themselves. Yet everyone seemed to share an unspoken purpose—to forget that last semester our philosophy professor had murdered a faculty member on campus.

Someone had thrown a tarp over half of the gym floor so our street shoes wouldn't scar the finish. The gym's bright overhead lights cast an air of unreality over everything. Perhaps because of them I started wondering what was real and what wasn't.

I stood alone at one side, battling the music in my head and grieving for receptions past before the death of my wife, Faith. We talked to everyone then. But now, as the campus recluse, I don't talk much at all. As always, I dreaded returning to my empty house and Faith's Steinway grand piano that has stood silent these past three years.

With any luck, I thought, I wouldn't have to talk to anyone. So I simply listened while the orchestra in my head played the overture to *Die Meistersinger*. This internal music came to me at Faith's death, and it's all I have left of her now. It's not just a tune here and there, but a torrent that floods my life with imagined sound. The clinical name is "musical hallucinations." They make my life like a movie that's been mismatched with the music score from another.

So I watched from the sideline, as neglected as the third stanza of a hymn, while the music, for once, assuaged my grief. Then a trustee walked up and broke the spell.

"Professor Barclay," he said. "I'm Steven Drisko." He put out his hand.

"I'm Preston Barclay." I took the offered hand. It isn't often a trustee seeks out a mere faculty member.

This one looked about ten years younger than I, which made him about forty. I only knew that, as CEO of Overton Technologies, Inc., he'd doubled his company's stock value. That made him Overton City's favorite son, and some thought it should earn him canonization. He wore a tailored suit that must have cost an arm and a leg, but in the economic sense he was rumored to be a centipede.

Drisko wasted no time on preliminaries. "Congratulations on solving the Laila Sloan murder. What will you investigate next?"

"Nothing," I said. I adjusted my trifocals and tried not to look self-conscious. "I just teach history." Everything in the gym seemed more unreal, a fantasy dreamed up by my subconscious.

Drisko smiled. "Won't you find that dull after your adventures last semester?"

"There's nothing dull about history," I said. "It's a wonderful panorama of human accomplishment and failure."

My internal musicians replaced Wagner with a pianist playing Paderewski's "Minuet."

"Well," Drisko said, "thanks for a good job that helped the college."

He returned to the crowd of trustees and administrators. None too soon, for his statuesque blonde wife seemed to be having too good a time with younger trustees who'd come without their wives.

"Press, I need to talk to you." The bold feminine voice belonged to Mitra Fortier, a physics professor who'd been a good friend to Faith. Mitra was a multi-talented woman of about forty, divorced long ago and devoted to her work. In past years she'd had carefully coifed golden hair that looked like combed corn silk. Tonight it looked like a haystack after a tornado passed through.

"Don't look so serious," I said. "This is a festive occasion."

"Don't hand me that, Press." Mitra's frown deepened. "You know as well as I do how everybody feels." She'd always been a just-the-facts realist.

"What do you want to talk about?" I asked. At the time, it seemed like a safe question.

"I need your help with an investigation."

"I'm through investigating," I said. "From here out I just teach history."

Mitra gave me a look like my drill sergeant gave me decades ago in basic training, and she snapped, "If you value your job, Preston Barclay, you'll help me out with this."

That got my attention. We work on annual contracts here with no provision for tenure. Since Faith died, my job is all the life I have left.

"Not here," Mitra said. She cast an apprehensive glance around the gym. "Come to my office when this thing is over." She spun on her heel and stalked away.

Suddenly, the scene in the gym seemed as surreal as a painting by Salvador Dali. The refreshments looked real enough, though. Beside their table I saw the slender figure and shoulder-length blonde hair of Professor Mara Thorn, my co-investigator from the previous semester. She was always very, very real. She wore a business-like navy pantsuit but no perfume or cosmetics. As I approached, her blue eyes flickered in friendship, then retreated into inscrutability as she moved out of earshot of the student servers.

I followed and said, "I see we're still the faculty pariahs."

"Yes, but we mustn't be seen together." A frown darkened the glow of her ivory complexion. "We can't afford those unsavory rumors. I need this job."

"Rumors are a constant on this campus," I said. "You just have to ignore them."

Mara speared me with her blue gaze. "I hear that our contracts come out in the week after the trustees meet. We both can forget about them if the administration finds out about you-know-what."

She could have meant the kiss she gave me in an emotional moment when our lives hung in the balance. Or the night we'd spent barricaded in a motel room hiding from the mob's professional hit men. Both events were innocent, but either could give the administration an excuse not to renew our contracts.

"All right," I said. "I'll take this cup of punch back to my side of the gym."

"Fitness Center," she corrected, then added, "How's the new phone?"

"I guess I'll get used to it," I said, "but I still use the voice recorder." I'm known as the campus Luddite because I carried an ancient cell phone that did nothing but send and receive. My first concession to modernity was a twenty-five-dollar voice recorder. But last week I gave in and bought an up-to-date model cell phone. I'm still struggling to learn all its functions. Meanwhile, I still use the voice recorder for quick notes on one thing or another.

Mara gave me a smile and headed back to her side of the gym. As I returned to my side, I glanced at the corner where members of the administration flitted from trustee to trustee like moths trying to choose among a plethora of light bulbs. I said brief thanks that I was only a professor.

"Hello, Professor Barclay. Do you remember me?"

A new feminine voice shook me out of meditation. I turned to the voice.

"Of course I remember," I said. "You're Cynthia Starlington. I'd heard they contracted you to teach philosophy." With a female philosophy professor, I'd have to lay off jokes about shaving with Occam's razor.

Cynthia was not the kind you forget. She'd come to Overton as a skinny sixteen-year-old freshman obsessed with making good, and she'd graduated *summa cum laude* four years later. She'd taken every one of my classes and aced them all. Her classic features and dark brown eyes naturally drew my gaze. I had to work at not teaching directly to her.

That was ten years ago, and she wasn't skinny now. With an olive complexion and waves of brown hair cascading over her shoulders, she'd turned into a real beauty.

"It's good to be back," she said. "It's wonderful to find Overton College grown into a university."

"Our administration calls it a university," I said, "but in truth it's still a liberal arts college. 'Only the name has been changed to hoodwink the innocent.'"

She laughed. "You always were quick with a quotation." She grew serious. "This is all new to me. To be honest about it, I'm scared stiff."

"I can see how replacing a murderer would worry you, but you've always done fine."

A frown furrowed her brow. "I'll need someone to show me the ropes. Will you do that for me, Press? Oh ... " She put her hand to her mouth. "Professor Barclay, I shouldn't have been that familiar ... "

"It's okay. All the faculty call me Press. I suppose I should call you Cynthia?"

She beamed like a kid with a new lollipop. "Call me Cyn."

"Is that original, Cyn?" I asked.

She laughed. "'Original sin?' I remember—you liked puns. So did Faith. Oh ... " Her hand flew to her mouth again. "I'm sorry."

"It's all right," I said. "She's been gone three years, so I ought to be used to it." I wasn't, but there was no use worrying Cynthia with my grief.

She touched my arm. "Thanks for agreeing to help. I'd better go meet more faculty now, but I'll be seeing you."

She glided away, tall and graceful. My gaze followed her as she circled the gym floor, smiling and speaking to everyone she met.

Except Mitra Fortier. When they approached each other, their expressions froze and they passed without speaking. For some reason, my gaze followed Mitra's haystack hairdo as she swooped down on Mara Thorn.

Mara and Mitra, I thought. I instantly associated them with M&Ms, the candy-coated chocolates. Not entirely appropriate: Mara could be sweet enough when she chose, but Mitra was more like anchovies.

Mitra engaged Mara in spirited conversation, and Mara shook her head. Mitra spat out a final statement and walked away. More unreality. Things like that didn't happen at a faculty reception.

Then another trustee accosted me. This one was Gordon Samstag, a gray-haired master banker, member of the board of half a dozen corporations and chairman of Overton University's board of trustees. If Steven Drisko's wealth made him a centipede, Samstag must be a millipede.

"Professor Barclay," he said, "I'd like to thank you for solving that ... um ... *nastiness* on campus last semester. That murder was a terrible blight on our reputation, but it's best that the moral rot has been excised."

"I hope things get back to normal," I said.

"We all hope so." He fixed a serious gaze on me. "Will you investigate something else now?"

"Only better ways to teach history." Why did so many people want to know what I was going to do next?

"Good." He showed a practiced smile. "No use stirring things up needlessly."

He patted my shoulder and made the trek back to trustee territory, where Steven Drisko's wife was laughing with Emory

Estes, owner of a local used car lot. If the college didn't renew my contract, I might have to ask Estes for a job.

With that thought I surrendered to unreality. The gym faded from my senses, and my internal orchestra caressed me with the slow movement of Mendelssohn's Piano Concerto No. 2. By the time its last chord subsided into silence, I could almost believe in human perfectibility.

My reverie must have lasted quite a while. When reality returned, the people had left. I looked frantically for Mitra Fortier, but she was nowhere in sight. I saw Mara stride briskly into the exit, head held high as if daring anyone to question her. I gathered my hat and overcoat and made my own exit through a nearer door.

Outside, I snugged my coat collar against the Midwestern winter. The remnants of last week's snow lay on the ground, slowly fossilizing into ice. A wind off the plains brought an Arctic blast that would freeze the hide off a fur-lined rhinoceros.

The gym ... uh ... *Fitness Center* ... sits on the back side of the campus, but the walkways are well-lighted. The wind sliced at my cheeks and sent shadows from the elm trees dancing along the walkways as I trudged back to the campus circle. There I had to decide—home or meeting Mitra Fortier in her office? I didn't relish returning to the now-silent piano in the home where Faith and I raised our daughter.

That and the prospect of losing my job decided me. So I followed the campus circle around to the Science Center and descended the stairs to Professor Fortier's basement office. Her door was closed, but the lights glimmering through its frosted glass window revealed Mara Thorn standing before it.

She looked up in surprise. "I didn't expect to see you here, Press."

"She told me to meet her here if I valued my job."

Mara wrinkled her nose. "She told me the same. She wanted me to investigate. I refused, but she said if I valued my job I'd meet her here. I knocked, but she didn't answer."

"That's not like her," I said. I knocked loudly and called, using the nickname Faith had given her. "Mitzi?"

Still no answer. With my gloved hand I tried the door and found it locked.

Mara's chin lifted a fraction of an inch. "Do you still have the pass key?"

She meant the one I'd pilfered from the dean's office last fall when both he and the police were falsely accusing me. I nodded and took out my key ring. The door opened easily.

I stepped through the doorway with Mara close behind. Shelves on three walls of the office were filled with books. A desk that had seen better days stood near the far wall with four hardwood chairs flanking it. A computer monitor rested on the desk, its cables leading to the computer underneath.

Protruding past one end of the desk lay a stockinged foot in a black high-heeled shoe.

I bounded around the desk and knelt beside the prone form of Mitra Fortier. There was no doubt she was dead. Sadly, I looked up at Mara and shook my head.

Without warning, my internal orchestra broke into the Can-Can sequence from *Gaite Parisienne*.

CHAPTER 2

Without a word, Mara took out her cell phone and withdrew to the hall. While she called 911, I made a final study of Mitra Fortier. Her yellow haystack-hair spread wildly on the floor around her head, but her body bore no obvious marks. Nothing in the scene suggested a struggle. Her heavy coat lay folded on a table by the door. She wore the same clothing she'd worn at the reception—a royal blue blouse with a modest, dark skirt. Her clothing remained in good array except for a small spot of dried blood on the blouse inside her left elbow.

Returning to the hall, I used my gloved hand to turn the door's spring lock to the "off" position. I couldn't admit I'd used an unauthorized pass key to enter the office. Mara handed me her phone in silent concession that I would know better than she when to call the college administration. I guess she'd forgotten that I carried a good phone now.

While we waited for the police, I tried to push Mitra's death from our minds. "How have you been?" I asked Mara. That sounded too trite, so I added, "I gather things haven't gone smoothly." How could they, with her recent conversion from Wicca piled on top of adjustment to a new teaching job and being accused, along with me, of both murder and immorality?

She sighed. "Any way but smooth. Department politics is bad enough, but those rotten rumors about us ... " Her lips pressed tightly together. "We've been bitten by the Blatant Beast."

Score another point for Mara's erudition. The Blatant Beast was Edmund Spenser's allegorical figure for slander. Few people have persevered as far into *The Faerie Queene* as Book VI, where Calidore, the Knight of Courtesy, seeks out and binds the beast.

She sighed. "Spenser advised the beast's potential victims to 'avoid the occasion of the ill.' Maybe the rumors will die down if we're not seen together."

"We can hope so," I said. But in Spenser's epic romance, no medicine could heal people who suffered the Beast's poisonous bite. To slanderous imaginations on campus, the absence of evidence against us would only prove we'd covered our tracks well.

I decided to change the subject. "You said something about department politics?"

She wrinkled her nose. "My boss, Dathan Hormah."

No wonder. Dathan had re-christened the Bible Department as the Department of Religious Studies during our college's Great Renaming. He was thick as crows on carrion with the college dean, his neighbor in the Meribah Valley suburb. He also had no sense of humor. I once asked him, "If a Christian hangs out in Starbucks, does that make him a Latté Day Saint?" His response was not a smile, but a five-minute lecture on theology.

Mara's blue eyes blazed. "Professor Hormah hired me as a Wiccan so he could diversify his faculty. He thinks I double-crossed him by converting to Christianity."

"And the other department members?" I asked.

"They're both married men afraid to show cordiality to a female former pagan. So much for that business about the lost sheep. They feel safer packed in with the ninety and nine."

"They're probably jealous of the way your classes fill."

She sniffed. "They needn't worry about that. Dr. Hormah limited my classes to twenty-five, and that forced students to enroll in other sections."

"Any sensible student would rather look at you than those other guys."

Her blue gaze gave me a mild scorching. "You're coloring outside the lines again."

"Hey, you've moved the lines," I said. "So now they're excluding compliments?" In the past, they'd only referred to her abhorrence of being touched, the legacy of her ill-fated teenage marriage. She'd broken out of that and served an enlistment in the Army, then clawed her way up through college to a PhD in Comparative Religion, an achievement few could even dream about.

Her voice softened. "I'm sorry, Press. The rumors and the contract situation have me on edge. You've been a good friend, but I've fought everything else out by myself. This won't be an exception."

Where were the police? While they dallied, my head echoed with a flute playing Mendelssohn's "On Wings of Song," and I brooded about the campus situation. All the efforts to make things normal again had been in vain. Another death meant that nothing would be normal for a long, long time. And Mara and I, innocent as we were, stood once again at the center of disruption.

As the first faint wail of police sirens reached our ears, she spoke in a soft voice. "I'm sorry about Mitra, Press, but you know the trouble this means for *us*."

I did know. The jaws of the Blatant Beast would savor fresh blood.

I knew our involvement would cause us trouble, but at the moment I was too submerged in emotion to think more about it. Despite my outward calm, finding Mitra Fortier dead had shaken me to the core. She'd been a close friend to Faith. We'd often made a threesome at concerts and restaurants. I hadn't seen much of her in the three years since Faith's death, but I still considered her a friend. With her death, I lost another part of Faith's world that I carried in my heart.

The police sirens drew closer.

"Press?" Mara walked into my line of vision. "Are you going to call someone or shall I?"

I dragged myself out of thought and dialed the home phone of the college dean. As I did, a premonition formed in my mind. It told me I'd again be forced out of my persona as history professor and into a self I'd left behind more than two decades before. I had no wish to revive that self.

I didn't want to talk to Dean Billig, either, but I had no choice. We'd learned at the reception that our president, J. Cleveland Cantwell, would leave town immediately after the reception on a fund-raising expedition. In his absence, Dean Billig would be in charge, a condition which always conjured up visions of the sorcerer's apprentice—the Disney version, not the original.

The Great Renaming in which Overton Grace College became the graceless Overton University also gave Billig the title "Vice President for Academic Affairs." Faculty wits made the obvious wordplay about his potential for affairs. Dean Billig is his actual name. Thus, in pre-university days when he was appointed dean, he became Dean Dean Billig, and the faculty promptly shortened that appellation (not entirely affectionately) to Dean-Dean. He received his PhD in psychology by correspondence without ever leaving our campus. So he grows self-conscious around faculty who earned their degrees in residence at major universities, going eye to eye with tenured professionals in cutthroat oral examinations.

Dean-Dean answered on the fourth ring with his high-pitched voice.

"Preston Barclay here," I said. "I have bad news. We've found Professor Fortier dead in her office."

Dean-Dean sputtered for several seconds. He is the only man I ever knew who could sputter in the pitch range of a contralto. As he did, my internal orchestra rollicked through a cheerful number with a bassoon in the lead. Something about Dean-Dean always calls up that bassoon.

When he got through sputtering, Dean-Dean gasped out a single word—"Again?"

"No, not *again*," I said. "So far as I know, this is the first time she's been dead."

There are reasons I'm the campus pariah, and Dean-Dean brings out the worst of them.

He sputtered again. "Professor Barclay …" He was breathing hard, like a lapdog chasing a cat on a hot day. "Don't you do anything but go around finding more bodies?"

"I use extra-body shampoo," I said.

He sucked in his breath. I could almost hear his synapses straining to make connection. "That … that is totally illogical," he said.

"So is your implication that I'm responsible for the body's being there to find."

He was silent for a while. "I suppose we have to call the police," he mused at last.

"We've already done that," I said. "The law requires it."

"I'm aware of that, Professor Barclay," he snapped. He paused, apparently ambushed by a thought. "You said 'we.' Who else is there with you? Is it that … that *Wiccan* again?"

"*Former* Wiccan," I said, "assuming you mean Professor Thorn. But yes, Professor Fortier asked us to meet her at her office after the reception."

Dean-Dean invoked the Deity, but not in a meaningful context. "You two bring me more trouble than all the rest of the faculty combined."

"Someone else brought the trouble," I said. "We merely announced it." I was glad he hadn't yet thought of shooting the messenger.

"I'll be right there," he said. "Don't go away."

For various legal and practical reasons, we weren't about to leave.

Mara showed a sardonic smile. "You're still running for Most Popular Man on Campus."

"I'm only running away from involvement," I said. "Speaking of which, remember to say we found the office door unlocked."

She nodded, no more eager than I to admit our pilfered pass key.

The basement hallway felt hot and stifling. I shed my overcoat and slung it over one arm. I wasn't looking forward to dealing with the police. It's said in a classic understatement that police procedures in Overton City are somewhat informal. A few of the officers are first rate, though. Maybe we'd luck out and get one of them.

The sirens arrived outside and lapsed into silence. Heavy steps clattered down the stairs and two uniformed policemen charged into the hallway.

My heart sank.

CHAPTER 3

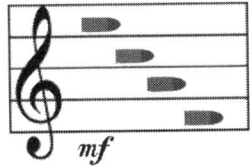

It sank like hot lead through tissue paper. The policeman in charge was Bruno Pinkle. He stood about my height, five-feet-ten, but carried a bulk at least twice mine. With a surly round face full of pockmarks, he looked like a boxer who'd retired ten years too late. To say he considered me no friend was like saying Stalin's Gulag was inconsiderate. In the distant past he'd taken one of my classes with less than favorable results.

Pinkle gave me a hostile stare and growled, "I might have known I'd find you here."

"The body is in the office," I said.

Pinkle opened the office door, efficiently confusing any fingerprints the doorknob might have contained, and clomped inside. His associate kept a suspicious eye on Mara and me. Actually, he kept both eyes on Mara. In his place I'd have done the same.

Mara, however, turned her blue gaze on me and raised an eyebrow. She must have wondered how I managed to be *persona non grata* to so many people at once.

Pinkle clomped back from inspecting the corpse and called for Homicide. His partner took Mara several steps down the hall to get her story while Pinkle listened to mine.

When I finished, he asked, "What did this female professor want with you this late at night?" He made it sound like a lovers' tryst.

"She didn't say." My answer was literally true. Mitra hadn't said definitely that the subject was about keeping my job. In any case, I wasn't going to raise that issue with Bruno Pinkle because I knew which way he would vote.

Pinkle shifted from one foot to the other and said, "Just remember, Professor. You ain't doing the grading this time."

"Just remember that neither are you," I said.

Fortunately, that conversation was interrupted when Weldon Combes, chairman of the Physics Department, emerged from the stairwell. He was a tall man of about forty, with short-cropped sandy hair, fighting a losing battle against an expanding forehead. Combes was good at physics, but not physiques. He was too skinny to make an hors d'oeuvre for the average cannibal.

Alarmed, he asked, "What's wrong, Press? I see police cars outside." Then he noticed Professor Fortier's open door. "Oh, no ... Not Mitra ..."

"She's dead, Weldon," I said. "I'm sorry."

"Oh, no," he said again and put a hand to his forehead. "How did it happen?"

"That's just what we plan to find out." Bruno Pinkle awoke from his customary stupor and placed a restraining hand on Combes' chest. "Now tell me who you are and what you're doing here at this time of night."

I also wondered what brought Combes there that late.

Pinkle closed Mitra's office door, took the bewildered physics professor by the arm, and guided him several steps down the hall.

"My office is right there," Combes said, pointing to the office next to Mitra's.

"We don't need no office," Pinkle said.

The other officer placed yellow crime-scene tape over the now-closed door and resumed his vigil over Mara and me. Behind his back, Freda Broyles came out of the stairwell and took three steps into the hall. Freda, chairman of the Math Department, was a heavy woman of about sixty or so with a personality like a horned frog. She was shaped kind of like one, too.

That made two professors who'd need to explain their after-hours presence.

Freda froze with a shocked expression as she saw the tape over Professor Fortier's door, then reversed course and disappeared back into the stairwell.

Our policeman guard whirled to look at the now-empty hallway. "What was that?"

I shrugged. "Maybe a rat or a cop."

"You have rats in this place?" He threw a worried glance around the premises.

"Without rats and freshmen," I said, "our psychologists would be out of business."

He muttered something derogatory about techniques of running railroads and muttered, "I don't like rats."

Mara watched with one eyebrow raised but said nothing. After that, we stood silently in the overheated hallway. My forehead beaded with sweat, and so did the cop's. Mara showed no sign of perspiration. I never learned how she managed that.

The approach of another siren outside announced the arrival of Clyde Staggart, Overton City's Captain of Homicide and no friend of mine. More than twenty years ago when he was my boss in Army Special Ops in Central America, I'd stumbled onto evidence he was taking kickbacks. Another lieutenant and I had testified to that under oath. Staggart was allowed to resign his commission in lieu of court martial, and he swore revenge against everyone who testified against him. Last fall he'd tried to pin Laila Sloan's murder on me, with Mara as my accomplice. The fact that Mara and I solved the case did not improve our relationship with him.

A heavy-set man with deep black eyes, Staggart charged in with his usual bull-like manner, followed by an entourage of four. One of these was the sloppily dressed medical examiner. Another was Staggart's constant companion, a man whose face bore an amazing resemblance to that of a basset hound. I didn't know his name, so I'd always referred to him as Dogface. But I'd found to my embarrassment that, in spite of his habitual silence, he could quote John Keats' poetry from memory. The other two detectives I didn't know.

When Staggart saw me, his lip curled in distaste. "You again, Press?"

I pointed to the office. "Not me again. Another body to keep you gainfully employed." My conscience winced at my referring to Mitra as a body.

"It's hot in here," he said. "With this heating bill, it's no wonder your college stays in financial trouble."

"*University*," I corrected. "Talk to your friend, the dean. I just teach history."

Staggart turned a contemptuous gaze on Mara. "I thought they'd have run you out of here by now."

More evidence of police informality.

Mara made no answer but turned her back on him and examined the junction of wall and ceiling.

Staggart and the medical examiner moved through the yellow tape into the office.

I called after them, "Check the left elbow."

That was when Dean-Dean entered. He threw nervous glances at the various policemen like a ball bouncing around in one of the old pinball machines. Then he homed in on me—"Professor Barclay—"

He got no farther. Dogface stepped in and put a hand on his chest. They must have seen someone do that on TV, I guess. Then the other two detectives took Mara and me separately down the hall. While I retold my story, I could see the other one listening to Mara. That one had sense enough not to touch her arm. Maybe he'd heard she was good at karate and judo.

Staggart and the medical examiner emerged from the office and conferred with the two detectives while Dogface kept Dean-Dean occupied. Then Staggart turned to me.

"How long did you wait in the hall?"

"No more than a couple of minutes," I said.

"A 'couple of minutes' with no answer and the office light on, and you didn't try the door?"

"Professors don't go poking into each other's offices."

"So why *did* you open the door?"

I shrugged. "It wasn't like Mitra to be unresponsive. I got worried."

He cocked his head to one side. "So you knew the deceased that well?"

"She and my wife were good friends." I didn't like the direction of his questions.

"And that friendship was your only relationship with the deceased?"

"That and our being members of the same faculty."

Staggart shifted his weight from one foot to the other. "What did you do when you left the reception?"

I answered as bluntly as I could. "I came straight here."

"But not alone…" Staggart turned his gaze on Mara and leered.

Mara showed him her own gaze of blue fire.

"Professor Thorn was already here," I said. "I didn't know Professor Fortier had asked her for a meeting."

Staggart leered at each of us in turn. "That's all for now. We'll be in touch when we need you."

Mara and I promptly re-donned our coats and headed for the stairwell. We almost escaped without talking to Dean-Dean. But Dogface released our glorious Vice President for Academic Affairs, and for a moment I thought we would suffer an extended interview. Dean-Dean glowered at us, but he only growled "I'll see you two later" and minced past us toward the spot where Clyde Staggart stood. They greeted each other like long-lost friends.

That couldn't mean anything good, considering the false stories Staggart had planted with him last fall.

Outside, Mara and I took deep breaths in the cold, fresh air, as if that could somehow purify the scene we had just witnessed. Under the flickering campus lights, the chill added color to her ivory complexion.

"That wasn't as bad as I expected," Mara said.

My now-familiar premonition asserted itself again, thrusting an icicle into my heart to match the frigid air.

"It will get worse," I said. "It will get much worse before we're through."

We parted then. I brooded about the Blatant Beast and that threatening future as I followed the narrow walkway from the campus down to the emptiness of my silent house.

CHAPTER 4

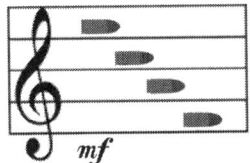

That night I dreamed of Faith again, a warm dream of companionship and love. I woke to a frigid February morning, the reality of an empty house, and a world gone stale except for teaching history. And I woke dreading the implications of Mitra Fortier's words—"If you value your job." They boded no good in the week before contracts were renewed.

Or maybe not renewed.

My internal musicians played sad melodies from Schumann's *Carnival* while I dragged through a ham-sandwich breakfast, put on my brown suit—I'd worn the blue one to the reception—and climbed the narrow walkway back up to the campus. My new cell phone made an unfamiliar bulge in my pocket, but, at least, it balanced my trusty voice recorder. Last night's razor-edge of wind had eroded to the dullness of a trowel, but the cold still seeped through my overcoat into my bones.

I paused before the Liberal Arts Center where my office is located and looked across the campus circle to the Science Center. Students wandered into it, and everything looked so normal it seemed I might have imagined last night's events. But I had a class to teach. In a kind of daze, I picked up my teaching notes from my office and headed into class.

My daze continued, so much so that I couldn't tell you what I taught. Fortunately, the news of Mitra's death hadn't gotten around enough for students to ask about it. That wouldn't last, but for now it let me escape back into my office. By noon, everyone on campus would know I was involved in something weird. That meant faculty members I hadn't seen in months would drop by my office to pump me for information.

So I shut my office door and turned out the lights. If anyone knocked, I'd pretend I wasn't there. I reviewed the situation while my internal orchestra played Brahms' *Academic Festival Overture*. By now, I'm brazened to the necessity of thinking and planning in spite of that music.

The first thing I wanted to know was how Mitra Fortier had died. The spot of blood above the veins inside her left elbow suggested some kind of injection. But so far as I knew, she'd never been a drug user. Besides, she was left-handed. If she'd injected herself, she would have held the syringe in her left hand and injected the right arm. That seemed suspicious, but the answer would have to wait for the police investigation. Mara's and my finding the body did not make us guilty of anything, though Dean-Dean's unique logic would blame us for bringing him more trouble. That couldn't be helped. But unless something unexpected turned up, even Clyde Staggart's enmity couldn't make me a suspect.

But Mitra had said that something threatened my job. Other than Dean-Dean, I didn't know who, or what, that might be. But I admit it worried me. Since Faith's death, I live for teaching history and, as I must have said a dozen times, I'd make a lousy used car salesman. I'd hoped that last fall's student demonstration in favor of Mara, together with our solving the Laila Sloan murder, had won us contracts for another year. But this was crunch time. The trustees had met, and contracts would be awarded within the next seven days. We would find them in our campus mailboxes.

Or not find them.

Just then, Brahms's overture ended with a rousing treatment of the student song "Gaudeamus Igitur" (Let Us Rejoice). I'd rarely felt less like rejoicing.

During my ponderings, I'd ignored several knocks on my office door. Through its frosted glass I could see masculine silhouettes against the lighted hallway. I ignored the knocks.

Then high heels clicked hurriedly in the hall. Shadowed slender fingers tapped on the door, and a feminine voice called, "Press, let me in. I have to talk to you."

I hoped it might be Mara. But when I clicked on the lights and opened the door, it turned out to be Cynthia Starlington.

Anxiety showed in her dark eyes.

"I have to talk to you, Press," she said. "I think I'm in trouble."

My internal orchestra cranked up again, this time with Artie Shaw's classic recording of "Begin the Beguine." The liquid tones of his clarinet in the lower register were perfectly suited to the meaning of the music. Or to the soft beauty of Cynthia Starlington.

"You don't look like you've committed crimes against humanity," I said. I motioned her toward one of the hardwood straight chairs aligned against the wall to the left of my desk.

When she'd disposed of her topcoat and seated herself, I pushed the door full open, eased a doorstop under it, and settled myself into a chair that faced hers. That put the width of the room between us. I'd admired Cynthia as a student and thought I could trust her, but in these super-sensitive times when an untoward word or gesture can get you accused of sexual harassment, I don't take chances. As I've commented before, music bounces around in my head, but I don't have any loose screws.

"Okay, Cyn," I said. "What's bothering you?"

For a few moments she said nothing but sat primly on the edge of her chair, knees pressed close together and hands clasped in her lap. She wore a brown blouse figured with darker brown leaves with a flowing brown skirt. For a poignant interval, her eyes searched mine.

"I ... I've heard about Professor Fortier, Press," she said at last. "That's why I'm in trouble."

I took time to straighten my necktie. I remembered that Cynthia and Mitra had snubbed each other at the reception, but I asked, "Why should her death involve you?"

Nervously, she rubbed her hands together. "We had a terrible row the other day. I'm afraid they'll say I killed her."

"You're rushing ahead of things," I said. "No one yet knows how she died. It could have been natural causes or even suicide." I thought I knew better but wasn't ready to admit it.

Cynthia shook her head. "She was murdered. I feel it in my bones."

"Hey, you're a philosopher," I said. "Aren't you folks supposed to demand a rational 'basis of belief'?"

Her eyes grew more earnest. "That's all fine and good for the classroom, but some things you just know because you know them."

I could have reminded her that if philosophy had no application outside the classroom, it wasn't worth the effort of studying. But she was young, hardly past thirty, so maybe that hadn't occurred to her.

"What kind of disagreement did you have with Professor Fortier?" I asked.

Cynthia looked at the floor. "It goes back to when I was a student. Her physics class was the only one I ever made a bad grade in. I made one teeny little error in calculation. I got all the principles right, but she wouldn't give me credit for that. She said if the answer wasn't completely right, the answer was completely wrong. So I made a *B+* in the course, and that knocked me out of being valedictorian."

"You were salutatorian, and that's quite an honor."

"But I'd set my sights on winning the top honor. I deserved it. You know I never shied away from the hard subjects. And Greg Willis—the boy that won it—never took anything but powder-puff courses once he got his required courses out of the way."

I winced at the idea that required courses constituted unnecessary obstacles in what students regarded as the superhighway to promised job credentials. But I was surprised at Cynthia's venom after all these years of academic success.

I took time to adjust my trifocals. "Tell me about this last incident."

A tear trickled down her cheek. "I went by Professor Fortier's office and told her what I thought of her. She raised her voice right back at me—you know what a loud voice she has ... *had* .... Anyway, while we were shouting at each other, Professor Combes and several others came out of their offices to see what was going on. And I said something I shouldn't have. I told Professor Fortier that anyone who'd do that to a student ought to be killed."

This Cynthia was not the skinny kid I'd admired as a student for being methodical and well-controlled. And it wasn't a great start on her faculty career.

"Who else heard you?" I asked. Weldon Combes had always been a stabilizing influence on campus, but there were others who might be trouble.

"Professor Broyles—from the Math Department, I think." Cynthia had tears on both cheeks now. "And that trustee—I think his name is Samstag."

I whistled. The aging Freda Broyles was a close friend of the deceased. She had a face like a prune and a temperament like boiled vinegar. And Gordon Samstag was chairman of the board of trustees. Cynthia couldn't have done worse if she'd threatened Mitra with an axe in the lobby of the police station. Now she looked at me with wide dark eyes that begged me to help her pick up the pieces.

"You've made a real mess," I said, "but that doesn't indict you for murder. What did you do after last night's reception?"

The soft clarinet music continued inside me supported now by the full orchestra.

Her eyes widened. "I drove straight home and went to bed."

I thought it best not to ask if she had a witness. The last thing I wanted was an outburst of the temper she'd been telling me about. Maybe if the police could trace Mitra's movements after the reception or find something on her computer or cell phone, the scene with Cynthia might never come up.

"We don't yet know how Professor Fortier died," I said again, still hiding my suspicions. "Until that's definite, no one can accuse you of anything except an impropriety." I avoided the obvious word *stupidity*. "Meanwhile, the best thing you can do is behave yourself and act as if the incident never happened."

She nodded silently and dabbed at her tears with a facial tissue.

"If the police do question you, don't hold anything back. They'll dig out the truth and throw it in your face. Their questioning won't be pleasant, but telling the complete truth is the best way out."

She nodded again.

"Another thing, it won't help your credibility with the police to be associated with me. My name has been mud with them ever since last fall."

Her eyes widened. "The Laila Sloan murder? They should be grateful to you for solving it."

Welcome to the real world, I thought. But I only said, "They don't see it that way." No use bringing up the long story of Clyde Staggart's enmity. It was time to end the interview, so I stood up. "Remember, be on your best behavior."

Smiling now, she also stood. As she crossed the room toward me, I admired the smooth perfection of her olive complexion. I'd never noticed before, but her dark brown hair grew lighter toward its ends, with little golden tips glinting like tiny jewels in the reflected light.

Artie Shaw's music climaxed in my head with a long clarinet glissando and, as always, he entered the final high note a bit flat.

"There's one other thing," Cynthia said. "I keep hearing about 'The Crisis,' but nobody explains ... "

"They should have told you when they hired you," I said. I tried not to go into lecture mode, but it still came out that way. "When you were a student, Overton Grace College was an under-endowed but respectable liberal arts college with about eight hundred students. But when enrollment suddenly dropped below seven hundred, it caused a panic and a change of presidents. The new one—President Cantwell—brought in a consultant to lead us back to economic health. So now we have a slew of 'relevant' classes to bring in hordes of students, we've begun a high-profile athletic program, and we've opened extension centers throughout the state to serve all kinds of special groups."

I could have said we chased money wherever it could be found, but Cynthia needed to make her own value judgments.

Again, her dark eyes widened. "That's why we're just Overton University instead of Overton *Grace* University?"

I nodded. "The consultant said our denominational identification would scare students off, so it's played down in all our publicity."

I didn't tell her the consultant had the crosses removed from the campus entryways until last fall when President Cantwell suffered a fit of conscience and ordered them restored.

Cynthia laid a hand on my arm. "Thank you, Press. I needed to know all that. And on the other thing ... I knew you could help."

She retrieved her topcoat and left without looking back. My arm tingled where she had touched it, and there lingered behind her a subtle perfume I didn't recognize. If she wore that to class, she'd have the male students too hypnotized to hear a word she said. And the female students too jealous.

My internal orchestra replaced Shaw's clarinet with a trio of muted trumpets. Somehow I pushed them into the back of my mind and considered my interview with Cynthia. Her foolish scene with Mitra Fortier wouldn't help her acceptance by the faculty. But if she was telling the truth, the worst she could expect was an unpleasant questioning by the police.

It didn't seem to change my situation in any way.

I was wrong again.

CHAPTER 5

I usually took lunch in the campus grill, but today that would provoke an inquisition about Professor Fortier's death. So, with the musicians in my brain tinkling a Chopin waltz, I followed the narrow walkway down the hill to my home and caught a ham sandwich. Then I returned to the campus for my class in Western Civilization.

I'd hardly walked in the door when a student asked, "Is it true that someone murdered Professor Fortier?"

My cerebral musicians responded with three toots from a kazoo. I would have done the same, but that would not have been scholarly. So I only said, "It's true that she's dead. Anything beyond that is up to the police."

Another student piped up. "Are you going to investigate?"

"We all are," I said. "We're going to investigate how Western civilization got us where we are today and why that is important. We'll begin by looking at an obscure but important turning point in early English history."

With resigned expressions at being denied their hot topic, the students settled back for a routine class in things they'd never heard of. The Synod of Whitby in A.D. 664 is one of those odd occasions when a few people's simple actions produced far-reaching results they never imagined. King Osby of Northumbria observed Easter by the Scottish calendar while his queen observed it a week later by the Roman calendar. King Osby called the synod to resolve the question. Hearing that Peter founded the church at Rome and that he was keeper of the keys in heaven, the king changed to the Roman calendar to remove a possible obstacle to his entry into heaven.

The unforeseen result over time was that the tiny, competitive kingdoms of Anglo-Saxon England moved toward unity under the influence of a vigorous church while Scotland remained fragmented and outside the civilizing influence of Rome.

These small historical events and their huge results suggest that a force greater than human intellects directs the major tides of history. But the question remains: Does the Providence that controls the tides also concern itself with individual waves? And what happens when the waves clash with each other? These are theological questions, so I don't tackle them in a history class.

Six or seven students showed genuine interest, and that's all it takes to motivate me. By the end of class, serotonin was flooding in my brain, and I could agree with Browning's Pippa that "God's in His heaven—/ All's right with the world."

But my uncooperative internal pianist kept playing something atonal by Poulenc that sounded like it would never get anywhere. It didn't, and I wasn't getting anywhere either with worrying about what Mitra Fortier had said about my job. If she'd shared her thoughts with anyone else, the most probable recipients were her colleagues. So I sought them out in the Science Center.

Mitra's office was locked, with yellow crime-scene tape almost obscuring the prominent **mf** that marked her door. I bypassed it and found Weldon Combes in the office just beyond. He looked up from his desk as I entered.

"Come in, Press." He waved a pipestem-thin arm toward a chair against a side wall. "I suppose you're here about Mitra's death."

"I guess so." I adjusted my trifocals and tried to look as confused as I felt. "She and Faith were good friends, and her death made me realize I didn't really know her."

Combes fidgeted. "I knew her only professionally, though my wife and I had her over for dinner a couple of times. She did a fine job of teaching, and she put all of us to shame on math, especially probability theory."

"Probability theory?" This wasn't going the way I'd hoped.

"Yes." Combes gazed off into space. "She worked out a system for winning at blackjack. It worked so well that they barred her from the tables in Las Vegas."

That got my attention. During spring break three years ago, about the time Faith was dying, a faculty group spent spring break in Las Vegas. Our philosophy professor got in debt and had to pay off the mob by directing its rackets from our campus computer system. That led to last fall's murder.

"I didn't know Mitra had struck it rich," I said.

Combes laughed. "They stopped her before she could break the bank. Two big guys escorted her into one of the offices. Several of us—faculty and trustees—waited outside the door, just in case. But she came out and said everything was all right."

"Trustees? I didn't realize any of them made the trip."

"Three that I remember. The used car dealer, Emory Estes—he was ready to take on every goon in the place if they laid hands on Mitra."

"And the others?"

"Gordon Samstag and his wife. They stayed pretty much to themselves, though he joined us while we waited for Mitra to come out of that office. So did Steven Drisko. That was soon after his divorce, so he'd come by himself."

"Did anyone in the group seem to win or lose a lot?"

"Mitra won enough to buy new furniture for her living room. Some people won a little, others lost a little. No one complained much one way or the other."

That wasn't much help. The philosophy professor had concealed his losses, so others might have done the same. I changed to the subject I'd really come to investigate.

"Did Mitra talk about anything unusual lately? Something she hadn't been concerned with before?"

He looked thoughtful. "Not that I can remember."

"Maybe something about the college?"

Combes shook his head. "Only the usual stuff. Nothing new."

I tried a different tack. "I heard someone had a real dust-up with her last week."

"That new woman in philosophy went off her rocker and accused Mitra of discriminatory grading or something."

"Were threats exchanged?"

"Not by Mitra. The other woman said something about Mitra … that she ought to be killed. She looked angry enough to try it."

"How did it end?"

"Both of them were shouting at the same time so you couldn't understand the words. The other woman saw several of us watching and just walked out. That was about it." He glanced at his watch. "I'd better get ready for my lab."

I stood up. "Thank you, Weldon. By the way, is there any reason you came to your office last night? You're notorious for staying away after suppertime."

He also stood, clumsily, and his chair tipped over. He caught it at the length of his long, thin arm, and yanked it upright—a surprising show of strength for anyone that thin.

"I came by to pick up something I'd forgotten," he said, not meeting my eyes.

"It couldn't wait until morning?"

He shrugged. "Sometimes it happens that way. Say, we have a faculty meeting Tuesday after the memorial service for Mitra. Rumor says someone may try to slip something by us."

Was that change of subject supposed to divert me from questioning?

"I'll vote, but I won't speak," I said. "I'm still in the doghouse from past skirmishes."

"Voting is good enough." He half turned, then added, "Be careful with your investigation, Press. You were lucky last time, but you may not be that lucky again."

"Who's investigating?"

I left before he could answer. I wondered if his warning had been friendly.

CHAPTER 6

Down the hall, I found Freda Broyles' office door open and her sitting at her desk like a spider in her web. She gave me the welcoming glance she'd give a leprous polecat and motioned me to a chair.

"I've been expecting you, Press," she said. "What took you so long?"

I didn't waste time wondering why she'd been expecting me. "I'd lost track of Mitra since Faith died. I thought you might fill me in on these last couple of years."

"Baloney." Her look now classified me as a misplaced decimal point. "You think she was murdered, and you're trying to find out who killed her. Be honest with me."

It was okay by me if she wanted to think I was investigating a murder. With enough talk, she might give me a clue toward understanding what Mitra meant about my job.

"All right," I said. "What can you tell me?"

Freda leaned her elbows on the desk. "I wouldn't know much about Mitra except that she lives ... *lived* ... across the street from me. We were both single women, so we checked on each other. She spent most evenings at home with the shades drawn. Maybe she read books, maybe she wrote letters, maybe watched TV—I never asked what she did."

I looked at the ceiling. "Maybe she worked math problems. I heard she was a whiz on probability."

Freda showed me a horned-toad scowl. "That was years ago. Her recent interest was …. Are you familiar with the term *nano*?"

"Not unless it's the children's nickname for their grandmother."

She repeated the leprous-polecat look. "It's a prefix meaning the one-billionth part of something. Mathematically, it's the factor of ten to the minus nine. She got interested in nano-technology."

"The study of very small things?"

"Very, very small. But before that it was accounting."

"Accounting?" That sounded more promising.

Freda relaxed a bit. "That was about a year ago when she was dating a CPA fellow down in Cloverdale. She was happier then than I'd ever seen her."

"He was teaching her accounting?"

"No such thing!" Freda sat straight up. "They were just dating. She studied accounting on her own so she'd know what he did for a living."

"What happened?"

She sighed. "Mitra was really happy for about six months—till July, I think. Then he got killed in that airplane crash."

"Tell me about that." It was provocative—both halves of a dating couple killed within six months.

"Not much to tell," she said. "Jerry had served in the Air Force and liked to fly on weekends. He and some others built their own airplane, but they must have done something wrong. A wing came off while he was flying, and he was killed. Mitra took it real hard."

I vaguely remembered reading about the crash, but I'd never heard Mitra had a connection with it. That would take some research—if something made it relevant.

"I never knew," I said. "She was a good friend to Faith."

Freda sighed again. "After Jerry's death, she turned back inside herself, though she kept going out somewhere on weekends. I never knew where and never asked." Freda's jaw hardened. "She didn't deserve what that young wench said about her."

"What young wench? What did she say?"

Freda harumphed. "Professor Starlington, and what *didn't* she say. Some garbage about a grading problem years ago. And she threatened to kill Mitra."

"Hold on," I said. "Did she say she was going to kill her or only that she ought to be killed?"

"What's the difference? But if you've heard about it before, you don't need to get a recap."

"It always helps to hear different viewpoints," I said.

"Well, you won't hear any more of mine. I have to go home and fix myself some supper."

I was grateful that she didn't ask me to dine with her.

"Thank you for the information," I said. "It gives me something to work on." I might as well pretend I was investigating a murder if that would keep her happy.

"You and Faith were good friends to her," she said. "Otherwise, I wouldn't have told you anything."

"Tell me one more thing, then." I stood up, hoping to increase the surprise of the question. "Why did you come to the Science Center last night, and why did you duck out when you saw the police?" That was two things, but I hoped she wasn't counting.

Freda took a facial tissue from a box on her desk and wiped an invisible tear from her left eye. Without looking back at me, she took another one and repeated the process with the right eye. Then she viewed the two tissues with disgust.

"They make these confounded things smaller every year," she said. "Before long, they'll have to sell them in sheets like postage stamps."

I said nothing and waited.

She spoke again with a look that demoted me from polecat to cockroach. "I'd forgotten a lesson plan I needed to look over before this morning. But if I got tied up with the police, they might keep me past midnight. I'm old enough that I need my sleep."

I returned her gaze. "Freda, you never needed a lesson plan in your life."

She dragged her bulk out of her chair to a standing position. "Old dogs can learn new tricks, Press. Shut the door on your way out."

I did shut the door. The fact that Freda stayed behind it told me her claim of fixing supper was a ruse to get rid of me. Such are the niceties of campus life.

I was halfway down the hall before I realized I hadn't asked her what Mitra was saying about the college lately. Freda's diversionary tactic had worked.

In the gathering dusk, a chilling wind off the plains reminded me that I'd left my gloves in my office. When I went by to pick them up, I found a student named Sally Finhatter waiting. She'd never taken one of my classes, but I'd noticed her on campus because her dishwater-blonde hair usually covered one eye and the other one never seemed to look straight at anyone.

"Professor Barclay?" Her squeaky voice reinforced the impression of uncertainty.

"That's me," I said. "How can I help you, Sally?"

"You know my name? Well, I ... I have a problem, and Arthur Medford said I should talk to you about it."

Arthur Medford was Mara's prize student. Last fall he'd organized a student demonstration in favor of Mara when she and I were on suspension. All bets were that he'd be next year's student body president.

"Come in." I unlocked the door, stopped it full open, and flicked the light switch on. I motioned Sally to a chair and took the chair opposite hers. "What's the problem?"

Her unobstructed eye focused momentarily on mine, then returned its gaze to the floor. "Well, the other day I was talking to Professor Fortier in her office about, you know, like assignments and stuff. While we were talking, I had an index card in my hand that had part of my bibliography on it."

I assumed she meant the bibliography was on the card rather than the hand, but I did not request confirmation.

"Well, I lay the index card on that table by Professor Fortier's door." She paused with a puzzled look. "I never can get that straight. Should it be *lay* or *laid*?"

"*Laid*," I said.

"Well, then, I *laid* it on the table. Like just to get it out of my hand, you know?"

I said I did know. I only knew it because she had told me, but it would have been unkind to remind her of that. Besides, I was getting interested.

"Well ..." She used that word almost as often as the news reporters on TV. "Well ... when I left, I went to pick up that index card, but there was another one just like it laying ... *lying* ... right beside it, and I got that one by mistake." Her eye flickered through another brief contact with mine before refocusing downward. "I didn't mean to. I didn't realize till later that I had the wrong card, and when I came back for it, Professor Fortier had went somewhere else. Now the police have her office taped off, and I can't get my card back."

"Do you have the other card?"

She removed it from her jeans pocket and handed it to me. It contained one word scrawled in Mitra Fortier's illegible handwriting. The word might have been Buspin, Ruskin, or something like that. Maybe even Rasputin, for all I knew. I wanted to study it further, but the police would need the card. So I led Sally into the department office and made a photocopy.

"You'll have to take the card to the police," I told her. "It may or may not mean something, but that's their call." She looked doubtful, so I added, "If you don't tell them, I'll have to. Withholding evidence is a serious offense. Besides, they might even let you have your card back."

That last comment seemed to decide her. She said she'd tell me what the police said, then headed off down the hall.

Back in my office, I made no more progress with the photocopy than I had at first glance. Best leave it to the police, I decided. As always before leaving the office, I evaluated the day's activities. There'd been plenty, and I'd collected many odd bits of information.

But none of them helped explain why Mitra Fortier thought my job was threatened.

CHAPTER 7

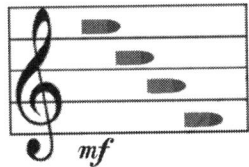

Full dusk had fallen, but if I hurried I'd have time before supper to visit my former chairman and mentor, Lincoln Sheldon, who would want to know about Mitra. In addition to being an excellent historian, Dr. Sheldon was a decorated Korean War veteran. Now in his eighties, he'd been wheelchair-bound in an assisted living center since a stroke cost him the use of his legs. But he still liked to stay abreast of campus affairs. His mind could still devour great quantities of information. His computer researches last fall had been invaluable to Mara and me in solving the Laila Sloan murder.

I always enjoy the drive across town to visit him. The Overton River isn't much, but it has a magnificent mile-wide valley with steep hills rising on either side. Overton City lies mostly in the valley, but its recent growth spills out into the hills. The college ... uh ... *university* ... dominates the valley and the city from the western hills. My long-time dream has been for our planned fine arts building to be topped with a cross to proclaim the college's Christian heritage to the entire valley. But President Cantwell's consultant says that heritage will drive students away. So the fine arts building will be just another red brick structure with another flat roof.

My mid-eighties Honda protested a bit going up the eastern hills but finished without a downshift. By all rights, it should have died by now, but a good mechanic named Manny Clampett has cured its periodic illnesses. I can't afford to replace it as long as I have a daughter in college.

I found Dr. Sheldon in his room in the assisted living center, already in conference with Mara Thorn.

"Come in, Press," he boomed, "I think you may have met Professor Thorn?"

He was goading me, so I answered in kind. "Professor Thorn and I have met on several occasions."

Seated nearby, Mara carefully studied the wall, but her smile showed she was part of the game. In these quarters we didn't have to worry about the Blatant Beast.

Dr. Sheldon raised a book from his lap and waved it at me. It was Mark Moyar's *Triumph Forsaken: The Vietnam War 1954-1965*.

"This is the most thoroughly documented history book I ever read," he said. "No journalistic bushwa. This will become the definitive study of the subject."

"I'll look forward to reading it," I said. It would have spoiled his fun to tell him I'd already read it and agreed with his assessment.

A frown clouded his leonine countenance. "Mara has told me about Professor Fortier. I know this comes as a blow to you. She was a friend to Faith."

"They were good friends," I said. "We did a lot of things as a threesome, but I haven't seen much of her since Faith died."

"If you feel like talking, Press," Mara said, "I'd like to know more about her."

"I do feel like talking," I said, partly trying to convince myself.

Mara focused her blue gaze on me. "When you knocked on Professor Fortier's door, you called her 'Mitzi'?"

"Faith's pet name for her," I said. "I've used it now and then."

"She had some kind of musical symbol on her office door. I don't know much about music." Mara's head was packed with more information than most people even knew existed, so she confessed this tiny unknown as if it made her a dunce.

"The symbol was **mf**, meaning *mezzo forte*, or moderately loud," I said. "There's a story behind it."

Mara raised her eyebrows expectantly while Dr. Sheldon for once sat silent. He knew the story because he'd watched it develop.

"It was odd for Faith and Mitra to become friends because they were so different," I said. "Faith was intuitive and emotional, as you'd expect a concert pianist to be. But she was also imaginative and playful. Mitra was a just-the-facts physicist. If you handed her a seashell, she'd try to compute the mathematical formulae for its curvature."

Memories flooded back to me as I talked. Mitra's singing brought her and Faith together, for Faith was a polished accompanist as well as a brilliant soloist. Mitra's strong voice made her in demand for entertainment at faculty dinners. She sang with vigor but without emotional nuances. As some people are mono*tones*, Mitra was a mono-*volume*. Everything she sang came out moderately loud, or *mezzo forte*.

So Faith in characteristic playfulness gave her a new name. *Mitra* became *Mitzi*, and *Fortier* got shortened to *Forte*. Mitra joined the game, proudly displaying the **mf** symbol on her office door. She was sometimes unpredictable. Who'd have thought the just-the-facts physicist would possess a well-honed sense of humor? I'd sometimes wondered if she had other hidden depths she never showed.

Mara cocked an eyebrow when I said Mitra often made a threesome with Faith and me. "Didn't that get awkward at times—two women and one man?"

I thought a moment before answering. "I guess it would in most cases, but Mitzi didn't have an ounce of flirtation in her. She'd been divorced before she came to Overton, and I guess that cured her of any romantic inclinations."

Mara looked a bit uncomfortable, and I remembered her history of early marriage to a dominating older man. She still had that aversion to being touched, and her fierce independence would choke off romance before it got started.

I thought it best to push ahead. "Well, Mitra wasn't *all* facts and logic. She had periods of moodiness. Then Faith would go spend a few evenings with her. After a few days, Mitra would snap out of it and be her confident self again."

I decided to close the subject. "The good news is that there's no way the police can involve either of us."

"Certainly not me," Mara said. "Professor Fortier and I hadn't exchanged a dozen words before last night."

Dr. Sheldon harumphed. "Don't sell Clyde Staggart short, Press. He's held that grudge against you for twenty years. He isn't about to drop it now."

"He can't do anything without evidence," I said. I hoped I was right.

Dr. Sheldon looked at Mara but spoke to me. "I understand Cynthia Starlington has come back as faculty. She always had a crush on you."

I adjusted my trifocals. "She was a good student, and she seemed to like history."

He snorted. "She liked *your* history. She never took a single course from me."

"Maybe it didn't fit her schedule," I said.

Dr. Sheldon answered with a sarcastic laugh. Mara had returned to her study of the wall, this time without the smile.

Dr. Sheldon looked at his watch. "Five o'clock. Let's see what our glorious friends in the Fourth Estate have come up with." He pointed a remote control at a TV on a table in one corner. It was a cheap set with poor color. TV was not one of his priorities.

The screen announced station KLYE's evening news program. Trumpets sounded a fanfare while colorful graphics gyrated around the screen, climaxing in a flaming nuclear explosion accompanied by a ringing bell. It was the only place I've ever seen A-bombs associated with bell ringing. The local news anchorette, Francie LaBouche, appeared out of the mushroom cloud like a stage magician emerging from a puff of smoke. She was dressed like a chorus girl, had brownish hair with bottle-born highlights, and wore enough grease on her lips to fry an egg. Her manner suggested she bore tidings more important than the Second Coming.

"Death struck once again at Overton University last night," Francie orated. The visuals shifted to police cars with flashing lights outside the Science Center while the anchorette's voice-over continued. "Last evening, physics professor Mitra Fortier was found dead in her office, and two of the same people involved in the Laila Sloan murder last fall were once again on the scene. The body was discovered by none other than professors Preston Barclay and Mara Thorn, shown in this footage from last fall."

I'd had some decent photos taken for past college annuals, but they might as well not have existed. The footage chosen for the TV's split screen had been taken the night we returned from a three-day investigation and found a decaying body stuffed into the trunk of Mara's car. As I walked forward to identify the body, the cameras caught me in the rumpled brown suit I'd worn for three days. In the glare of TV lights I looked like something out of a Frankenstein movie.

Mara fared no better on the other half of the screen. The cameras showed her, grim-faced, being loaded into a police car for questioning at headquarters.

"For the latest details," Francie announced, "here is KLYE's Cissy Ferret *live* on the Overton University campus."

"I'm glad she's not dead," Dr. Sheldon said.

Mara scorched him with her blue gaze.

The cameras focused on the Science Center exterior, where another chorus-girl/newsperson—apparently the aforementioned Cissy Ferret—interviewed Captain Clyde Staggart, with a distraught Dean-Dean dithering around in the background. Dean-Dean's image inspired a reprise by my internal bassoon. Though the interview had obviously been pre-arranged, it was presented as spontaneous.

"It's too early to suggest any theories," Staggart began. "All we know right now is that we have a dead body. We won't know the cause of death till the autopsy is complete."

The reporter was not to be denied. "Was the deceased fully clothed?"

Staggart glowered. "Yes, but like I said, it's too early for any theories." His tone implied that someone might have sneaked in and dressed the corpse.

"I understand the professors who discovered the body are the same ones who found Laila Sloan's body last fall. Does that suggest anything?"

"Well, they're the same two." Staggart's face showed disgust. "But we can't draw conclusions based on their character alone. We'll have to follow the evidence to find the extent of their involvement."

Dr. Sheldon clicked the remote control and the screen went blank. He made a noise like "Arrgh!" I think he'd have spit if he'd had a cuspidor.

Mara sat grim-faced and tight-lipped.

"It's nice to have friends in the bureau," I said.

We sat in silence, not looking at each other.

After a while, Dr. Sheldon cleared his throat. "Well, children, what will you do now? You're credited with being involved whether you are or not."

"There's nothing we can do," I said. "In cold fact, we have no involvement beyond finding the body. We have to wait for the police to reach that conclusion."

Mara stood up, still stony-faced but quite attractive in spite of it. "I know exactly what I'm going to do. I'm going to go find some supper."

"I hope he's worthy of you," Dr. Sheldon said.

Mara bristled but left without further comment.

I confess that I felt a little stab of jealousy. I would have asked her to join me for supper, but she hoped our avoiding each other would scotch the rumors of an illicit relationship. Tonight's newscast knocked that plan into a cocked chapeau. Until Mara got used to that, I would have to stay away from her.

I gave her a few minutes' head start, then said, "I guess I'd better go, too."

Dr. Sheldon gave me a something-you-ought-to-know look. "She's going to dinner with Emory Estes, the trustee who owns those used car lots."

"Maybe it's a job interview," I said. "Contracts come out next week."

Dr. Sheldon acknowledged with a grunt, his head already back in his book. No one ever accused him of being indefinite.

*****

I drove back across town while my internal orchestra played a Brahms Hungarian Dance, and I debated whether I should have briefed Mara and Dr. Sheldon on my interviews with Malcolm Combes and Freda Broyles. I decided I was right in not briefing them. I hadn't learned anything significant and certainly nothing about my prospective job loss.

I drove by the campus and picked up a list of research questions I'd left on my desk. I would need them for my trip to the state university's library tomorrow. With them in hand, I turned toward the door and found it filled by a uniformed policeman.

Fortunately, it was my former student Sergeant Ron Spencer, who'd made the actual arrest of Laila Sloan's murderer. His embarrassed scowl showed this wasn't a social call.

"Doctor Barclay, I thought you ought to know you're still on Captain Staggart's hit list. He's given Bruno Pinkle a full-time assignment. He's supposed to find evidence that will justify indicting you for a felony—any kind of felony."

CHAPTER 8

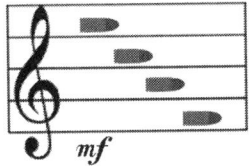

Sergeant Spencer's glad tidings should have kept me awake, but Friday had been a tough day. I slept the sleep of the just without wondering if I was qualified.

Saturday morning broke cold and clear. The sun reflected glaringly from all directions, but the roads had been swept clear of snow. I pointed my old Honda eastward on the Interstate for the hundred-mile drive to the state university and its Humanities Research Center. The car had lost a fender and wheel last fall in Mara's and my flight from the mob's hit men, but Manny Clampett had returned it to reasonably good shape. I could probably pay the repair debt off in four or five months if I lived frugally.

I love research, and a few hours of reading Marsilio Ficino's *Commentary on Plato's Symposium on Love* had me exhilarated. My spirits were still high when I joined my daughter, Cindy, for late lunch at a restaurant near the campus. She has Faith's light brown hair and clear complexion, and her soft voice always reminds me of Faith. Cindy radiated her usual high spirits, and she had a surprise for me.

"Daddy, I want you to meet Mark Weston," she said. "He edits *Voice of Reality*, the alternative newspaper on campus."

The young six-footer behind her had clear gray eyes and a steady gaze, both reinforced by a firm handshake. "I'm glad to meet you, sir," he said.

I returned the gaze and the greeting and reminded myself not to adjust my trifocals or my necktie. Those mannerisms had always irritated Cindy. We found a table where the canned music wasn't too oppressive. For once, my cerebral orchestra cooperated by shutting down. I ordered a grilled cheese sandwich with my coffee. Cindy and Mark ordered hamburgers and Cokes.

"Alternative newspaper?" I asked Mark as the server departed. "Do you always swim upstream?"

Cindy answered for him. "He always does. He's another dropout from the university's Residence Life Education Program."

Mark grinned. "If I'm going to be brainwashed, I'll do it for myself and not surrender my mind to some half-trained dorm assistant."

Cindy had run afoul of that program last fall when it taught that chastity was part of an oppressive patriarchal system, and one of her dates tried to act on that instruction. Her Residence Life group turned on her, but she finished the semester with head held high, moved off campus, and formed new friendships through her church.

She laughed at Mark's comment. "He's probably going to brainwash them. Last week, he wrote that if diversity made society better, we could further improve it by importing headhunters, cannibals, and terrorists."

Now it was my turn to grin. "He'll be the most popular man on campus."

"You should see what he's coming out with next week," Cindy said.

Mark blushed but said nothing. The server preempted further conversation by bringing our food and commanding us to enjoy it.

"Thank you," Mark said. "I shall endeavor to do so."

The server gave him a what-planet-do-you-come-from look but departed without comment. I could see what had drawn Cindy to Mark—his reflection of her own stubborn streak that she'd unfortunately inherited from me. I hoped it wouldn't land them in too much trouble with school authorities.

The food proved edible, and we attacked it without talking while the babble of student conversations, loud music, and clatter of dishes echoed around us.

While we relaxed over refills of Cokes and coffee, Cindy brought up the subject I dreaded. "Daddy, today's paper told about your finding Professor Fortier. What's that going to mean for you?"

I sighed. "Nothing, I hope. It's a police matter, and I really don't know anything about it."

She gave me a stern look. "You're not going to investigate it, are you? I came close to losing you last fall."

"The only plan I have is to keep teaching history." To change the subject, I asked, "How's the car?"

She drives Faith's decade-old Camry. To keep Cindy in school and give her a small nest egg on graduation, we have to keep the old car working.

"Oh, *Daddy*." She wrinkled her nose. "The car's doing fine. Oil and filter change aren't due for another thousand miles."

Not a bad answer, even if she spoke it in that special tone daughters reserve for overly protective parents.

Cindy turned to Mark and said, "If my father lived on Pike's Peak, he'd buy flood insurance."

"But not on Everest," I said. "That would be overdoing it."

Mark greeted the exchange with a smile.

"Will you be home for Valentine's Day?" I asked Cindy. Schools in our state take a holiday on the Monday closest to Valentine's Day. No one seems to know why.

Cindy looked at Mark before answering. "I don't know, Daddy. It depends on a lot of things …"

"It's fine either way," I said. "You're always welcome, but do what's best for you."

I parted from them then with a hug for her and a handshake for Mark, thinking privately that he looked like a pretty good specimen.

As my old Honda purred westward along the Interstate, my orchestra returned with the dramatic opening chords to the Grieg Piano Concerto No. 1. I used my voice recorder to make notes for further research, but my mood followed the sun on its downward path. Cindy's nonconformist streak was bound to work against her with the university administration.

She'd shown that streak at her high school graduation. Her principal forbade her mentioning God or Jesus in her valedictorian speech and required her to submit a verbatim copy for approval. She fumed about that at home, but at school she showed sweetness and light. She submitted a speech filled with the usual graduation clichés, ending with pabulum patriotism and an admonition to live lives worthy of our national anthem. Her manuscript closed with the note, "Quote one stanza of 'The Star-Spangled Banner.'"

Her principal assumed she meant the first stanza. But she actually quoted the fourth, with its plethora of religious references: "the heav'n rescued land ... praise the Power that hath made & preserv'd us a nation ... this be our motto—'In God is our Trust' ..." So despite the principal's censorship, Cindy reminded the audience that our nation's religious heritage was not merely stated, but flaunted, in words established as our national anthem by act of Congress.

There was nothing the principal could do about it without exposing himself as a politically correct idiot. But Cindy would have no such leverage against the state university, so I worried about where her stubbornness might lead.

I tried to shake off the depression by recalling the pleasures of fruitful research and meeting with Cindy and her friend. But maybe I don't have enough imagination. Each mile of highway brought me closer to the lingering threat of Clyde Staggart, the unresolved circumstances of Mitra Fortier's death, and the unanswered question of why she thought my job was threatened.

My emotions hit bottom about sunset as I parked the Honda in my driveway. They stayed on bottom when I went inside. The empty house and its silent piano made life seem devoid of purpose, with my teaching history the only slender thread of hope. Beyond that, I felt again that disturbing premonition of unseen powers forcing me in directions I didn't want to go.

Then the doorbell rang.

I opened the hardwood main door and looked out through the transparent storm door at Cynthia Starlington. She wore a caramel-colored coat with an ocelot collar. The waves of her hair cascaded over her shoulders. Her late-model Lexus rested at the curb.

My internal orchestra switched immediately to a reprise of Artie Shaw's liquid clarinet.

Cynthia's lipstick was smeared where she'd been biting her lip. "Press, I have to talk to you. The police have been just awful."

"Not here," I said. "The campus rumor mill mustn't find out you visited me at home. Especially this late in the day."

Her hands flew to her hips. "I'm a grown woman, and I'll go wherever I like."

I made no effort to unlatch the storm door. "You don't know the local gossips. I'll meet you on neutral territory. Do you know Goolock's? Find a table there, and I'll meet you by accident in about fifteen minutes."

Goolock's was a combination donut shop, grill and convenience store halfway between the campus and downtown. The owners were a middle-aged couple who'd immigrated from China about thirty years ago. The name came from their selling of lottery tickets. Mrs. Lee always wished the lottery customers good luck, but in her imperfect English it came out "Goo' lock." The customers began calling the shop Goolock's, and the owners adopted the name in good spirit. Their children, of course, had assimilated with perfect English. Their son was valedictorian of his class at Overton and, in his valedictory speech, had brought down the house by claiming that the name Lee qualified him as one of the First Families of Virginia. Their daughter, now in our junior class, was well on her way toward honors.

Cynthia's tight-clamped jaw showed disapproval, but she marched back to her Lexus and drove away. My internal clarinet was replaced by a grotesque duet by a bass violin and a piccolo.

I stood there with mixed feelings. I didn't want to get involved in police business, even as an advisor. But behind me I felt the sadness of the silent piano, and in spite of my better judgment, I knew I'd enjoy talking with Cynthia. She had a quick mind, and she wasn't a bit hard to look at. A vision of light reflecting from the golden tips of her hair appeared before me. I spent the next ten minutes mentally kicking myself, but then I cranked up the Honda and headed for Goolock's.

After exchanging pleasantries with the Lees, I bought donuts and coffee and joined Cynthia at one of the four tables. A plastic cup of Sprite sat in front of her, and she'd nibbled at something that looked like a cream cheese sandwich. I didn't like our table's location in front of a plate glass window, but the convenience store's shelves shielded us from internal observation. At the sight of Cynthia, my soft clarinet music returned.

Cynthia looked at me through worried eyes. "The police questioned me today, Press. It was awful."

"It's seldom fatal," I said. "What did they ask?"

"They asked me about my ... my quarrel with Professor Fortier." Cynthia toyed with her sandwich. "I told them everything I could remember, but they kept trying to make me say there was more to it than there was."

"It's their way to keep you talking," I said. "Sooner or later, a guilty person will slip up. You have nothing to worry about if you're innocent. Besides, Professor Fortier may have died of natural causes." I tried very hard to believe what I was saying.

Cynthia made a face. "They certainly questioned me as if it were murder. And that man—Staggart, I think they called him. He looked at me like ... like he was going to attack me physically."

"He likes to lean on people," I said, "but he can't do anything without evidence. If there's nothing more than your shouting match with Mitra, you're home free."

My soft clarinet kept weaving quiet melodies.

Cynthia looked at the floor. "There is one other thing." She looked up, anxiously searching my eyes. "After my ... *scene* with Professor Fortier, I mailed her a letter. I said I meant every word I'd said to her, and I'd carry that feeling to the grave."

My internal clarinet glissandoed into something high, shrill and squeaky.

"For a salutatorian," I said, "you have an unusually low quotient of common sense."

A tear rolled down from one of her dark eyes. "I know it was a dumb thing to do. I wouldn't have done it if I hadn't been so angry."

I knew what Staggart would say: *You wouldn't have killed her if you hadn't been so angry.* But I didn't say it. Cynthia looked at me like a hurt child, so I asked instead, "Did you post it in the campus mail office or downtown?" I might be able to finagle an unstamped letter out of a student mail clerk.

"In the main post office downtown," she said. She knew as well as I did what that meant.

I grimaced. "Then you'll have to wait for the police to question you about it. When they do, tell them that was your way of dissipating your anger and that once you'd done it, the anger was gone." The police might even believe that story if she batted those dark eyes often enough.

She turned them on me now as she reached over and squeezed my hand. "Thank you, Press. You're a good friend."

My hand tingled and my mental clarinet resumed its liquid tones.

I was about to tell Cynthia she should start being a friend to herself, but a carload of young people drew up in front. Fortunately, they were too busy bantering among themselves to look inside the store.

"Some of those kids are students," I said. "There's no telling what kind of rumors they'll start if they see us together."

While the students stood around ragging each other, I dumped my coffee and uneaten donuts into a receptacle and ducked behind a row of shelves. Armed with a candy bar, I arrived at the cash register as the students entered.

"No lott'ry ticket?" Mrs. Lee asked as she checked me out.

"Not tonight," I said.

She knew very well that I never bought one, but she always asked, and I always gave the same answer.

"Goo' lock anyway," she said.

As I drove away into the night, Cynthia Starlington still sat by the window, nibbling at her cream cheese sandwich and looking like a beautiful orphan. I didn't know if I was angrier with her for getting into trouble or with myself for being foolish enough to sympathize with her. At home, I solved the supper problem with another ham sandwich. At least I had the candy bar for dessert.

Afterwards, while my musicians plinked away at something oriental that I didn't recognize, I chided myself for even listening to Cynthia's story. The lingering fragrance of her perfume on my hand where she'd squeezed it didn't improve my mood. I consoled myself, though, that listening to her did not constitute involvement.

Then I did another dumb thing. I turned on the television to station KLYE. The same bright graphics raced around the screen to the same fanfare, climaxed by the same explosion and the same incongruous bell-ring. Then Francie LaBouche emerged from the nuclear cloud. Tonight she wore a different chorus-girl outfit and a different color of grease on her lips. She spoke with the voice of one crying in the wilderness, "Make straight the way of the media."

"Here is the latest on the mysterious death of Professor Mitra Fortier," she orated. The visual changed to a still photo of Clyde Staggart, whose black eyes glowered at the camera.

Francie's voice-over continued, "Captain Staggart of Homicide said this afternoon that, pending the autopsy, they have to keep open the possibility of murder. Officially, he remains neutral on that question, but he says the deceased had a suspicious bump on the back of her head. Reliable sources, though, say he has identified several 'persons of interest' in the event the autopsy indicates foul play."

I didn't have to ask who one of those persons would be.

My internal musicians responded with the mocking growl of blues played Clyde McCoy-style on a wah-wah muted trumpet.

CHAPTER 9

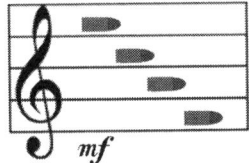

Sunday morning brought more sub-freezing weather with another ear-slicing wind off the plains. Still depressed, I fumbled through breakfast and skimmed through the Sunday paper. I skipped the front-page coverage of Mitra Fortier entirely. Between the funnies and the sports, I found a report that a company called Western Admini-Med was under investigation for Medicare fraud. Nothing unusual, except that the company was a subsidiary of one that had Gordon Samstag as Chairman of the Board. Samstag was quoted that his companies would cooperate fully and appropriate action would be taken.

After that, I inspected my two suits. The blue one needed more touches from a Sharpie to disguise its frayed cuffs, and the brown one wasn't far behind. I made a note to buy a brown marker pen to keep that one up to snuff. I'd have to buy new suits sooner or later, but the later I could make it, the better for Cindy's education and my solvency. Monday, Wednesday, and Friday were brown-suit days this week, which made Tuesday and Thursday blue-suit days. That meant I should wear the blue suit to church today.

Eleven o'clock found me in a rear pew in St. Mark's Grace Church. That church figured in many of my cherished memories, for Faith and I used to attend it together. During the hymns and prayers, we would hold hands and feel close to God in a way I haven't felt since her death. Going there without her brought so much pain that I'd stayed away until a couple of months ago.

Providentially, my internal musicians usually take a break during church. I hope they listen and learn something. Today, as always, the solemn organ music, the prayers and the deep harmonies of hymns renewed my consciousness of the eternal truth, order, and goodness that hold as firm bedrock beneath the transient evils of daily affairs. That knowledge doesn't make the evils less painful, but it does put them in context. I was resting in that assurance by the time Pastor Urim Tammons delivered his homily.

He began by reading from Proverbs—"A man's heart deviseth his way: but the Lord directeth his steps." He went on to say that we devise in our minds what we want to be true, and we try to build our dreams into reality. But in this fallen world, our minds are also corrupt, and what we want reality to be is often far removed from what reality actually is. So we all live to some degree in imaginary worlds, and our fantasies collapse when they collide with the Lord's reality.

That reminded me of my difficulty, at the reception, in telling what was real and what wasn't. By the time Pastor Tammons finished, he had me wondering how much of my world as I perceived it was real and how much was fantasy.

After the final "amen" today, several people stopped by to express sympathy about Mitra Fortier. Some asked if I was going to investigate, and I gave my stock answer that I only taught history. Everyone gave way as Pastor Tammons approached. He is a bit past sixty and a bit overweight, thoroughly knowledgeable and poised in his calling. I'd describe him as always sympathetic and never overbearing, but a bulldozer couldn't move him one millimeter off of principle. He was proving the ideal mentor for Mara since her conversion.

"I'm sorry about Professor Fortier," he said, "but how are you doing, Press?" He meant my whole process of grief, not just my response to the momentary trauma of Mitra's death.

"About the same," I said. "We all owe God a death."

His eyes twinkled. "What we worry about is the due date."

He is a well-read man, and we both knew we were paraphrasing an exchange between Shakespeare's Falstaff and Prince Hal.

"The process continues to unfold," he said and moved on to another parishioner.

I knew what he meant. From time to time in my grief, he'd reminded me that God wasn't through with me yet. So now he meant that I shouldn't take up residence on my present plateau.

Then the full question hit me. Did his contrast of our imagined wishes and reality mean my claim that "I just teach history" was not my final destination but only a rest stop along the way?

My musicians returned with soft strings as, across the sanctuary, Mara Thorn moved into the aisle without looking in my direction. I knew she was fighting the rumors about us, but I still felt a twinge of regret. I'd enjoyed our brief partnership last fall, and our present avoidance of each other brought its own kind of emptiness. Then Cynthia Starlington engaged Mara in conversation and made a conspicuous nod in my direction. Mara shook her head in definite negation.

I beat a quick retreat before complications could arise. I also changed my plan for lunch at a good restaurant in favor of a hasty sandwich at home. For variety, I had cheese along with the ham. My euphoria from church prevailed throughout lunch, and my internal organist cooperated by playing *Panis Angelicus*. But the phone rang as I downed my second cup of coffee. Dean-Dean's high-pitched voice sounded from the receiver.

"Professor Barclay, I want to see you in my office tomorrow morning between classes. When are you free?" It would never occur to him to look at the schedule.

"Ten o'clock," I said. "What are we going to talk about?"

His voice climbed to a higher pitch. "There's no preparation needed. I'll tell you when you get here."

"Okay," I said, and he rang off.

That was not good news. Our annual contracts would be in our campus mailboxes sometime this week. Would Dean-Dean tell me I had no contract for next year? Or had he scheduled the meeting to make me worry about it? In either case, he'd make sure he had witnesses.

I decided not to let it worry me, but I worried anyway. Since Faith's death, teaching history is my life. And as I keep saying, I'd make a lousy used car salesman. For consolation, I kept telling myself that even if I lost my job, there was nothing to get me entangled in the investigation of Mitra's death.

Nevertheless, that insidious canker of worry remained as I tried to lose myself in professional reading, in this case the late M. Stanton Evans' *Blacklisted by History*. I was shocked by the fact that essential documents about the Joe McCarthy hearings had disappeared from the National Archives. Documents are subject to interpretation, but each document itself is a historical fact. With original sources for that important study removed, we might never achieve accurate understanding. Maybe that's what someone intended.

Hours later, at sunset, my worry still goaded me like a steel cocklebur in my brain. Then I heard a car drive up outside. It stopped right in front of my house.

Flashing red and blue lights reflected through the windows and a heavy pounding sounded at the front door. I opened the hardwood door and saw, through the transparent storm door, the angry face of Captain Clyde Staggart. The basset-faced detective I knew only as Dogface stood behind him.

Staggart pounded again on the door.

"You still haven't discovered doorbells?" I asked. "There's one three inches to the right of the door." That had been a contention the last time he came visiting.

"Open up," he bellowed.

"Do you have a warrant?" I asked.

He glowered. "I don't need a warrant to talk to you."

"Then talk," I said. "I can hear you through the door."

"No go," he said. "We can talk inside, or you can come down to the station."

"I'll meet you halfway," I said. "If you turn off the flashing lights on your kiddie-car, you can come in for the purpose of conversation." The lights were his way of getting me in bad with the neighbors. They'd already accomplished their mission, so turning them off was a belated effort at damage control.

Staggart looked like he wanted to argue, but Dogface headed out to the car and doused the lights.

"Welcome to my humble abode," I said, and opened the door.

Staggart marched in and took one of the two comfortable chairs. Dogface took the other one. I pulled up one of the straight-back hardwood chairs and straddled it backwards, resting my chin on my hands on the chair back. Staggart stared at me for several seconds with a malevolent grin.

"You didn't come to play gin rummy," I said. "What's your business?"

"Business, Press?" Staggart's grin widened. "You're known all over town as a good family man. Now tell me about your long-standing affair with Mitra Fortier."

CHAPTER 10

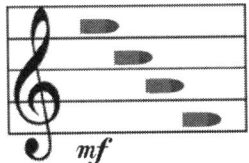

I admit being stunned. It's one thing to be accused of something within the bounds of possibility. I expect people to scan my essays on history for plagiarism, and I expect every year or two to be accused of unfair grading. I stand prepared to defend myself against logical claims like those. But it's quite another thing to be accused of something that never crossed my mind. So I sat there with my mouth open while Staggart watched me with a knowing leer.

After a long silence, he spoke again: "All right, Mr. Virtuous Professor. What do you say to that?"

I took a deep breath and answered with a calm I didn't feel. "Two things. First, I have never had an untoward relationship with Professor Fortier. Beyond that, I exercise my Fifth Amendment right to remain silent."

Staggart tried again. "I suppose there was nothing 'untoward' between you and your little Wiccan last fall?"

"Fifth Amendment," I said.

Still leering, Staggart turned to Dogface. "This guy is a regular Casanova, Don Juan, and Bluebird all rolled into one."

With rare presence of mind, I refrained from correcting either his mispronunciation of Bluebeard or his confusion of that mythical

61

wife-murderer with mere seducers. Silently, I awarded myself a medal for discretion.

Dogface also made no comment, but he did look uncomfortable.

Staggart stood and fired a final rhetorical shot. "You'll tell us all about it, Lover Boy, at a time and place of our choosing."

He stalked out with the unspeaking Dogface close behind. This, in itself, was a minor victory for me. In our last few encounters, Staggart had left with a warning to "Keep your nose clean, Press," and I had said, "I always do—I thought you'd remember that." I suppose he got tired of my reminding him of our contrasting departures from the active Army—me with an honorable discharge and him with a forced resignation in lieu of a court martial.

When I heard the door close behind them, I went over and locked it. They drove away with lights flashing, but at least they didn't turn on their siren. I searched under the chair cushions to make sure they hadn't planted anything, then plopped down in the chair Dogface had vacated. With my musicians playing something dissonant, I reviewed what I knew of Clyde Staggart.

As I'd known him long ago, he was corrupt and vengeful but technically competent. So I had a formidable adversary in his accusation of an affair and in the attempt to have Bruno Pinkle pin a felony on me. So why couldn't he solve the Laila Sloan murder last fall?

I sat and brooded about Staggart's new accusation until full darkness sent the outside temperature nose-diving into a freezing Midwestern winter night. I had no idea where the accusation had come from or how to fight it. I'd never touched Mitra Fortier except perhaps to help her on with her coat. She was not a hugger, and she certainly was no flirt. On the other hand, plenty of people had seen her with Faith and me at concerts and dinners. So the campus gossips would interpret what they had seen as evidence of much more they had not seen.

Staggart's accusation also raised a new possibility about my interview with Dean-Dean tomorrow. Just thinking about Dean-Dean called up my internal bassoon. Our glorious Vice President for Academic Affairs always believes the person who gets to him first, and no amount of evidence can convince him of anything different. Staggart had taken advantage of that last fall to plant several poisonous accusations against me.

I could do nothing about that, so I focused on the story linking me romantically with Mitra. I could find no reason the story should have started and no way for me to fight it.

Several hours later, I realized I really didn't know much about Mitra Fortier. All the conversations I'd shared with her and Faith never reached beneath the surface. The two of them would chatter about other faculty members or about music, or maybe Mitra would mention a research project. But never once, so far as I could remember, had she ever talked about herself. For all I knew, her life might have begun the day she joined the Overton University faculty.

The one source where I could begin filling that vacuum was her college personnel record, but the only way I could examine it required unauthorized entry to the Executive Center. Getting caught would cost me my job, and the one time I'd done it, I'd almost gotten caught.

Once again, I felt unseen forces crowding me in a direction I didn't wish to go. So I retrieved my running shoes from my closet and my black jogging suit from the washing machine. Last fall, the police had searched my house for that suit, hoping to prove I was the black-suited runner who'd violated crime-scene tape at Laila Sloan's house. But they didn't look in the washing machine. I still couldn't afford for them to find it, so I kept it there, taking it out only when I washed other clothes. The latex surgical gloves I'd used then to avoid leaving fingerprints were still in the pockets.

At midnight, dressed in that black jogging suit and a black toboggan cap, I eased out my back door and through midblock garbage-truck alleys to the walkway up to the campus. At the campus circle, I checked to see that the college's one night watchman, Elmo Koonz, was nowhere in sight. Then I moved through unlighted areas to the back door of the Executive Center. My cheerful musicians accompanied me with the funeral march from Chopin's B-flat Minor Sonata, which might turn out to be appropriate for my employment prospects.

The pass key I'd lifted from Dean-Dean's office last fall opened the door without a problem. So far, so good. If I were discovered at this point, I could claim I found the door open and went to investigate. But that excuse would evaporate the second I entered Mrs. Dunwiddie's office between the dean's and president's offices.

I took a deep breath and inserted the pass key into the office door. It turned easily, and the door opened without a sound. I silently thanked the janitor ... uh ... *Custodial Associate*, as he is called since the Great Renaming ... for astute use of graphite and oil. Gingerly, as careful of each step as I'd been long ago on night patrols, I eased into the office.

One step ... two steps ... three ...

Then everything happened at once. A dark-clad form leaped out of nowhere, seized my arm in a judo hold, and threw me face down on the floor. My breath went out with a whoosh. Before I could move, the assailant was on top of me with my arm twisted up behind my shoulders and a knee boring into my kidney.

A whispered voice hissed, "Don't make a sound."

Pain wrenched through my shoulder as my arm twisted higher and the knee dug farther into my kidney. My lungs struggled to draw breath but lost the battle. I sank into oxygen debt.

"Who are you?" the voice hissed. "What are you doing here?"

CHAPTER 11

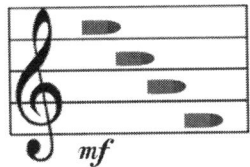

"Who are you?" the voice hissed again. The knee ground deeper into my back.

My lungs broke the expansion barrier, and I gasped several deep breaths. The pain in my twisted arm and back held steady but did not increase. I took several more breaths and decided I would live.

"Who are you?" the voice whispered again.

"I'm Walter Gieseking," I said. "I'm a concert pianist, and I'm looking for a Steinway grand piano." As if on cue, my internal musicians drummed out the percussive opening to Beethoven's *Waldstein* Sonata.

"Press, you idiot," whispered Mara's voice, "Gieseking died in nineteen fifty-six." Trust her to remember details like that.

"I'm his ghost," I said.

"You'll be a ghost if you keep burglarizing buildings and not paying attention to your surroundings."

"I suppose you're here on night watchman duty," I said. "Now if you'll give me back my arm and extract your knee from my kidney, let's decide what we're both doing here and get it done before we get caught and thrown in jail."

The knee moved and the pressure disappeared from my arm. I sat up and tested my extremities. They all worked, so I decided I'd suffered no permanent damage. Except to my ego. I'd been pinned by a woman five inches shorter and fifty pounds lighter than I.

She moved, quick and lithe, into a kneeling position beside me.

"How did you get in?" I asked. "I'm the one with the pass key."

"You lent it to me last fall. Did you think I'd be foolish enough not to duplicate it?"

"I stand corrected," I said.

She laughed softly. "On the contrary, Cupcake, you are not standing. You are sitting, which is a promotion from your previous position." She was as much a nit-picker for exact detail as I was. And she'd used the nickname given me last fall by a waitress who'd trumped my wisecrack with a better one. Another shot to my ego.

"Whatever we're doing here," I said, "we'd better do it before Elmo Koonz's conscience prods him into making his rounds. I'm interested in Mitra Fortier's personnel record."

"That and maybe a few others," she said. "You go first, and I'll keep watch."

My limbs creaked a bit as I stood, but Mara sprang up like an Olympic gymnast and took her post at the window. I put on my trifocals, which fortunately had been in a plastic case in my pocket, and I fished a penlight from another pocket. I'd put a red filter on it so as not to interfere with my night vision and to make it less likely to be seen from outside the building. I found the filing cabinet keys in Mrs. Dunwiddie's desk drawer and soon had Mitra Fortier's record in front of me.

Its contents were routine, nothing more. She was forty years old. She'd been born in Iowa but grew up and finished high school in Cloverdale, just south of Overton City. She'd earned a B.S. degree at our state university. Afterwards, she was out of school for a couple of years, then re-entered and worked straight through to her PhD in physics. All her recommendations came from graduate school, none from any employers during her out-of-school years. She'd joined the Overton faculty ten years ago, and that was that.

The only unusual item was that the surname Cochran had been added to her undergraduate transcript and then lined out. I knew she'd had a short marriage that ended in divorce, but I'd never heard any details. No documents in the file shed any further light on the subject.

I laid the file on Mrs. Dunwiddie's desk and relieved Mara at the window. My musicians played something soothing with strings. The well-lighted campus circle showed no movement, proving that even student night owls had sense enough to come in from the cold. I could hear the quiet sibilance of Mara's shifting papers and the occasional opening of another file cabinet. She had a red-filtered flashlight, too—another relic of her military training, I supposed. She seemed to be taking forever.

"How many files are you reading?" I whispered. "If we stay much longer, we'll have to pay rent."

"Last one," she whispered back.

I heard the file cabinet close. When I turned, I saw her returning the keys to Mrs. Dunwiddie's desk.

"Look," I said, "I know why I'm here, but why are you doing this?"

"I could ask you the same," she said.

"I asked you first." Trust me to find a brilliant comeback.

She sighed. "It's complicated. But let me tell you now that I enjoyed working with you last fall. You've been a good friend, and—I'll admit it now—I'm going to miss you."

Her words struck like hammer blows. I struggled for calm as I asked, "Which one of us is going somewhere?"

Another sigh. "Didn't you know? Faculty contracts were in the campus mail office yesterday. I didn't get one, and I'm meeting with Dean-Dean at ten Monday morning. It looks like I've been terminated."

A familiar hot brick took up residence in my stomach. "I'm meeting with him then, too. I didn't check my box Saturday."

Even in the dark, I could tell she spoke through clenched teeth. "I haven't been this angry since he accused us of ... of you-know-what."

I did know what—Dean-Dean's Staggart-inspired accusation that we'd had a one-night stand at my house. But a different thought occurred. "I don't think Dean-Dean has nerve enough to fire both of us in the same meeting. Not even with handpicked witnesses. Let's take a look."

My pass key opened Dean-Dean's office, and I moved to his desk. It was not locked, and I opened the main drawer. It contained two nine-by-twelve manila envelopes, fastened with clasps but not sealed. One was addressed to me, the other to Mara.

I gave her hers without comment. Each of us withdrew the contents and studied them with our filtered lights.

"I'm new to this, Press," she said. "What does it mean?"

She handed me some papers, and I made a hurried glance through them. "It means we're both contracted for another year," I said. "Both contracts are signed by President Cantwell, and they're binding as soon as we sign them. They even gave us the ten percent raise the trustees voted for faculty last week."

She breathed angrily in and out. "So Dean-Dean is making us think we've been fired, and then on Monday he'll give us a warning and hand us our contracts. I'd ... I'd like to catch him in a dark alley."

I had never seen her so angry. I knew she'd studied judo and karate, but I'd never seen her use either until my ill-fated encounter with her tonight. Thinking what she could do to Dean-Dean, I could almost pity him. Almost, but not quite. I was as angry as she was.

"I have a better idea," I said. "These contracts are binding the minute we sign them. So we sign them now, keep our copies, and put the return copy in the campus mail office first thing tomorrow ... uh ..." I looked at my watch, which showed one-thirty. "... Uh, this morning. Our contracts will be returned with everyone else's, and who's to say someone didn't slip up and put ours in the mail office?"

Mara laughed, quietly. "That plan is worthy of Machiavelli."

I joined the *sotto voce* laugh. "He said it was better to be feared than loved ..."

"Because 'men love as they please,'" she quoted, "but 'fear as the prince pleases ...'"

Trust her to be able to quote anything she'd ever read.

We signed the contracts and returned them to their envelopes, then restored the dean's office to the condition in which we'd found it.

"We're pushing our luck," I said. "We've got to get out of here."

"All right," she said, "but there's something else you need to know. Staggart is spreading the most awful story about you and Professor Fortier."

The hot brick in my stomach turned to lead. "He questioned me about it earlier this evening. I pled the Fifth."

Her voice grew earnest. "I need to talk to you about it. I have to know what's going on."

I knew better than to ask why, and I felt time and our chances of escaping undetected ticking away.

"Not here," I said, "and I know you'll rule out my house or your apartment. So where and when?"

I could hear her breathing impatiently. "Go to the alley behind your house. I'll pick you up there in about twenty minutes."

"All right," I said, "but why does Staggart's story that *I* had an affair with Mitra Fortier have *you* upset."

Her voice grew impatient. "That's easy. He claims I was involved in it."

CHAPTER 12

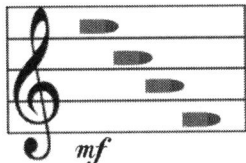

My ears were only half frozen when Mara drove up in her used Buick. Some of the trustees had gotten together to replace her car that the mob destroyed last semester. They may have been intimidated because the students held a mass demonstration in her favor, but in any event they gave her wheels. They told her to choose any car on the lot at Emory Estes Experienced Autos, owned by the trustee the lot was named for. She rejected the Cadillacs and BMWs and chose a five-year-old baby Buick.

"I didn't know they made Buicks this small," I said as we drove away. My musicians launched into something tempestuous from Gustav Mahler.

"This car does everything I need," Mara said.

"Where are we going?" I asked.

"Where we can talk without feeding the Blatant Beast." She drove across the river and up the eastern hills. There she turned into the familiar park at the edge of the bluffs, the one with a magnificent view of town and river valley and the university in its commanding position on the opposite hills.

"I think you've been here before," she said as she parked facing the view of the valley. It now showed only scattered lights on a blanket of black.

Credit her with understatement. I'd brought her up here last fall for a take-out donut breakfast between the two burglaries we committed en route to solving the Laila Sloan murder. I'd introduced her to the view and my dream of a highly visible cross atop the planned fine arts building, and she'd explained Wicca to me with chocolate donut smudges on her face. There'd be no donuts now at two-thirty in the morning. The park had a few lights, but I saw her only as a silhouette against them. My musicians abandoned Mahler and shifted into some playful pizzicato by Benjamin Britten.

"Tell me about you and Mitra Fortier," Mara said.

I made a face, not that she could see it in the dim light. "All I know is that Staggart accused me of having a long-standing affair with Mitra. I denied it and then took the Fifth Amendment. That's all I know."

She turned to face me, her tone accusing. "But you told Dr. Sheldon and me that you and she and Faith often went out together."

"Mitra was Faith's friend. That's all there was to it."

"Staggart made it sound like a *ménage à trois*."

"Faith wouldn't have put up with it if Mitra had ever flirted with me."

Dimly visible in the faint light, Mara pointed her forefinger at me. "You swear that there was nothing between you and Mitra?"

My anger surged. "I swear there was nothing untoward between Mitra and me—or between Faith and Mitra, for that matter. And if you keep bugging me about it, I'm going to swear like you never heard before."

She laughed and settled back in the driver's seat. "I didn't think there was, but I had to know."

My anger still spoke. "All you know now is that I've denied it."

She grew serious. "No, Press. I know you're telling the truth because I know you."

A deep basic honesty in me wanted to argue that she didn't know me that well. In an absolute sense, there's a lot of dishonesty in me. Maybe that's why I struggle so hard to learn and teach what is actually true instead of what I would like to believe. And in this fallen world, there's scarcely a day I don't have to suppress jungle impulses. But this was no time for total confession.

So I said, "Now tell me how Staggart thought you were involved."

"It's so silly." She shook her head. "He claimed again that you and I had an affair last fall and Mitra got jealous. He said she confronted me, we had a shouting match, and I threatened her life. I don't have to tell you that none of it ever happened."

"What did you say to Staggart?"

"I asked him which insane asylum he visited to get those ideas. He laughed and said he had good evidence. I told him he couldn't have evidence of something that never happened, and then I took the Fifth."

"He's not above manufacturing evidence," I said. "I suppose he brought Dogface with him?"

"The man who quoted Keats to you?"

"That's the one. He not only looks like a dog, he follows Staggart around like one."

"You're too hard on him. He looked pained while Staggart was questioning me, and at times I thought he would intervene." Her voice softened. "His name is Duggan Hahn."

"How did you find that out?" What I really wondered was why.

"I asked Sergeant Spencer. When a Homicide detective can quote Keats, it's worth knowing who he is. Spencer says he's a good man who doesn't go along with everything Staggart does."

I grunted. "If he doesn't, he gives a good imitation of it. Look, we need to figure out what this new situation means for us."

Even in the dark I could tell she looked away. "It means the Blatant Beast is loose, and there's nothing we can do to cage him. Staggart will leak those stories. People will invent other things beyond that ..."

"There's one thing we can do. We can find out where Staggart got his information. We started that at the only place we knew to start—Mitra Fortier's personnel records."

Mara sighed her disgust. "I didn't find anything there."

"Neither did I, but I can question a few faculty members about her. I've already talked to Weldon Combes and Freda Broyles."

"What did you learn?"

"They weren't forthcoming, but I think there's more to forthcome. I'll try again. Meanwhile, why don't you see if you can get anything out of Sergeant Spencer."

Her head snapped around to face me. "Why me? I have no special 'in' with him."

She seemed as defensive as she'd been in our first meeting last fall.

"Division of labor," I said. "I'm interviewing faculty because I know them better than you do. You and Sergeant Spencer finished the Laila Sloan case as allies."

"Maybe Dr. Sheldon can help with computer research," she said.

I gathered that meant the Spencer issue was settled. "Dr. Sheldon will love it. He's bored stiff except for reading." I pointed my penlight at my watch. Three o'clock. "We'd better call it a night and catch a couple of winks before classes tomorrow. Not to mention our glorious interview with Dean-Dean."

She turned the car around and headed back across town. "Where do I drop you? Same place?"

"Same place," I said, "and keep it quiet. Don't forget to post the return copy of your contract in the mail office before class."

"I'll remember." She ground the answer out between clenched teeth.

*****

She eased the car to a stop at the mouth of the alley behind my house. I hopped out and pushed the door almost shut. She leaned across and held it, driving with the other hand until I lost sight of her around a corner. I never did hear the door close.

Inside, a few minutes later, I considered the night's work. Mara and I had gotten by with another burglary, and it felt good to work with her again. The pleasure was short-lived, for the odds against our success rolled over me like the tread of a tank.

The campus gossip mill, the college dean, and the entire Homicide Division were arrayed against us.

And we didn't even know what we were looking for.

CHAPTER 13

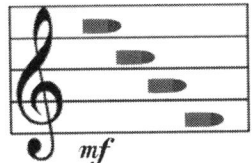

The alarm clock jangled me half-awake at seven the next morning. A shower lifted me to three-quarters. A dazed look at the calendar told me it was a brown-suit day. I had a nine o'clock class in Renaissance History of Ideas and—oh joy!—a ten o'clock session with Dean-Dean. Once on campus, I dropped the return copy of my contract in the mail office.

My mailbox contained a notice reflecting Dean-Dean's unusual approach to the English language:

> *A memorial service for Professor Mitra Fortier will be held in the old auditorium at 10:45 Tuesday, all faculty must attend because a faculty meeting will follow. If any faculty member has a conflict they must cancel and attend.*
> Dean Billig
> Vice President for Academic Affairs

By noon, some phantom grammarian would post that message on the mail room board with the errors circled in red. I don't know who does that, but Dean-Dean thinks I do.

In my nine o'clock class I tried to introduce the students, gently, to the fact that people haven't always gone about the business of thinking in the same way. That's because the Medieval and Renaissance picture of the universe was perceived mostly by comparison while our modern picture is approached largely by cause and effect. I was just getting started when Cynthia Starlington slipped into the classroom and took a seat in the back. But I persevered, drawing my usual blackboard diagram of the Ptolemaic cosmos, the centerpiece of the Renaissance body of knowledge.

For once I had the students' complete attention. They'd never heard that the Ptolemaic system had any relevance to the way they'd been taught to think. The idea that there were other ways to go about thinking came as a shock. So it was a good class right down to the summary, during which Cynthia slipped out as quietly as she'd come in.

My cerebral orchestra celebrated the class with trumpets and timpani while I dragged my reluctant carcass to the Executive Center and my interview with Dean-Dean.

Mara was there before me in Mrs. Dunwiddie's office. Mrs. D is a gentle late-middle-aged lady who does her job and tries to stay out of trouble. She busied herself shuffling papers on her desk. That was not a good sign.

Dean-Dean's door opened presently, and the little man himself beckoned us in. My internal orchestra promptly launched into a bassoon concerto. Something about Dean-Dean always brings up that bassoon. I've wondered if my cerebral musicians associate the words *bassoon* and *buffoon*, but that is a question beyond my expertise.

As we entered, I pressed the "Record" button on my voice recorder. Two hardwood chairs awaited us in front of Dean-Dean's desk, and Mara's boss, Dathan Hormah, was seated to our rear. My chairman was not present, presumably because he is not as cooperative as Professor Hormah. It looked like bringing the recorder was a good idea.

From behind his desk, Dean-Dean glared at Mara and me in turn. He began in his high-pitched voice, "I've brought you here to talk once again about your job performance."

Mara preempted. "I would like to talk to President Cantwell."

Dean-Dean blinked and said, "That's not possible. President Cantwell is in Minnesota on a fund-raising tour."

"I didn't realize he'd taken up ice fishing," I said.

President Cantwell is an ardent fisherman. He spends weeks away from the campus on fund-raising tours. He does raise money, and he's making good progress toward funding the planned fine arts building. But he always takes his fishing tackle, and it's suspected that he spends more time catching fish than catching funds.

At my comment, Dean-Dean pointed a finger at me. "I am fed up with your facetious obstructionism."

"*Bon appétit*," I said.

Dean-Dean's mouth opened and closed, but no sound came out. Behind me, Dathan Hormah cleared his throat. Call me a knight out of season, but my main objective was to draw fire away from Mara.

Dean-Dean finally got his voice back and started in on me again. "You've been uncooperative ever since I've known you—"

"Could you please clarify?" I asked.

He cited my role in the faculty's defeating an administration proposal to abolish our core of required courses and make all courses elective. Then he mentioned my leading opposition to the administration's attempt to drop chemistry from the nursing curriculum. Faculty voted to keep the required chemistry course, but the administration subverted it by taking the course away from the Chemistry Department and bringing in a high school teacher to teach it separately.

There are reasons I'm the campus pariah. But after the nursing problem I've mostly tried to stay out of the line of fire. Teaching history is my life, and I wouldn't be much good at anything else.

Dean-Dean was just getting warmed up. "When President Cantwell told your department that we were 'on the very cusp of history,' you asked if that made us cuspidors ..."

A suppressed giggle emerged from Mara.

Dean-Dean glowered at her and plunged on. "When we modernized the names of things on campus, you satirized it with that idiotic contest. And you sabotaged our requiring faculty to take that personality test—"

"Wait a minute," I said. "I didn't do anything about anyone's taking that test."

Dean-Dean pointed his finger again. "You marked answer *A* to every question on it."

"You told the faculty we had to *take* the test," I said. "You didn't say we had to *pass* it."

He was breathing fast now. "And you led other people to do what you did."

"No, sir," I said. "I made no effort to influence anybody. A couple of people looked to see why I'd finished so quickly, and they talked to their neighbors. I never said a word to anyone."

"But the end result was that more than half the faculty turned in papers with nothing except answer *A*. How do you expect me to know my faculty if the tests are invalid?"

"You might try talking to them," I said.

Dean-Dean knew when to change the subject. "I also want to talk to you two about your personal conduct."

"What's wrong with my conduct?" Mara demanded.

"Please." Dean-Dean raised a hand. "Overton University is on the annual budget of more than one hundred churches. We cannot afford anything that might lead them to drop us."

"Then scuttle your plan for coed dorms," I said.

Dean-Dean tried to draw himself up to full height, which proved difficult while he was sitting down. "Our consultant says coed dorms will bring in more students."

"Then fire the consultant," I said. "We all know the trouble kids get into."

"You still haven't answered my question," Mara said.

Dean-Dean looked pained. "We have previously discussed your spending the night in Professor Barclay's house."

Mara's eyes blazed. "You know very well I found him unconscious on the floor and stayed to take care of him through the night. Nothing else happened."

Dean-Dean put his nose in the air. "Be that as it may, there are new stories circulating about you two and … and the late Professor Fortier."

"Those stories are false," I said, "and you could only have heard them from Captain Clyde Staggart. You ought to know by now that everything he's told you about me is false."

"I have no reason to doubt Captain Staggart's veracity," he said.

"The next time you talk to him," Mara said, "ask him why he had to leave the Army." I'd confided my story to her, and now she was defending me.

Dean-Dean blinked again. "That's immaterial. The subject of this discussion is your conduct. On questions of morality, we have to draw a line in the sandbox. I'm putting you on notice that no improper conduct by any member of this faculty will be tolerated."

He leaned back with an air of satisfaction. "Have either of you wondered about your contracts for the coming year?"

Mara and I exchanged elaborate shrugs. We looked back at Dean-Dean and said nothing.

Uncertainty appeared on his face. "Did you check your mail boxes on Saturday?"

Mara smiled. "I did, and my signed contract is on its way back to you."

"Mine is, too," I said. "Thanks for the raise."

Dean-Dean looked down and yanked his desk drawer open. He looked like he'd stumbled into a plague house.

"Did you want to talk to us about anything else?" Mara sounded all sweetness and light.

Dean-Dean sat speechless. Then he looked down and muttered, "N-n-no, I guess not." Mara rose and said, "Thank you again." She smiled at her amazed department chairman, "Have a nice day, Dr. Hormah."

I ignored Dean-Dean and followed Mara out of the office. As if on cue, my musicians turned off the bassoon and changed to soft strings. Mara and I said nothing until we cleared the Executive Center.

We rounded a corner, checked to make sure we weren't observed, and let our laughter explode. It went on and on, and I recalled the companionship of our laughter together last fall after the waitress had named me Cupcake. It was a good feeling.

When we finally stopped, Mara asked, "What do we do now?"

"We each do what we agreed on last night. Then let's meet with Dr. Sheldon tonight."

Mara nodded and headed across the campus circle to her office. I held in place, deciding what to do next.

The euphoria of our small victory over Dean-Dean faded quickly.

Clyde Staggart still threatened our reputations and perhaps our freedom.

Our investigation still lay ahead, but we had not the slightest idea of what we were investigating or how we should go about it.

CHAPTER 14

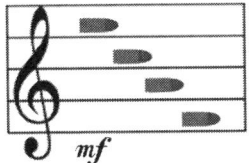

I didn't know what I was looking for, but the ticking clock told me I'd better start looking. As before, the most probable sources of helpful information were Mitra's colleagues. But it was lunch time, so the best place to find them was the campus grill.

Weldon Combes was coming out of the grill as I was going in. He stopped me and said, "Something you ought to know, Press. A couple of trustees were talking about you earlier in there."

"Which ones?" I asked.

Combes checked to see that we weren't overheard. "Emory Estes and Gordon Samstag."

Strange that Samstag should turn up this soon after I read his name in the paper. But stranger yet that two trustees would still be on campus in the week *after* their meeting.

"Were you in the group?" I asked.

"I was at the next table, but they talked pretty loud."

He paused, apparently expecting me to prompt him. I tried to wait him out, but he out-waited me. So I did prompt—"I suppose I should know what they said."

Combes resumed with enthusiasm. "They agreed that you had great talent for stirring up a hornets' nest. They wished you'd lay off and let the police handle it."

He paused again. "That's all I heard because Samstag left and Emory Estes went across the room and sat by Professor Thorn."

"Thanks," I said. "I don't know why people think I'm investigating."

He showed an I-know-better-than-that expression and headed out across campus.

Inside, I ordered a grilled cheese sandwich and coffee. The only open seat was directly across the table from Mara Thorn. She appeared deeply engaged in conversation with the husky trustee Emory Estes, who sat beside her. The other two persons at the table were composition specialists, one male and one female.

"Have a seat, Press," Estes said, his voice too loud for the occasion. "Always room for one more."

I sat and Mara recognized my presence with a nod. Nothing more. I felt a little pang inside, though I understood her reason. I looked for ways to give the Blatant Beast a false scent.

Before I could find one, the female composition specialist chimed in. "What do you think about that rocket failing in California?"

"What rocket?" I asked.

"You haven't heard? One of those multi-million-dollar things went out of control after takeoff and blew up over the Pacific. I heard it on the news a few minutes ago."

Estes made a wry face. "Our hard-earned tax dollars at work."

I wasn't interested in rockets, so I asked him, "How's the used car business?"

Estes launched into blow-by-blow descriptions of his latest sales. Accent on the *blow*. I listened with half a mind while giving primary attention to my sandwich and coffee. I'll never know how long his epic would have continued because Cynthia Starlington came by and rubbed a few circles on my back. Estes stared in unbelief.

"Hello, Cyn," I said.

"Hello, Press." Cynthia's long eyelashes fluttered a few times. "I hope you didn't mind my visiting your class. It was always one of my favorites, and I couldn't resist the temptation to hear that lecture again. You've added some new things." She rubbed a few more circles while everyone at the table watched.

"There's been some good work done in that field lately," I said.

"Got to go now." She stopped rubbing and flashed everyone a smile. All eyes followed her as she glided out of the grill.

"The last pose of summer," Mara said.

"The word is *rose*," I said.

She pushed back her chair and stood. "You take your word, and I'll take mine." She left with Emory Estes trailing close behind.

The female composition specialist filled the conversation gap. "You won't believe what one of my students wrote." I had no chance to say if I would or wouldn't because she continued, "He wrote, 'The editors of the student newspaper are not illiterate. Every one of them has a mother and a father.'"

"Remarkable," I said.

We seemed headed for normal faculty chit-chat when Steven Drisko and his wife occupied the chairs vacated by Mara and Emory Estes. Another trustee in the grill? Drisko spoke directly to me. "Professor Barclay, I don't think you've met my wife."

I stood and said, "I'm happy to meet you, Mrs. Drisko."

"Call me Brill," she said. She looked bored with everything except the cheeseburger in front of her and not too happy with that. I couldn't blame her about the cheeseburger. One drop of the grease oozing from it was enough to spoil the elaborately casual slacks she wore. They must have cost a leg or two at Neiman-Marcus or Saks Fifth Avenue, but a centipede like Drisko could spare a few appendages.

Until now, I'd only seen Brill at a distance. Here at close range she was impressive. The term "big blonde" leaped immediately to mind, but there was nothing phlegmatic about her. Every move she made showed strength and coordination. Her most distinctive features, though, were small black eyes and tightly-curled bottle-blonde hair.

I didn't have to wonder long what had brought Drisko to the grill.

He looked up and grinned. "Still not investigating, Press? I'd think another mysterious death would get your curiosity going."

I shrugged. "It's a police case. They'll make an announcement when they know something."

His grin broadened. "TV news says they've already got you and the Wiccan woman involved."

"*Former* Wiccan," I said. "We're not involved. We just happened to find the body."

Brill Drisko intervened, her voice a bit too loud. "That's getting to be a habit with you, isn't it? I learned long ago not to get involved in things that don't concern me."

"We're not involved," I said again.

Steven Drisko gave a satirical laugh. "The TV people implied a lot more than that."

"Then they implied wrong." I pushed back my chair. "Sorry, but I have to teach a class." I added as an afterthought, "I'm glad to meet you, Mrs. Drisko."

"Call me Brill," she said around a mouthful of cheeseburger.

Brillo would be more like it, I thought as I crossed the campus circle toward class. Her tightly-curled blonde hair reminded me of the spun metal swirls of a Brillo scrubbing pad, and her manner suggested she'd be just as abrasive. I don't worry much about people's private lives, but Steven Drisko's situation seemed provocative. I'd never met his first wife, but I wondered about their divorce. And I wondered where he'd latched onto a classic trophy wife like Brill.

My department chairman met me in the hallway outside my office. He looked worried. "Press, I guess you've heard about that rocket failure in California."

"Someone mentioned it in the grill," I said. I had more pressing things to think about. A line from *The Rubaiyat of Omar Khayam* leaped into my mind: "Nor heed the rumble of a distant drum!"

My chairman frowned. "That rocket may be important to the university. It belonged to one of Gordon Samstag's companies."

CHAPTER 15

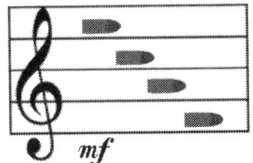

Samstag's company? That got my attention. My former distant drum now exploded like the thunder of timpani. Gordon Samstag was chairman of our board of trustees, and Overton University's solvency depended as much on trustee generosity as on government-subsidized student tuition. Any crisis that threatened a trustee therefore threatened the university. Yet from my point of view, I wondered why I kept stumbling over Samstag's name every time I turned around.

It turned out later that the rocket belonged to the U.S. government rather than one of Samstag's companies. But his company Pegasus Electronics had provided the guidance system that failed, so that amounted to the same thing.

But I had a class to teach. Still working on obscure turning points, I talked about the Peace of Wedmore. Invading Danes played havoc with the tiny kingdoms of England until King Alfred of Wessex defeated them in A.D. 878. In the peace that followed, he launched a cultural revival and the beginnings of English language literature. The small ripple of that single event grew into a tide that swept far beyond what those involved in it could imagine—yet another suggestion of a higher guiding force at the helm of history.

As always, my adrenaline was flowing by the end of the class in spite of my internal pianist's grinding out a Mozart sonata without enthusiasm. My own enthusiasm remained high, though, as I turned into my office for my scheduled office hours. I usually do professional reading unless a student shows up, and few of them do this early in the semester. But that day I only sat and worried about my nonexistent affair with Mitra Fortier. A couple of hours later, I'd still found no way to defend myself.

I was about to leave when the phone rang. This time my daughter Cindy's voice contained no sweetness.

"Daddy, I'm so mad I could ... could do something foolish."

My parental caution asserted itself. "Don't do anything until you calm down. What's wrong?"

Her voice remained tense. "You remember Mark Weston? His editorial came out in today's edition of the paper."

"I remember you said it would be better than his last one." The last one had been heretical enough.

She laughed. "It *was* better. You know how the diversity crowd talks about society as a tossed salad? The more diverse the ingredients are, the better the salad?"

"And we're not supposed to ask questions about the ingredients."

"Exactly." Cindy's earnestness overshadowed her anger. "So Mark proposed that students hold a tossed salad celebration sale."

I could see where this was going, but I waited for Cindy to tell me.

"The basic salad with lettuce and tomatoes would sell for one dollar a bowl. A serving with cat hair added would cost a dollar and a half. With cat hair and buffalo chips it would cost two dollars, and a serving with those and quinine would cost three."

"Once one grants the premise, the logic is unshakeable." My admiration for Mark soared. "But he isn't going to be very popular."

Cindy sucked in her breath. "Word leaked out in advance to some of the Residence Life Education Groups. They stole all the papers out of the campus racks and burned them right there on campus. So now nobody gets to read Mark's editorial."

"What is the university administration going to do about it?" I already knew, but thought I'd better ask.

"Nothing!" Cindy seemed to grind out her words between clenched teeth. "Not one thing! We told them it was larceny and violation of our newspaper's right to freedom of the press, and that the fire was a danger to everybody." She paused. "Do you know what they said?"

"Something about 'You have to understand the provocations,' I'd guess."

"How did you know, Daddy? That's exactly what they said. And they're not going to do one ... one *cussed* thing."

Her use of the pronoun *we*, as in "we told them," sent up the red flag, so I decided it was time for parental guidance. "Administrations rarely do anything in cases like this, honey. More to the point, what are you going to do?"

"We haven't decided yet, but we're not going to let them run over us."

"The best thing you can do is find a sympathetic alumnus who'll pay for republishing the paper."

She sighed. "We're already working on that, but the PC mob will just steal them again."

"The smartest thing you personally can do is to stay out of it. You don't need to get in trouble halfway through your junior year."

"I know that, Daddy, but it's a matter of principle. I think you've made a few decisions like this."

"That's why I'm the campus pariah," I said. "You'd be smart to sit this one out and graduate on time next year."

Her voice grew sad. "I'll think about it, Daddy."

She said she loved me and we hung up.

So now her troubles were piled on top of mine. Nothing weighs on a parent's conscience so much as seeing his own shortcomings reincarnated in the lives of his children. And Cindy had inherited my worst qualities of stubbornness on matters of principle.

The afternoon continued its slide toward winter night as I drove across town to meet Dr. Sheldon and Mara. She was there before me, and she did not look happy. I wondered if it had to do with Cynthia Starlington's visit at lunch. It isn't every day a beautiful woman rubs circles on my back.

"Well, children," boomed Dr. Sheldon, "let's cut to the chase. You first, Press."

I summarized my interviews with Weldon Combes and Freda Broyles, emphasizing that the faculty's ill-fated trip to Las Vegas was rearing its head again. I named the trustees who made the trip and mentioned Combes' warning that might or might not have been friendly. For good measure, I threw in Steven Drisko's question and Brill Drisko's not-so-subtle suggestion that I mind my own business.

"Did Freda tell you about her difficulties with the police?" Mara asked.

"What difficulties?" I asked.

Mara looked smug. "I did talk to Sergeant Spencer. He says when the police went to mark off Professor Fortier's house as a crime scene, they found Freda Broyles coming out of it carrying several dresses. She claimed she'd loaned them to Professor Fortier and just wanted to get them back before the police got them tied up as possible evidence. Thursday night—while police were investigating—do you remember that she came into the Science Center hallway and left before the police saw her?"

"I asked her about that," I said. "She claimed she'd forgotten a lesson plan and had to go back home for it. I never knew her to teach from a lesson plan."

Mara smiled, presumably at having learned something before I did. "Sergeant Spencer says the officers involved claimed that two of those dresses didn't contain enough material to make a girdle for Freda."

"She is rather large." Dr. Sheldon loved understatement.

With the dress incident, it looked like I'd have to talk to Freda again. We moved on to other things. I produced my photocopy of the card from Mitra's office, but Mara and Dr. Sheldon could make no more of it than I had.

I then gave more detail on Freda's story about Mitra's dating interest and its sad ending with the aircraft accident.

Dr. Sheldon leaned forward in his wheelchair. "I read about that accident last summer. I'll get on my computer and see what I can find out."

He'd always been an avid researcher, and his boredom provided a wonderfully powerful incentive.

"While you're at it," I said, "would you check into Gordon Samstag and the rocket that failed today? For some reason, his name keeps turning up."

Dr. Sheldon rubbed his hands together. "Another subject to research? That'll keep me off the streets and out of trouble. Now, Mara, it's your turn."

Mara's blue gaze had always seemed a kind of marvel to me. It could change from ice to acetylene torch in half a second, or it could radiate all temperatures in between. Now as she looked at each of us in turn, it registered in the moderate range—warm for Dr. Sheldon, cool for me. I could usually read her moods but not the reasons behind them.

"Something else from Sergeant Spencer," she said. "Beyond the Freda Broyles thing, he wasn't enthusiastic about giving us inside police information—at one point, said flatly he wouldn't do it. But he understood why Press and I were worried about Captain Staggart's accusations, and he said they didn't sound like anything either one of us would do."

A tiny smile lifted the corners of her lips. "I thanked him for that. Then he said he'd seen several policemen laughing over some kind of book in the evidence room where they shouldn't have been at all. They were leering at it as if it was pornography. He didn't know if it had any bearing on our situation, and he didn't offer to find out. So where do we go from here?"

I grimaced. "I'm not sure. I've already talked to each of the professors who saw the quarrel between Mitra and Cynthia Starlington."

Mara raised her eyebrow. "Just what are you investigating, Press?"

I gave her my patented blank stare. "Anything involving Mitra in the days before she was ... before she died."

Mara nodded. "So I'm not the only one who thinks she was murdered."

"I suspect it," I said, "but we'll have to wait for the police to confirm or deny."

"There's something else I want to know." Her gaze warmed a bit. "Dean-Dean said something about your holding a contest about the names on campus ..."

Dr. Sheldon pounced like a puma. "That happened during the Great Renaming, Mara, right after the new administration took over. The library became the Media Center, the gym became the Fitness Center, and Student Affairs became the Office of Student Services. Everything on campus became either a 'center' or a 'service.'"

He grinned broadly. "Our distinguished professor proposed that they rename other things, too. We still have a few ministerial students, so he organized a campus-wide contest to find a new name they could use for hell."

Mara's eyes sparkled.

"The only requirement," Dr. Sheldon continued, "was that hell had to become either a 'center' or a 'service.' I've forgotten a lot of the crazy suggestions that came up, but our glorious professor provided the winners." He paused for effect, then said, "The runner-up was 'Universal Retribution Center.'"

Mara laughed out loud.

"But the winner was ... " Dr. Sheldon again rubbed his hands together, "'Non-temporal Thermodynamic Services.'"

I felt the hot rush of blood to my face as he and Mara laughed together.

"It's no wonder you're the most popular man on campus," Mara said. Then she looked embarrassed. "I'm sorry to break this up, but I have to meet somebody." She avoided my eyes.

As the door closed behind her, Dr. Sheldon said, "I'm glad to see her launching some kind of social life." Before I could reply, he checked his watch and said, "News time." He clicked his remote control.

From station KLYE, the customary graphics chased each other around the TV screen, culminating in the requisite nuclear explosion and bell-ring. Tonight, the makeup artists had given

Francie LaBouche, the chorus girl/anchorette, a fairer complexion than usual. I was happy that the rocket failure bumped Mitra's death out of the lead story slot. The clip showed a solemn Gordon Samstag promising a thorough investigation followed by appropriate corrective action.

Then came the part I dreaded.

"Tonight the police announced the cause of Professor Mitra Fortier's death," Francie intoned. "The autopsy showed that she died of a massive overdose of cocaine." The visual image jumped to another peroxide pop-tart standing in front of the Overton City police station and looking important.

"Hi, Francie," the reporter said. "Well, police declined to state how the cocaine was administered, but their conduct makes it clear they're treating this death as a homicide. And there's apparently more to come. A police source who declined to be named said the deceased had recently had an angry conflict with another faculty member. Beyond that, however ..." (Here the reporter came close to drooling.) "Beyond that, Professor Fortier seems to have been involved in a long-standing romantic relationship with a male member of the faculty. But last fall she ran into competition from a younger female professor, and an angry confrontation between the two women resulted."

Virtue radiated from the reporter's face as she concluded, "Police declined to name the faculty members involved."

I didn't have to guess who they were or who had leaked the information.

CHAPTER 16

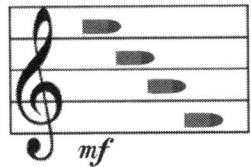

I drove home with spirits lower than a deep sea diver's toenail. It was just a matter of time before Mara and I would be identified as two sides of the alleged triangle involving Mitra, and I had yet to find a defense. How could I when no one had mentioned specific times and places? I worried about my daughter, too. Cindy didn't realize she was playing against a stacked deck, and it might be too late when she found it out. Even in bed I worried, but worrying brought no solutions. Hours later, I dropped off to sleep, my last memory the raucous mocking of Clyde McCoy's wah-wah-muted trumpet.

In dreams I couldn't even make a clean job of falling on my face, so I welcomed the alarm clock's jangle on Tuesday morning. I managed to shave without amputating my nose, and the calendar reminded me this was a blue-suit day. A glance at the newspaper headlines revealed that investigation of the rocket failure continued, but without further comments from Gordon Samstag. Fortunately, the TV-news rumors about me and Mitra Fortier had not made the papers.

I swallowed another ham-sandwich-and-coffee breakfast and followed the narrow walkway up to the campus before eight-thirty. I found my office door standing open. Seated at my desk and ransacking its drawers was Patrolman Bruno Pinkle. More evidence that local police procedures are somewhat informal.

Pinkle looked up with a sadistic grin. "Hello, Professor. Who's doing the grading now?"

He would never forget flunking my course. Several years ago, soon after The Crisis, our new administration created extension campuses in every location where money could be found. One lucrative source was a federally-funded law enforcement program. And on our short-lived campus at Sprague's Crossing, twenty miles west of Overton City, government funds found a small-town cop named Bruno Pinkle.

My assignment was to drive over there one night a week and teach a three-hour session of Western Civilization to our boys in blue. Most of them did well, but a few thought federal funds bought them an automatic pass. Those few included Bruno Pinkle, who had now turned up as a patrolman in Overton City.

Some failed the course but came close enough to pass next time around. But Pinkle flunked it flatter than a drop of sweat from the brow of a tall archangel. He earned a string of zeros that would have made him a millionaire if they'd had an Arabic number one and a dollar sign in front of them.

He held me responsible, of course. So now he sat at my desk, greeting me with a taunt.

I reached in my pocket, flicked my voice recorder on, and said, "I guess I'm not supposed to ask what you're doing in my desk, Patrolman Pinkle."

His grin widened. "You won't never have to ask, Professor, because I'll tell you. Your dean, Mr. Billig, said we could search any offices and any computers we wanted to."

"Does that mean I'm suspected of something?"

"Your affair with Mitra Fortier makes you a person of interest in our investigation of her death. It'll go easier with you, Professor, if you tell us all about it." His hands fumbled with my computer under the desk.

"There was no affair," I said. "What are you doing under my desk?"

He scowled. "I was trying to get into your computer, but you've got it rigged some way so I can't."

His hands remained out of sight, but his right arm moved toward a drawer where I store three CDs that back up the class and research notes on my hard drive. I heard the drawer close, and Pinkle stood up.

"Open that computer for me," he said. "I want to see what you have in it."

"I don't have time now," I said. "I'm due in class." I took my folder of class notes from the file cabinet.

"Have fun," I said as I left the office.

Pinkle did not look happy.

In the hall, I turned off the voice recorder and almost collided with Arthur Medford.

"I need some advice," he said.

"What's the problem?" I asked.

"Well, Dean-Dean ... uh ... Dr. Billig in psychology class is asking how everyone *feels* about one thing or another—"

"Wait," I said. "It's not ethical for me to comment on how another faculty member runs his class."

"I know." Arthur looked pained. "But when he calls the roll, we're not supposed to answer 'here' or 'present.' We're supposed to say how we *feel*. He ought to know no one's going to tell a professor how he actually feels."

"How *do* you actually feel?" I asked.

Arthur's eyes lit up, and I wondered what kind of genie I'd let out of the bottle.

"Say," he said, self-consciously changing the subject, "is it true that Professor Billig really thought the hippocampus was a zoo?"

"Don't believe everything you hear about faculty." I moved the two of us down the hall toward the classroom.

Leaning against a wall nearby stood a huge man who didn't look like a student. Still talking to Arthur, I nodded to him and moved to pass by. Suddenly, the hulk put his shoulder into me, knocking me against Arthur and both of us against the opposite wall.

"Why don't you look where you're going?" he muttered as he advanced on us.

Arthur had his mouth open for a reply when my grip on his arm warned him to silence.

"I'm sorry, sir," I said to the hulk. "I'm unusually clumsy today."

Surprise appeared on the man's face as I guided Arthur past him and into the classroom. I shut the door behind us. I took a deep breath, mentally shifted gears and launched into the topic of the day—America's entry into the Spanish-American War. Class went well, and by its end I'd almost forgotten the incident in the hall.

Arthur hadn't. He was the first student to the door and, after a glance outside, he threw me a quick nod to say the hulk had gone. I nodded back.

Arthur came back to me and asked, "Who was that guy?"

"I don't know," I said. "I never saw him before."

A smile spread on Arthur's face. "I was going to take him on and get myself killed, but you did something he didn't expect. So we got past him before he knew he'd been had."

"It probably won't work again," I said.

One corner of Arthur's smile quirked a bit higher, as if he had a secret thought. He seemed full of those lately. But he asked, "Do you think that guy was trying to stop your investigation of Professor Fortier's murder?"

"According to the news, the police aren't completely convinced it was murder. And in any case, I'm not investigating it."

"Sure." Arthur rolled his eyes. "And in any case," he mimicked, "thanks for listening to me about ... uh ... Professor Billig."

I still had a few minutes before the memorial service, so I went back to my office to see how much damage Bruno Pinkle had done. There was no sign of Pinkle. Nothing seemed out of place, so I went to my bookshelf and took out the well-worn King James Bible. From behind it, I removed my "personal biometric USB pod fingerprint reader" my computer-guru friend Richmond Seagrave had given me last fall when he debugged the campus computer system.

Seagrave was the other witness who'd testified against Clyde Staggart twenty-odd years ago in our Special Forces days. Since

Staggart had sworn to get even and had tried last fall to frame me for murder, Seagrave gave me that fingerprint reader for anti-Staggart insurance. He also gave one to Mara, my fellow framee of last fall.

I keep the gadget hidden because there's no reason for anyone's knowing I have it. But Pinkle couldn't have used it if he'd found it because it's set for my fingerprint only.

I put the device in my pocket for safe keeping and examined the desk. Pinkle hadn't been wearing gloves, so his fingerprints would be everywhere. He was there legally, but caution told me not to override his prints. So I avoided the drawer knobs and opened the desk drawers by their edges. In the bottom drawer with my three plastic-encased CDs of class notes I found a fourth CD in a different style plastic case.

Using a number-two lead pencil, I verified my three. The fourth was a stranger and had no label.

I still had a few minutes before the memorial service, so I phoned Sergeant Ron Spencer at home. He was not home, but his wife agreed to have him call me. I thanked her and hung up. I didn't like it, but later would have to do.

I was a minute or two late to the memorial service and slipped into one of the rear seats while a lady from the Music Department sang the last stanza of "Abide with Me." The auditorium was packed, but I made a quick survey for any strange faces.

All the faculty were there, of course, with many students and a sprinkling of trustees. Emory Estes, Steven Drisko, and Gordon Samstag were there. Lately that trio seemed to show up everywhere I went.

In all the congregation, I saw only one stranger. He was a small man hunched on an end seat on the back row at the opposite side of the auditorium. He had ill-combed dirty-blond hair and wore a dun-colored suit that hadn't been pressed since the Treaty of Versailles. He gazed at the bench ahead of him, and his face held an expression that might be either grief or boredom. I made a mental note to talk to him between the memorial service and the faculty meeting.

When the singer finished, Dathan Hormah from the Department of Religious Studies spoke a universalist prayer designed to accommodate any Sufis, Sikhs, or Shintoists among us and offend no one except his fellow Christians.

Then came the eulogy by President J. Cleveland Cantwell, newly returned from his fund-raising tour in Minnesota. His face lacked color, and he paused often to cough into his sleeve. My suspicion that he'd gone ice fishing when he should have been schmoozing monied alums around a fireplace might have some truth to it. I confess I don't know what he said, for I was concentrating too much on that stranger and plotting to get out quickly and intercept him.

During the second stanza of the final hymn, he slipped out the far door of the auditorium. But he'd scarcely moved when I bolted out of the door nearest me.

And ran smack into Gordon Samstag. I was about to say "Pardon me" and continue my chase when Samstag put a restraining hand on my shoulder. I don't make a habit of shaking off the hands of trustees. Not that many of them have a habit of laying a hand on me.

Collision or no, Samstag held me with a glance that made me feel like the wedding guest in Coleridge's *Ancient Mariner*.

"I've been wanting to talk to you, Press," he said. "We need you to stop your investigation and let the police do their job. Many things are going on behind the scenes, things that mean a lot to the university. We can't afford to have you banging around in ignorance like ... well, if you'll pardon the cliché, like a bull in a china shop."

He held me a moment longer with his gaze, then asked, "Do you understand?"

"I understand," I said. I think he meant did I understand the importance of what he was doing for the college ... uh ... *university*, but what I actually understood was that my name was mud if I kept doing what I was doing.

He nodded. "Good. Please tell Professor Thorn this applies to her, too." He pivoted and walked away.

I looked beyond him but saw only a multitude of students streaming out of the auditorium.

The man I wanted to talk to had disappeared in the swarm of bodies.

CHAPTER 17

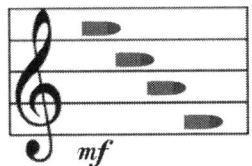

When I got back inside, Dean-Dean had launched into his customary admonition about keeping our enrollment up, and my internal bassoon provided appropriate accompaniment.

"It is imperative that we maintain the highest academic standards," Dean-Dean said in his scratchy voice, "and, above all, we must always continue the pursuit of excellence. But keeping our students satisfied is also essential. That's really what it's all about. And if you'll pardon my quoting Shakespeare, everything else is just gelding the lily .."

At the faculty's subdued twitter, Dean-Dean looked around in confusion.

"*Gilding*," Dathan Hormah prompted.

I glanced at the chairman of English, whose lips formed the words "to paint the lily."

Dean-Dean thrust out his chin. "Just as I said: *gilding*. That's what it's all about." He called the meeting to order before anything else could go wrong.

I glanced around to see if the same three trustees were present. But for once they were absent. Mara sat grim-faced in her usual seat on the left side of the auditorium, directly across from where I usually sat on the right.

Dean-Dean had published no agenda, his usual ploy when he wants to slip something through before we have time to think about it. With all the wonderful possibilities of campus life, you'd think college teaching would be like living in Shangri-La. But the stinky reality is that it often resembles recess time at an unsupervised schoolyard in a tough neighborhood.

The vice president for student services announced creation of a Learning Center where students could get tutoring. That brought up the usual questions about who would man the Center and what would prevent tutors from doing students' work for them. The answer to the first question was that juniors and seniors would man it. Because of vagueness, the effective answer to the second question was:

Nothing.

One new faculty member asked if creating the Learning Center meant that the faculty had become the Learning Periphery. Dean-Dean promptly ruled him out of order. He also said that this was an administrative matter not subject to faculty vote.

That done, the chairman of the Education Department moved the approval of two new courses for his department. The first was to teach students how to use techniques of "transformative learning" to alter people's basic ideas and attitudes. The second was a practicum in which students would use these techniques, essentially variations of drama, in presentations in the dormitories.

Which ideas and attitudes were the courses supposed to alter? Under questioning, the chairman said that the objective was eradication of societal evils like racism, sexism, classism, and lookism.

Also under question, the chairman defined "lookism" as the prejudice that some people were more pleasant to look at than others. Displeased with the resultant laughter, Dean-Dean gaveled the meeting back to order.

It soon became evident, however, that Dean-Dean had made a tactical error by scheduling the meeting after the faculty received their contracts rather than before. Freed from the threat of contract non-renewal, the faculty felt free to engage in genuine debate.

The chairman of the Sociology Department objected that the courses would practice sociology, and he questioned the Education faculty's qualifications for that. The Education chairman responded that no special qualifications were required to fight racism, sexism, and similar evils—this time he omitted lookism—and one of the coaches asked why the two courses were needed if no special qualifications were required.

Dathan Hormah then voiced the cliché that the courses would put our students "on the cutting edge," and a faculty nurse offered to provide tourniquets for those who got cut.

It was becoming just another routine faculty meeting when my internal musicians intervened. The piano began softly, high on the keyboard, and with a pang in my heart, I recognized Faith's expressive touch. Instantly, I was with her in our house again, holding her hand as we watched the classic movie that featured that haunting melody. The movie was *Enchantment*, a poignant story of love denied by jealousy in one generation and mysteriously fulfilled in a later generation.

The movie's *leitmotiv* song was the plaintive nineteenth-century ballad "Pretty Polly Oliver," repeated on strings and soft flutes. Faith wept freely and my own eyes teared up as the young lovers pledged to each other in the present and the older lovers were reunited in the life beyond. We watched that movie often, with Faith squeezing my hand each time the melody returned.

In the years that followed, I would be reading in my study while she practiced on her Steinway, and she would play the melody exactly as I was hearing it now in the faculty meeting. It meant she thought we'd been apart too long. I would rush to meet her, astonished as always by the miracle that someone like her could need someone like me. An embrace and a few kisses would restore us, and we could return to our separate work.

Some mornings I would wake with her face close above mine as she sang that song:

> *Nor father nor mother*
> *Shall make me false prove,*

> *I'll live for a soldier*
> *And follow my love.*

At least, that was her version of it. The actual word was *'list* rather than *live*, but Faith changed it to suit her purpose. Thus, over the years, that song wove itself into the golden fabric of our marriage.

My internal music stopped as suddenly as it had begun, returning me to the drab reality of our faculty catfight.

"Who gave us the mission of telling students *what* to think?" Weldon Combes was saying. "The mission of a college ... uh ... *university* ... is to teach them *how* to think and expose them to a sampling of the best that has been thought in all ages."

"Amen to that," Freda Broyles said, laboriously pushing her bulk into a standing position. "We're not supposed to run a Midwestern version of Hitler youth."

Dathan Hormah took issue with the Hitler comparison and asked, "What's wrong with filling students' minds with socially useful ideas?"

"Everything," said a younger member of Hormah's religion faculty. "Which one of us has the moral authority to decide *for them* which ideas are useful, or useful toward what end?"

Dean-Dean again gaveled for order, and in the ensuing silence Mara Thorn called the question and moved for a secret ballot. That was a bold move for a first-year faculty member. My white-knight impulse was to second her motion, but someone beat me to it. Dean-Dean looked like a man eating green persimmons as the faculty voted overwhelmingly for a secret ballot.

A scowling Dathan Hormah gave each faculty member an index card for a ballot, and Dean-Dean reluctantly named four faculty as a counting committee.

While the committee was out, one of the nurses asked when the faculty would vote on the question of coed dorms. Dean-Dean answered that it was an administrative matter not subject to faculty vote.

The counting committee returned and announced that the Education Department's motion had failed by a vote of 22 in favor, 35 against. A mixture of cheers and muttering followed until Dean-Dean's gavel stopped it. Without waiting for a motion, he adjourned the meeting *sine die* until the first Tuesday in March.

Yes, Dean-Dean has a problem with Latin. Faculty have explained to him that *sine die* translates "without day," meaning "indefinitely," and to follow that with naming a time to reconvene creates an oxymoron. Dean-Dean dismissed that correction and continues his undeclared war on logic and the Latin language. Nevertheless, I give no credit to the rumor that he thought *carpe diem* meant *fish today*, though that might well be true of a piscatory enthusiast like President Cantwell.

At lunch in the crowded campus grill I ended up again directly across from Mara and the inevitable Emory Estes. The two composition specialists were also there.

"I don't see what's wrong with telling students what to think," the female composition specialist said. "How are they going to know if we don't tell them?"

Emory Estes joined in. "It's a good idea. I wouldn't ever sell a car if I couldn't convince the customer what to think."

Mara caught my eye briefly, but her stony expression gave nothing away to anyone else.

"Some of these students!" the composition specialist exclaimed, seemingly unaware she was changing the subject. "One of mine wrote that William Wordsworth, as a boy, had found 'splinters in the grass.'"

Mara showed an innocent smile. "Does that mean he was a 'barefoot boy with cheeks of tan'?"

The composition specialist frowned. "Actually, I think someone else wrote that." Then, in case we didn't know, she added, "The word Wordsworth actually wrote was 'splendor,' not splinters."

Mara repeated her innocent smile. "I don't suppose that would hurt his feet as much."

"I suppose not," the composition specialist said.

I don't know what else was said, for my mind got busy reviewing the faculty meeting for anything meaningful. Last fall, my internal musicians preempted a faculty meeting with the music score from a movie, and the first faculty statement I heard afterward was the key to solving the Laila Sloan murder. Today's occurrence was only the second time my trickster musicians had thrust a movie music score upon me in a faculty meeting. Could this be a lead toward solving ... Solving what? The source of my alleged affair with Mitra Fortier, certainly. But her unexplained death? I didn't know.

I searched my memory for anything in the meeting that might point toward a solution for either problem, but I came up empty. I couldn't even decide whether to suspect faculty members or those three trustees who seemed to pop up all over the place. Why should I expect a solution from the music when the three trustees weren't even present?

At length, I gave it up and found myself alone. My lunch companions had left without a word. Some of them would no doubt spread more stories about my reclusiveness, but that was nothing new.

My real worry was that word of the alleged affair was bound to leak soon, and I was in no position to defend myself.

Nor did I have a clue as to how to proceed.

CHAPTER 18

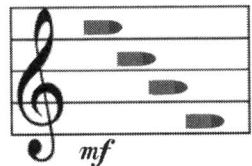

Outside, I hurried toward my one o'clock class. The midwinter wind tried to amputate my ears but, fortunately, had only limited success. The campus circle was filled with students moving quickly to get out of the cold. But three students whom I recognized as football linemen were hanging around the exit to the grill, and another group of three lingered some fifty feet farther along.

The group at the exit spoke as I passed, and the farther group turned and moved toward the Liberal Arts Center ahead of me. When I looked back, the first group was following. The leading group passed my classroom door and stopped a few feet beyond. I went straight into the classroom without looking to see what either group did next.

Soon I was totally absorbed in repeating the Peace of Wedmore bit that I'd taught the other class section on Monday. More students seemed to be interested this time, and I was on my usual high by the time class ended.

The two groups of football players had disappeared, but four new individuals of similar build stood around in the hallway. They nodded as I passed, and I proceeded down the hall to my office. As I entered, I glanced back and found them still watching me. I was too immersed in my own problems to ask what the game was.

So I sat at my desk and sought in vain for some way to rebut the rumored affair. You can fight an accusation if you know its basis, but how can you fight it if you don't? I must have sat for forty minutes or more as the day declined toward winter evening. Then high heels clicked in the hall, and a distraught Cynthia Starlington catapulted into my office.

"Press, I need help." Her voice was almost a sob.

"What is it, Cyn?" I rose and came around my desk. "Sit down and tell me about it."

I mainly wanted to get rid of her because I had enough problems of my own. But letting her talk might calm her down, and I could shoo her out of the office so I could get on with my worrying.

Cynthia hung her ocelot-collared coat on my coat rack, then turned to face me again. She wore a loose-fitting figured blouse with a lot of brown in it, the perfect complement to her olive complexion and flowing brown hair. The winter chill put a pleasant color in her cheeks, matching the light tint of her lipstick. With her entry, my internal musicians settled into the now-familiar liquid tones of the clarinet. They played something slow and easy from the big band era. Its languid movement contrasted starkly with Cynthia's frenzied entry.

She made no move toward sitting down, so I had to remain standing.

Anxiety was written on her face. "The police have questioned me again, Press. They think I murdered Professor Fortier."

"Have they said that?" I asked.

"Their questions pointed to that. They'd found that letter where I wrote that I meant everything I'd said, and they kept waving it in my face."

"They're trying to panic you into saying something they can use against you." Secretly, I felt glad the police suspected someone besides me. "How did you answer them?"

A frown creased her forehead. "I admitted writing the letter but said I had no intention of doing anything beyond that. They kept asking, and I kept saying the same thing over and over." She paused, thinking. "They did ask one other thing—if I was jealous of your ... *romantic relationship* ... with Professor Fortier."

My temper flared. But I suppressed it and asked, "What did you tell them?"

"The truth—that I'd never heard of anything between you and Professor Fortier." Her dark eyes asked an unspoken question.

"There never was anything," I said. "I don't know where they got that stupid idea." *But I'd better find out pretty quick.*

"I didn't think there was," she said. A smile flickered across her face and was gone. "Oh, Press, you've got to help me prove I didn't do it."

Alarm shot through me. "Hold on, Cyn. How on earth can I do that?" I was doing a lousy job of getting rid of her. She was like a hurt child. A beautiful child.

"Why ..." Her dark eyes widened. "You'll prove I didn't do it by finding out who did. That's what you did with that Wiccan last fall."

"*Former* Wiccan," I said. "We just got lucky."

A smile formed at the corners of her lips. "I know better than that, Press. There's not another professor on this campus that has your brains."

"I could name several," I said. All of them were smart enough not to become pariahs. But Mara Thorn's brilliance stood out above them all. She'd solved problems last fall that I couldn't begin to solve.

Cynthia's voice rose to near panic. "You've got to help me, Press. I don't know where else to turn." Under her dark gaze I felt the full impact of her beauty.

"No promises," I said, "but I'll see what I can do." That seemed vague enough to be safe.

"Thank you, Press." She smiled and her eyes sparkled. "I knew I could count on you."

With one step, she closed the distance between us. She stood for a moment gazing into my eyes. I grew increasingly aware of her delicate perfume. Then she put her arms around my neck and kissed me.

The liquid clarinet moved again to the forefront of my consciousness.

Cynthia kissed the same way she'd done her schoolwork as a student—thoroughly and with great attention to detail. I confess that I gave it equal attention.

After a while, she stepped back and gave me a shy glance. "I might as well tell you, Press. I've been in love with you since that first day in your class ten years ago."

I hope I didn't look as stupefied as I felt. "I ... I never had any inkling of that, Cyn. I'm glad you kept it to yourself. Just knowing it would have been awkward ..."

"That's why I never told anyone. You were married, and everyone knew you and Faith were head over heels in love. If she were ... still here, I'd never have taken this job."

I felt increasingly stupid. No, *terrified* was a better word. Conflicting impulses battled each other in my mind. On the one hand, I was too much aware of Cynthia's closeness and soft femininity. On the other hand, the twenty years' difference in our ages posed an apparently insurmountable barrier. And all the while, that soft clarinet in my mind played its seductive melody.

"I ... I don't know what to say," I stammered.

"You don't have to say anything, Press." Cynthia's smile hovered close before my face. She seemed as calm now as she'd been distraught when she came in. Then her smile gave way to deep seriousness. "I believe in you, Press. I know you'll find the murderer."

I wanted to say that I'd only committed myself to see what I could do. But I couldn't say anything. Cynthia's sudden change of mood had me too confused.

Just as suddenly, her smile returned. "I'm glad I waited for you, Press." She touched her left forefinger to her lips and then touched it to mine. "I know you'll find him."

Before I could reply, she whisked her coat from the coat rack and was gone. So was the soft clarinet music, for my internal orchestra sounded the opening chords of Beethoven's Piano Concerto No. 4.

It occurred to me that I'd done a lousy job of getting rid of her. Instead, I'd let myself get halfway committed to doing two things I'd had no intention of doing before she came in. And there was no telling where either one of them would lead.

"Professor Barclay."

I looked up and found Sergeant Ron Spencer standing in the doorway.

"My wife said you called," he said. "It seemed just as quick to come by on my way home."

"I'm glad you did," I said. My mind shifted out of stupefaction and back to business. "Bruno Pinkle searched my office earlier today—legally, of course—but after he left I found a CD in my desk that wasn't there before."

Spencer looked skeptical. "You're saying he put it there?"

"I'm saying only that it isn't mine, and it wasn't there before. I don't want to touch it, and I'd hoped you could find out what was on the disk."

Spencer frowned. "You're suggesting that Pinkle planted some kind of false evidence on you. That will be hard to prove, and I'm not sure I'd like to try."

In the past, he'd always maintained good eye contact, but now his gaze focused on my face below eye level.

"All I'm asking you to do is check the fingerprints and learn the content of the CD," I said. "Pinkle wasn't wearing gloves, and I haven't touched the thing."

Spencer looked pained. "You're asking me to investigate a fellow officer. I won't do that unless you file a complaint against him."

"You know what will happen if I file a complaint. Word will get to Clyde Staggart, and the evidence will disappear. This has to be kept quiet until too much is on record for it to be suppressed. Or do you want to help them frame me?"

"You don't have to put it that way, Dr. Barclay."

I admit I'd given Ron an unfair shot. He'd been one of my better students. Last fall, he'd played along with Mara and me, heard the murderer's inadvertent confession, and made the actual arrest.

Only a few days ago, he'd warned me that Staggart had assigned Pinkle to get me indicted. But now, I was straining his friendship to the limit by asking him to take my word over that of a fellow policeman.

If he had looked pained before, he now looked like a man suffering Comanche hospitality. Like hot coals poured onto his abdomen.

"All right," he said at last. "I'll take the disk and have it fingerprinted, and I'll find out what's on it. Beyond that, I won't make any commitment."

"That's all I ask, Ron," I said. "Let the evidence lead wherever it will."

While he watched, I used the erasers of two pencils to lift the offending disk's plastic casing out of the drawer and onto the surface of my desk. From another drawer I took a Ziploc bag full of rubber bands and dumped the rubber bands back in the drawer. I again used pencils to slide the encased CD into the Ziploc bag.

"There'll be plenty of my fingerprints on the bag," I said. "But headquarters should have them on file from last fall."

Still gazing somewhere below my eyes, Spencer nodded and zipped the bag shut. "I don't understand the game about this CD," he said, "but you ought to know that I'm having a harder and harder time believing you."

"How's that?" I asked.

"The business about you and Professor Fortier."

My stomach tensed. "What business? I found her dead in her office. That's all."

His lips drew tight. "That's far from all, according to her. She kept a journal."

I stood stunned into silence while Spencer fixed his gaze on my face. I finally managed to stammer out, "A journal?"

"A journal in Professor Fortier's handwriting." Spencer's jaw tightened. "I managed to get a look at it in the evidence room. It tells of her ... uh ... *romance* with you going back for years—several years before your wife died, as a matter of fact."

"That can't be," I said. "Nothing like that ever happened."

His gaze stayed focused on my face, still somewhere below the eyes. "Like I said, Professor Barclay, I'm having a harder and harder time believing you." He waved the Ziploc bag with the CD inside. "But I'll go with you this far. The physical evidence will tell its own story. We won't have to take anyone's word for that."

When he left, I had the feeling I'd lost a good friend.

CHAPTER 19

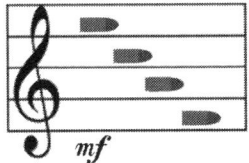

Sergeant Spencer's news of a journal by Mitra Fortier had stunned me so much that I forgot to ask details of its contents. Mitzi had been Faith's friend and confidante, but she'd never sent so much as a flirtatious glance in my direction. So what was this nonsense about the journal of an affair? I couldn't fathom it. Nor could I fathom Cynthia Starlington's unexpected declaration of love. The two hitting in quick succession had me totally confused.

So I sat and brooded. The more I considered the idea of a journal, the less sense I could make out of it. So I shifted into worrying about Cynthia. Of course, I was attracted to her—what male wouldn't be? And her kiss awoke impulses in me that I thought had died with Faith.

As I remembered the kiss, my internal musicians gave a reprise of that soft clarinet—a pleasant memory.

I didn't love Cynthia. But if letting her love me would make her happy, why not go along with it? So what if I was twenty years her senior? Why shouldn't I seek happiness for whatever years were left to me?

Before my imagination gained control, reason crept in like a rancid tide. I knew very little about Cynthia. Her emotional tirade directed at Mitzi Fortier was hardly a good character reference. All I knew of Cynthia's years between her graduation here and her return as faculty was that she'd earned a doctorate in philosophy. But I did know that her words this afternoon weren't entirely truthful.

It might be true that she'd been in love with me from her first day in my class. But she'd also said, "I'm glad I waited for you, Press." She'd given me a truly remarkable kiss. And it could possibly be true that she had waited for me.

But she'd been practicing while she waited.

My internal clarinet departed its lower register with a long Artie Shaw-style glissando that hit the keynote a quarter tone flat.

Feminine heel-clicks in the hallway startled me out of my brooding. Had Cynthia come back for another installment? Half of me hoped she had, and the other half wanted more time to think things out.

Neither half got its wish, for the woman who stood in the doorway was Mara Thorn. Surprisingly, my gloomy mood vanished—perhaps because I was glad to see her or, perhaps, because my cerebral orchestra changed to a feisty trumpet concerto by Telemann. The feistiness fit Mara's personality, and I found myself smiling.

But Mara wasn't. Her eyes focused below mine the same way Sergeant Spencer's had, and her voice came as hard and metallic as her blue steel gaze.

"Dr. Sheldon is fed up with that assisted living place, and I'm taking him to Goolock's for supper. He has new information and wants you to join us."

"I'll be there," I said. I should have known better than to ask my next question. "Say, is something wrong with my appearance? You're looking at me the same way Sergeant Spencer did."

Mara's eyes became the acetylene torch she'd shown me several times in the past. "You're going to get looks like that until you wipe the lipstick off your face. Whose lipstick is it? The brunette bombshell that massages your back publicly in the campus grill?"

I took out my handkerchief and wiped my lips with it.

She burned me with another glance. "How do you always manage to get it on your teeth?"

"What do you mean 'always'? It only happened once before."

I knew what she meant. During our investigation the previous fall, a female suspect tried to bribe me with a kiss. The evidence of it had incensed Mara so much that our partnership almost ended before it began. Mara thought I'd been pursuing pleasure while she risked her job by searching the suspect's office.

"You mean once that I know of," she said, "and that's once too often."

"It could have been twice," I said, "except that you don't wear lipstick."

Her acetylene torch became a blast furnace. "That is a dead issue, Professor Barclay." She pointed a finger at me. "Now. Can you contain your libidinous impulses sufficiently to continue this investigation, or shall I tell Dr. Sheldon you're too busy with personal *affairs* to participate?"

No one in this world is more stuffily officious than an angry professor who's trying to be impersonal. I didn't dare tell her that. Her blast furnace had scorched me enough, and I had no desire to see if she could generate a supernova. So I made another mistake just as bad.

"All right," I said. "So she kissed me. And what's going on with you and your used car salesman?"

"Not anything you imagine," she snapped. "Either join Dr. Sheldon and me or not. I don't care."

With that, she pivoted and swept out of the office.

I retreated to my desk and rested my head in my hands. Mara was the closest thing to a friend that I had on this campus, and I'd hurt her by reminding her of our one kiss. Despite all the rumors, that *was* the only time we'd "colored outside the lines," to use Mara's phrase. It happened in our darkest hour, when both our futures hung on what happened in the next ten minutes. She'd kissed me not as an enticement but in appreciation of what we were going through together.

Now I had tarnished it by giving it a meaning neither of us intended. That made me question my feelings toward both Mara and Cynthia. I was still pondering when the phone rang.

My daughter's voice sounded tense. "Daddy, I had to let you know what's going on."

"What is that, Cindy?" I could tell it wasn't going to be good.

"You remember that the university administration refused to do anything about the Residence Life Groups' stealing our newspapers ... " She paused, apparently to see how I would respond.

"I remember." I also remembered advising her to stay out of the conflict.

"Well," she continued, "Mark and I organized a demonstration protesting the administration's failure to act. More than five hundred students joined us ... "

"I imagine that made you as popular as a polecat in a polling booth."

"That's the understatement of the year, Daddy. Some of the Residence Life crowd yelled insults and began pushing some of our people around ... "

"Did your crowd do anything to provoke it?"

"Nothing at all. Mark and I had briefed everyone that we had to be above reproach. We carried signs with slogans like, 'Punish theft, not free speech.' But there wasn't one word to provoke trouble."

"Some people regard disagreeing with them as sufficient provocation."

"I can't help that," Cindy said. "All we were doing was exercising our right to free speech and peaceable assembly."

"What is your administration doing about it?" As if I didn't know.

"Six of us—including Mark and me—have to face a disciplinary hearing tomorrow. We're charged with 'hate speech' and 'inappropriate conduct.' They said our actions constituted a 'clear and present danger' to everyone on campus."

I could have told her something like that would happen. But I only asked, "Do you need a lawyer?"

"They won't let us have one, Daddy. They said this is an administrative procedure, not a court of law."

I'd heard that dodge before. "That's correct as far as it goes, Cindy, but the law can come into it after the university makes its administrative ruling. Have you ever heard of CIRCA—the Council for Individual Rights on Campus?"

"The what?"

"Council for Individual Rights on Campus. It's a non-profit organization that helps students defend their constitutional and legal rights. They've straightened out quite a few situations like yours. Contact them."

I heard Cindy draw in a breath. "I don't think we need them yet, Daddy. Mark and I are ready to defend ourselves before any fair-minded group."

"It won't be fair-minded, Cindy. You need to contact CIRCA right now." I gave her the URL for the organization's website.

Her sigh sounded through the phone. "I'll talk to Mark about it, Daddy. Right now I have to go help organize our defense."

She said she loved me and rang off.

Few things weigh more heavily on parents than knowing their children are in trouble beyond their experience and that the parents are helpless to intervene. In her innocence, Cindy still thought she'd get a fair hearing, but I knew different. I'd watched for a couple of decades as administrators had either joined the political correctness mob or been intimidated by it. Universities' "speech codes" and other coercive measures had been repeatedly struck down by the courts as unconstitutional, yet these same universities continued to misuse their administrative authority to suppress students' right to free speech and peaceable assembly.

I knew that Cindy and Mark would be suspended, but I could do nothing about it. So I went home, picked up my old Honda, and drove to Goolock's. Mara and Dr. Sheldon had not yet arrived. I ordered my usual grilled cheese sandwich and coffee.

Mrs. Lee cocked an eyebrow at me. "No lott'ry ticket?"

"Not tonight, Mrs. Lee."

She showed me the same smile as always. "Goo' lock anyway."

During this exchange, Mara and Dr. Sheldon arrived outside, and she got him established in his wheelchair. After a casual wave to the Lees and me, he wheeled directly to a table facing the window. Mr. Lee went to the table to take his order.

Dr. Sheldon's great voice roared out an order for a double cheeseburger and French fried onion rings—one of his periodic rebellions against his anti-stroke diet.

Mr. Lee showed a conspiratorial grin. "You order drink?"

Dr. Sheldon grinned back. "Sprite or Mountain Dew."

Mara ordered her usual Reuben and Coke. Her averted glance told me I was still in trouble. We joined Dr. Sheldon at the table.

"Well, children," he boomed, "what have you been up to?"

Mara's blue gaze speared me from across the table, so I gathered it was up to me to answer.

"I have been brooding," I said, "brooding unsuccessfully on how to fight scandalous rumors that have no basis in fact."

Mara spoke in a metallic voice. "You might try thinking about how to avoid further scandal."

"Children, let us not squabble," Dr. Sheldon said. "We have more substantive things to think on. I have been gainfully employed with my little laptop."

He paused for effect, but Mara and I were too busy glowering at each other to respond properly. Fortunately, our orders arrived and saved us the trouble. Dr. Sheldon's drink came in an innocuous-looking pop bottle, but it smelled suspiciously like beer. It shouldn't have because the Lees were not licensed for on-premises consumption. I learned later that Mr. Lee would give Dr. Sheldon a bottle of Heineken out of his personal supply, but he'd pour it into a pop bottle for camouflage.

Conversation waned while Dr. Sheldon made a starved-lion's attack on his food. Mara and I were still eating when Dr. Sheldon took a final swig from his pop bottle, drew a satisfied deep breath, and launched into the evening's lecture.

"I have researched the aircraft accident of Mitra Fortier's late fiancé," he said. "Jerry Vaughan was flying a home-built aircraft that he owned jointly with several other men. It seems he enjoyed aerobatics the same way some men enjoy golf. He'd successfully performed several rolls and a spin that day. But while he was pulling out of an ordinary loop, his left wing came off and the aircraft simply fell out of the sky."

"Had he done aerobatics in that aircraft before?" I asked.

"Many times," Dr. Sheldon said. "I phoned one member of the accident board. He said Jerry flew the aircraft every Saturday morning—always early, when the air was smooth. And he often performed maneuvers that placed greater stress on the wings than the one when the wing collapsed."

"Then why didn't the wing come off sooner?" Mara asked.

"Ah, my dear." Dr. Sheldon launched into full lecture mode. "With that question we exceed the degree of precision of which accident investigations are capable. My informant says it's next to impossible to tell when a particular part is going to fail. If the aircraft had been overstressed in the past, the likelihood of failure under lesser conditions is increased. The upshot is that no one knows if the aircraft had been overstressed. If it had, Jerry's catastrophe could be easily explained. And there is no way to determine which of a hundred possible scenarios actually happened."

"So we reach a dead end," I said.

"Not quite." Dr. Sheldon beamed. "Because the wing was improperly installed, the board found that to be the primary cause of the accident."

"Do we know who installed the wing?" Mara asked.

"The board was unable to determine that," Dr. Sheldon said. "All five of the owners helped put the plane together, and no one remembered who secured the left wing. Any one of the five might have done it."

"Who were the owners?" Mara asked.

"One of them was Ralph Dornberg. He lives in Cloverdale, where the accident happened."

"I never heard of him," I said.

Dr. Sheldon smiled as if he were announcing the winner of the Miss America contest. "The other owners were Jerry Vaughan, Emory Estes, Steven Drisko, and Gordon Samstag."

Estes, Drisko, and Samstag again. They kept turning up everywhere.

CHAPTER 20

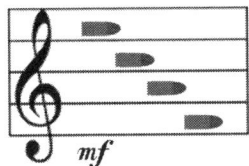

We couldn't pursue that thought because the Lees' son interrupted. Robert Sun Lee was as Americanized as a child of immigrants can get. His parents said they'd named him Robert, after the revered Confederate general, to emphasize how American they wanted him to become. I once asked Mr. Lee why he chose Sun as Robert's middle name. He said it was because Robert was not a daughter. I asked no more questions.

Robert was about my height, five-foot-ten, but more solidly muscled from his student days as a gymnast. He had strong features and a broad forehead, and he kept his black hair cut short in the old-fashioned flat-top style. Now he stood between Dr. Sheldon and me, and spoke perfect English in a well-modulated voice.

"I heard you talking about Jerry Vaughan," he said. "He was a good friend of mine."

Dr. Sheldon seized the initiative. "Can you tell us anything about his plane crash?"

Something in Robert's eyes shifted. "We were both CPAs," he said. "Jerry had his own company, and when I worked for Overton Technologies he used to audit us."

Drisko's company. Drisko again.

"Past tense?" I asked. "I thought you still worked there."

"Until last year. Gordon Samstag made me a better offer. Jerry audited several of his companies, too."

"How about Emory Estes?" I asked. Might as well make a clean sweep of it.

Robert grinned. "If he ever had an audit, I never heard of it."

"When was the last time you talked to Jerry?" Mara asked.

"We had lunch together about a week before he died. We talked some about the usual CPA stuff, but mostly about his engagement to Professor Fortier. Too bad he had to die before they got married. And now she's dead, too."

"Did Jerry say much about flying?" I asked.

"That wasn't something we had in common."

Dr. Sheldon cleared his throat like a thunderclap. "What was that 'usual CPA stuff' you talked about?"

Robert scratched his head. "He told me his audit schedule for the next month—three of the Samstag companies and Overton Technologies. The Samstag companies included Pegasus Industries, the one that had the rocket failure."

A frown furrowed Dr. Sheldon's brow. "No more details than that?"

"I don't remember any." Robert looked toward the cash register. "My parents need me."

"One more question," I said. "Why did you change jobs from Drisko to Samstag?"

Now Robert frowned. "Like I said: Samstag made me a better offer."

Something in his eyes said he wasn't telling everything he knew. That was the second time tonight.

After he left, we three silently eyed each other across the remains of our supper. We didn't know what to do with the information we'd received. Actually, Mara looked mostly at Dr. Sheldon. I was still in the doghouse.

"Well, children," Dr. Sheldon said at last, "where do we go from here?"

Mara made a face. "Home, I suppose."

"One thing first," I said. "This morning, a big guy I'd never seen before bumped Arthur Medford and me in the hall of the Liberal Arts Center. He looked like he wanted to start something, but we got past him before he could."

"Arthur Medford?" Mara showed her first smile of the evening. "That explains a lot. A tough-looking fellow I didn't know gave me the evil eye today, but some football players cordoned him off, and I went on my way. I'll bet Arthur has been fixing things again."

"Come to think of it, I had a convoy, too," I said.

"But what does it mean?" Mara asked. "It's like the mob threats against us last fall, but we haven't done anything since then that would justify it."

"From what I hear," I said, "they don't take revenge this long after the fact. And if they did, they wouldn't just bump into us. They'd bump us off."

Mara showed a pained expression at my archaic pun.

"Be careful, children," Dr. Sheldon warned. "Don't assume that anyone would act according to logic."

"I don't understand any of this," I said. "Mitra Fortier warned us about losing our jobs, so she must have heard a hint about Dean-Dean's game with our contracts. Maybe she didn't hear the whole story and thought we were getting fired. But it looks like that got settled when we received our contracts."

Alarm showed in Mara's face. "Not just *our* jobs. Her exact statement was, 'We're *all* going to lose our jobs if something isn't done.'"

I whistled. "That's a horse of a different dolor."

Mara slapped the table. "That's enough of your puns, Preston Barclay. If Professor Fortier was right, we're dealing with something that affects the entire college."

"*University*," I said. "But you're right. It has to be a much broader problem."

Mara burned me with another blow-torch gaze. "And while everything goes smash around us, you sit in your office and play hands and ... and *whatever* with that ... that brunette Lorelei."

"I wasn't sitting," I said. "We were both standing, and we weren't playing hands."

I knew when I said it that I shouldn't have. Mara's face reddened. I feared I was going to get the star heat I'd feared that afternoon.

"Now, children," Dr. Sheldon began. "Let us not—"

He got no further, for a grim-looking Robert Lee returned. He spoke in a low voice. "Don't look out the window, but there's a car full of tough-looking characters hanging out across the street. They keep looking this way."

CHAPTER 21

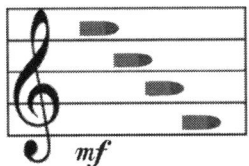

It taxed my willpower to keep from looking out the window. In contrast, Mara managed it without a trace of strain. She smiled up at Robert Lee and said something about the winter weather. Dr. Sheldon beamed up at him as if he'd announced apple pie for dessert.

Robert grinned as if making polite conversation and said, "My dad has called the police to check them out. He thinks they're waiting for you to leave before they rob the place."

Dr. Sheldon made a ceremony of drinking from his empty pop bottle, then said, "What we need is a joke. Press, I've never known you to be short of one."

I searched for one but came up empty. Still looking at Robert Lee, I shrugged.

Dr. Sheldon looked at Mara, who duplicated my shrug.

"All right, then." The older man assumed the attitude of a storm-tossed sailor taking the helm when the rest of the crew fell seasick. "Press, what were some of those notices you posted on your office door in the old days?"

He referred to the days when he was still active and Faith was alive.

"I don't remember," I said.

"Well I do." Dr. Sheldon rapped on the table. "There was one that said, 'Turtles crawling under high tension wires may suffer from shell shock.'"

A look of wonder crossed Mara's face. "Press, did you actually do that?"

"When I was young and foolish," I said.

Dr. Sheldon rapped the table again, obviously enjoying my embarrassment. "There was another one. 'Naked steam engines may be arrested for indiesel exposure.'"

Mara suppressed a laugh. "That's definitely coloring outside the lines."

"The administration thought so," Dr. Sheldon said. "Dean-Dean called him on the carpet, and that was the end of his office-door levity."

The police saved me further embarrassment.

Dr. Sheldon had the best view. "That was neat," he said. "Two police cars sandwiched the other car between them before they turned on their flashers."

"You'd better leave while the cops keep them busy," Robert said.

Mara led, Robert wheeled Dr. Sheldon's chair after her, and I brought up the rear.

"Goo' lock you all," Mrs. Lee called after us.

Robert and I stood by while Dr. Sheldon hoisted himself into Mara's car. Then we folded his chair and tucked it onto the floor behind his seat. Mara backed out of the parking space and drove toward the assisted living center. She did it hastily but without squealing tires.

"Thanks, Robert," I said. As I moved to my Honda, I threw a quick glance at the parked car. The police had the attention of its occupants, with the exception of one mug who gave me a malevolent look. That told me his group had no plans to rob Goolock's. He was the guy who'd bumped me in the hall.

With commendable self-discipline, I managed a quick departure without leaving rubber on the pavement. At the first corner, I turned in the opposite direction from my home. Then I circled back to cross their street behind them and make sure the police still had their attention. They did, so I headed direct for home while my internal pianist gave a reprise of Schumann's *Carnival*.

Appropriate, for my life was becoming a carnival, complete with sideshows.

But why would those toughs be interested in me? They looked like underworld strong-arm types, but how could I be a threat to organized crime? If they wanted revenge for last fall, they'd simply shoot me and be done with it. Yet their actions thus far looked more like an attempt to scare Mara and me off.

Scare us off from what? So far as we knew, we weren't looking into anything connected to organized crime.

I half-expected some surprise to be waiting for me at home. I inspected my front door carefully before I opened it. When I did, nothing happened. One night last fall, I'd walked right in and gotten slugged by an intruder. So this time I let my eyes check the entryway before I let my body enter.

The entryway was empty, and the house was quiet. The only noise came from inside my head, where a music box was tinkling away at "The Anniversary Song," one of Faith's favorites. Inside, I locked the door behind me and checked every room before I relaxed. Only then did I realize how fully my life had changed.

In our home territory, we tend to take personal safety for granted. But one hallway bump and tonight's stakeout had made that assumption obsolete. For reasons I couldn't fathom, people I didn't know were trying to frighten me.

They were doing a good job of it.

For a distraction, I turned on the ten o'clock news. When the graphics quit scrambling around the screen, Francie LaBouche announced that police had released further information about Professor Fortier's death. The cause of death was a massive overdose of cocaine, but the autopsy also revealed traces of chloroform around the mouth. The police, therefore, had declared her death a homicide. They were now questioning the deceased's close acquaintances, Francie said, especially those known to have spoken with her on the night of the reception. Police declined to name names, but Francie remedied that deficiency by announcing that Mara and I were surely among them.

My premonition of things closing in on me seemed to be working out in real life. Too real. To avoid brooding about it, I saturated myself in routine. I took off my brown suit and camouflaged the frayed cuffs with a brown marker pen so it would be ready for the next brown-suit day. That done, I turned in and, remarkably, fell instantly asleep.

I woke on schedule in pre-dawn darkness with my internal musicians playing Prokofiev's "D-Minor Toccata." To be charitable, it sounds like an army of jackhammers performing at random inside a boiler factory. I ignored it, swallowed my ham-sandwich-and-coffee breakfast, and headed up the hill for my nine o'clock class, Renaissance History of Ideas.

Two sleepy-looking football players met me at the point where the walkway begins at the foot of the campus hill. Both grunted a "Good morning" and I replied with the same. They followed about ten feet behind me.

At the top of the hill, I stopped and beckoned them forward. "I appreciate what you're doing," I said, "but I'm not sure one bump in the hallway merits this kind of precaution."

They showed pseudo-puzzled expressions.

"I don't know what you mean, Professor Barclay," said one. "We was just out breathin' the fresh morning air."

"And I'm the reincarnation of Benjamin Franklin," I said.

The other one showed a discreet leer. "I heard you had several things in common with him. But like Jeb says, we was just out takin' the morning air."

I laughed. "Have it your way, but make sure this word gets around—if you see anybody carrying a weapon, run the other way. I don't want anyone hurt on my account."

They both looked remarkably innocent, and the first one said, "Okay, we'll do it. But I still don't know what you're talkin' about."

We walked together into the Liberal Arts Center, where neither one of them had set foot since "getting his required courses out of the way," and we parted amicably at my office door.

Inside, my phone was ringing. It was Mrs. Dunwiddie.

"Professor Barclay, President Cantwell would like to see you in his office at eight-thirty this morning."

All I needed to start the day with a bang was a meeting with the president. I checked my watch. Eight-twenty-five.

I struggled not to grit my teeth, and said, "I'll be there."

A new pair of football players trailed me to the Executive Center, and I saw two more following Mara Thorn toward the same destination. We met in the entryway.

"Do you know what this meeting is about?" she asked.

"I hope I'm wrong," I said, "But I'd guess the Blatant Beast is salivating."

Her jaw tightened. I hoped President Cantwell could read the warning signs.

In the secretary's office, we found Mrs. Dunwiddie trying to look inscrutable, another sure sign of something unpleasant. The only favorable sign was that Dean-Dean's office door was closed and no light showed under it. That meant he was probably somewhere else. I flicked my pocket voice recorder on as Mrs. Dunwiddie showed us into President Cantwell's office, where two hardwood straight chairs awaited us, facing his desk. She herself slipped into a chair somewhat behind us, apparently to take notes. The president himself sat resting his elbows on his desk with his face hidden in his hands. This was a J. Cleveland Cantwell I hadn't seen before.

Our president is a tall, impressive man with a long, thin face like John Carradine in the classic movies, and a resonant voice well-suited to formal rhetoric. Like Dean-Dean, he'd received his doctorate in an unusual manner. He was enrolled in an elementary education program when the trustees brought him in as president. His lack of a doctorate proved no obstacle, for our sister institution in the next state promptly awarded him an honorary degree. In the following year, Cantwell awarded one to that college's un-degreed president. Thus the amenities were served, at least nominally.

When our president straightened up to acknowledge our presence, he showed a face so pale it had a greenish tinge. His eyes were red. Overall, he looked like the guest of honor at last week's funeral.

He spoke in a hoarse voice. "I've asked both of you in because of certain information I've received about your recent activities, some of which occurred while I was in Minnesota raising funds for the university."

At this point, I would normally have asked how he enjoyed the ice fishing, but today I didn't. I held back because the situation was too threatening for levity, and Cantwell looked too ill for needling.

I didn't have to ask what his information was or where he'd gotten it. Staggart to Dean-Dean to Cantwell was the expected course.

Mara sat forward in her chair. "And just what *information* have you received?" I think she'd have leaned across his desk except that she didn't want to catch whatever disease he had.

"Please." Cantwell raised a restraining hand, coughed into his sleeve, recovered, and proceeded in his customary rhetorical manner. "It is said that *both* of you were *Involved* with each other and Professor Fortier in ... in what I must call ... An Unsavory Relationship."

As always, the president's words were so formal they seemed to me to roll off his tongue largely in capital letters.

Mara burned him with her ocular blow-torch. "*It* doesn't say anything, President Cantwell. *Someone* has said it. I demand to know who is spreading vicious rumors about me."

Cantwell recoiled before her onslaught. "Please," he said again. "I believe the original source of the information is the police ... "

"You mean Captain Clyde Staggart," Mara said, eyes still blazing. "Last fall, Richmond Seagrave told you exactly why Staggart hates Pre ... uh ... Professor Barclay. It's because twenty years ago in the Army, Professor Barclay and Richmond Seagrave testified against Staggart and he had to resign his commission. Staggart tried to pin Laila Sloan's murder on Professor Barclay—and on me because I was associated with him. And now he hates both of us all the more because we solved the murder he couldn't solve."

President Cantwell erupted in a fit of coughing, some into his sleeve but some toward the room in general. At that moment, I might have sold my soul for a gas mask.

He took a gasping breath and tried again. "Professor Thorn, I hear that you are only Peripherally Involved in the ... ah ... Difficulties ... between Professor Barclay and Professor Fortier ... "

I thought she'd carried our case long enough, so I jumped in. "Sir, those supposed 'difficulties' between me and Professor Fortier never happened. There has never been a romantic or other improper relationship between us. Nor has there ever been an improper relationship between Professor Thorn and me."

Cantwell coughed again, thankfully only into his sleeve, and resumed his formal rhetoric. "Professor Barclay, I'm aware that No Official Information on this ... ah ... Matter...has yet been received. But As You Know, we are on the Annual Budgets of More Than One Hundred Churches. Any further derogatory information could cause a Serious Decline in that support."

Mara attacked again. "I would hope a respectable church would act upon truth rather than scurrilous rumors. I demand my right to face my accusers."

Cantwell roused himself momentarily. "You both may have that opportunity, Professor Thorn. I have asked Dr. Billig to determine if there is Any Substance to the rumors and to Initiate Appropriate Action if he finds that there is."

He coughed into his sleeve again. I wondered if the dry cleaners could ever sanitize it.

"In the Meantime," he said, "I expect you to Conduct Yourselves in the Exemplary Manner expected of faculty at This Institution." He stood, signaling that the meeting was ended.

Mara also stood, eyes blazing. "President Cantwell, I have always conducted myself that way, and I don't plan to conduct myself any differently now."

With my history as faculty troublemaker I couldn't make that boast, so I only said, "I understand."

Mrs. Dunwiddie remained with the president and closed his door behind us. Mara still had a full head of steam, but she held it until we reached the hallway. Then she exploded.

"How *dare* they spread that vicious drivel about us! And how *dare* President Cantwell believe it!"

"Welcome to the college faculty," I said. "Here everyone lives by his own fantasy about the way things are." I wondered if that included my claim that I "just teach history."

Mara spoke between clenched teeth. "I can't wait to confront the people who started those rumors." She marched out toward her classroom, her chin elevated in the manner that meant trouble for someone.

I realized with a shock that I hadn't told her about Mitra's journal.

CHAPTER 22

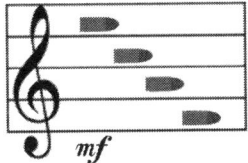

I hadn't told Mara about Bruno Pinkle's attempt to get into my computer, either. I'd intended to brief her on both, but the appearance of the toughs at Goolock's interrupted. I decided I'd try to bring her up to date at lunch. If she would listen, that is. Cynthia Starlington's lipstick had made her very angry—more than the occasion warranted, I thought. Mara had chosen to fight rumors by avoiding me, so why was she complaining if someone else didn't?

By the time I began my nine o'clock class, I was feeling quite self-righteous about it. The class itself is my favorite—Renaissance History of Ideas. And today I talked about the Renaissance view of the Imagination, often called Phantasie, Fantasy, or Fancy. All of these words referred to the same link in Renaissance psychology's hierarchy of human faculties. For it was believed that everything in the cosmos, including human beings, was organized in related hierarchies. (Admittedly, I gave an abbreviated version.)

At the bottom of the hierarchy came the five outer senses, with touch at the bottom and sight at the top. Above them came the inner senses, the Memory and the Imagination, and above those came the Reason, or Rational Soul. The important thing for our discussion was that the function of the Imagination was to convert data from the outer senses into images and pass these images to the Reason. The Imagination could also originate images. It was believed to be particularly powerful in poets and other creative artists. Consequently, everything the Reason did was based on the images fed to it by the Imagination.

But the Imagination did not always present accurate images. If it empowered creative artists, it also presented lunatics with their delusions. Imagination also presented the lover with the image of his beloved. Thus the variations in those images among individuals explained why different men fell in love with different women.

These variations in Imagination appeared to explain much about love, creative artistry, and insanity. As always, I concluded by quoting that wonderful passage from *A Midsummer Night's Dream* in which Duke Theseus explains that "The lunatic, the lover, and the poet/Are of Imagination all compact ..." I quote the entire passage, including the lines in which an errant Imagination causes the lover to believe an ugly woman is beautiful.

By the time I finished, about half the class recognized the majesty of the idea while the other half was giving me the Visiting-Professor-from-the-University-of-Pluto look.

When the class ended, I was on another high, with my internal musicians playing trumpets and timpani, and with Clyde Staggart and Bruno Pinkle only small clouds on a distant horizon. So much for *my* Imagination. But reality waited for me at my office in the form of Sally Finhatter.

"Professor Barclay," she said, "I did give that index card to the police. They decided the word was 'Ruskin' because I'd picked it up right beside a book by somebody named Ruskin. Something about painting."

"John Ruskin's *Modern Painters*?" I asked.

Her face lit up. "That's the one. I came back to tell you because I know you had a hard time reading Professor Fortier's writing."

"Thanks for telling me," I said.

She turned to leave, then threw a few words back over her shoulder. "The best part is that the police gave me back my own card."

That encounter returned my mind to disproving my own scandal. I wasn't satisfied with what Weldon Combes and Freda Broyles had told me, so I headed over to the Science Center. Combes' office was locked, so I tried Freda. She was sitting at her desk like a giant toad waiting for a fly to come within tongue-lapping range.

Her glance made me as welcome as a scorpion. "What brings you back to science territory, Press? Looking for another body?"

"Only a body of fact," I said. "You didn't play straight with me last time, Freda. You told me you went home to get a lesson plan, but the police caught you taking dresses out of Mitra's house. What were you trying to do?"

Her glance demoted me from scorpion to West Nile virus. "For heaven's sake, Press. That terrible homicide policeman keeps pestering me, and now you come along. Are you trying to pin a murder on me?"

"I'm just trying to get a few facts straight," I said. "What's with the dresses?"

"They were mine. I didn't want them tied up forever in some police evidence room." She made such deliberate eye contact that I knew she was lying.

"I hear that the dresses wouldn't fit you."

"Of course not," she said. "They were costumes from the Regency period. I don't wear them. I collect them, so the sizes don't matter."

"What were they doing in Mitra's house?"

Her shoulder gave a half-shrug. "I lent them to her. Last summer—before Jerry's death—she talked about going to a costume ball with him. After he got killed, I didn't want to ask for them back. She would have returned them when she got around to it."

"Why Regency?" I asked. "Or do you collect from other periods, too?"

"That's a special period for women readers," she said. "It's made famous by that romance writer, Georgiana Lowe."

"I didn't know you were a fan of romances," I said.

This was the first time I'd ever seen a horned toad flutter its eyelashes. "We all have a bit of romance in us. We scientific women can't spend all our time chasing decimal points."

"Which book is your favorite?" I asked.

"Uh ..." Freda's bold façade wobbled, but she quickly shored it up. "I think it's called *Ajax Revisited*."

"How did you like the one called *The Bad Lady of Bath*?"

Her discomfort returned, "Ah ... that was good, too."

"Faith liked the bedroom scenes in that one," I said.

"Yes, they were quite ... ah ... *daring*, I suppose you'd say."

"Where did you say Mitra went on weekends?" I hoped the sudden change of subject would shake some information loose.

Instead, the impenetrable fortress façade returned. "She never said, except that she was doing research. And once she mentioned the School of Business library at the state university. The only relative she had was an aunt that raised her. Mitra sometimes visited her in a nursing home down in Cloverdale."

"Did you ever hear of any love interest besides Jerry Vaughan?"

Freda again showed the overly-straight gaze that told me she was either lying or holding something back. "Not a trace of anything like that. She was very self-contained. I was surprised that Jerry even got to first base with her."

"How many bases did he touch?"

"That's something she would never have told me. Suffice it to say they planned to be married." Her eyes shifted momentarily. "Well, Professor Combes had his eyes on Mitra right after Jerry's death, but she wasn't having any."

Combes was married, and untoward conduct would get him in trouble with the administration almost as quickly as it would me. So I asked, "Did he make any overt advances?"

"You'll have to ask him about that." Freda looked at her watch and laboriously heaved her bulk into a standing position. "Now, if you're through playing Torquemada," she said, pronouncing the Grand Inquisitor's name with an English *d* sound rather than the Spanish *th*, "I have an appointment. And I'd advise you to quit bulling around like you're doing. You know what almost happened to you last fall."

"People who tell me the whole truth have nothing to worry about," I said, and left before she could reply.

Actually, my statement wasn't the full truth, either. There was a murderer loose, and truth could be fatal to him or her. My statement was aimed at Freda's deceptions. For Georgiana Lowe never wrote a book called *The Bad Lady of Bath*, and she prided herself on never writing bedroom scenes. Aside from the fact that Freda was lying, the only useful thing I'd learned was that Mitra had an aunt in a nursing home in Cloverdale.

Then it hit me. Freda had said "that terrible homicide detective" was still pestering her. So the police were still interested in Freda. I'd failed to follow up on that because I got tunnel vision about the dresses. Another opportunity missed.

When I got back to my office, the phone was ringing.

"Professor Barclay," said a husky female voice on the line, "this is Brill Drisko. We met in that campus hamburger joint the other day."

"I remember," I said. "I gather you didn't like your cheeseburger."

"It was the pits," she said. "It got grease all over my mouth, and I had to do my makeup over again."

"Life's tragedies," I said.

She shifted topics without missing a breath. "Professor Barclay, I've got to talk to you before this thing gets too far."

"What thing?" I asked.

"Your investigation of Mitra Fortier's death."

"That's a police matter," I said. "I'm not investigating it."

"That's not what I hear." Her voice became huskier. "Can you come by here this afternoon?"

"Where is 'here'?" I asked. My caution went on red alert.

"Steven's and my house," she said. "It's a couple of miles out on the Caneyville Road."

"I'm sorry," I said. "I'm tied up this afternoon with office hours."

"Some other time, then," she said. "But I do have to talk to you about your investigation."

"I'm not investigating anything," I said, but she had hung up.

It was almost noon, so I rang Mara's office in hopes of catching her before lunch. She didn't answer, so I headed to the grill. I found her there with the seemingly inevitable Emory Estes and the male and female composition specialists. Today, though, Mara's chairman, Dathan Hormah, had graced us with his presence. As I joined them, Hormah was speaking in lecture mode.

"This whole idea of romantic love is hogwash," he said. "In biblical times, love was either lust or a matter of having children to carry on the family name. Romantic love didn't exist until medieval fiction made a fetish of it, and no one knows if people actually practiced it even then. That fiction has overshadowed reality ever since. The whole concept of romantic love is imaginary, a mythology our culture indoctrinates us with. The truth is that we're well-designed physical organisms genetically programmed to propagate the species."

He paused for effect, and Mara responded, "You're saying that 'This is what men called love until the Freudians taught us to blame it on the glands.'"

Score another point for her erudition. She'd neatly adapted Maxwell Anderson's *Winterset* to the present occasion.

Dathan Hormah looked taken aback. "That's a rather blunt way of putting it, Professor Thorn, but it's essentially correct." He showed no awareness that she was quoting anything or that she was using irony to refute him.

I usually stay out of these discussions, but this was too good to miss. "Back to your biblical claim," I said, "from Genesis through Revelation, marriage is the earthly image of man's right relationship with God."

Hormah smiled. "Those writers also let their imaginations override their reason. It's taken two thousand years to cut through the horseradish and fantasy. All metaphors are imaginary. In the real world, you have to deal with physical facts." He heaved himself out of his chair and said over his shoulder as he left, "Come to my church in Meribah Valley, and we'll give you the real facts."

"I'm glad I'm not his wife," the female composition specialist said.

Emory Estes looked confused. Mara had gone suddenly quiet when I mentioned marriage. Hers had been short and unpleasant.

"I hear you're a weekend aviator," I said to Estes. This wasn't the place to question him, but I hoped to open communications.

"I was until Jerry Vaughan cracked up our airplane," he said. "It will take us a while to build another."

"Isn't building one more dangerous than buying one off the lot?"

"They don't keep them on lots like cars," he said. "They keep used airplanes on ramps at airports."

"Off the ramp, then."

"That's not always safe, either." He scratched his head. "If you buy one used, you never know what's been done to it. Some people treat their airplanes pretty rough. When a used car turns out to be a bummer, you pull it over and park it. But you can't park defective airplanes up there in the sky."

"So you guys built your own," I said. "But it still quit on Jerry Vaughan. What do you think happened?" Mara gave me a don't-go-there look.

"The accident investigation board said it was structural failure."

"They found that the wing was not properly installed," I said. "How do you think that happened?"

Estes' eyes narrowed. "The board never figured that out, and neither have I. Look, Professor Barclay, that's a settled issue, and it's dangerous to go poking around in things you don't have the qualifications to understand."

"It just seems strange," I said. "Jerry Vaughan and his fiancée both killed under mysterious circumstances within six months."

"Coincidences happen," he said. Anger showed in his eyes.

"Say," said the female composition specialist, "you wouldn't believe my students in Introduction to Literature. Some of them couldn't figure out why Hawthorne's Hester Prynne wore the scarlet letter."

"Maybe she was a cheerleader for the University of Alabama," I said.

That was an old one, apparently too old for the comp specialist to have heard it. Her mouth hung open. Emory Estes looked blank. Mara shook her head and suppressed a laugh.

Before anything else could develop, I felt a soft touch on the back of my neck. Everyone's eyes focused on something above my head, and when I turned and looked up, I found a smiling Cynthia Starlington. Her hand moved softly on the back of my neck. Fortunately, she used her long fingernails to stroke rather than scratch.

"Hello, Press," she said. "Have you found the murderer yet?"

"I'm not investigating anything," I said.

Emory Estes broke in. "You were giving a good imitation of it a while ago."

"Idle curiosity," I said.

"I hope you catch him." Cynthia gave a final stroke on my neck and left with her characteristic gliding walk.

"Gosh, Press," said the female composition specialist. "You must be a real favorite."

"'A favorite has no friend,'" Mara quoted.

Incomprehension showed on everyone else's face, but I knew exactly what she meant. She'd speared me with a line from Thomas Gray's "Ode on the Death of a Favorite Cat, Drown'd in a Tub of Gold Fishes." I could almost feel my unhappy corpse soaking in the water.

Before I could answer, Mara stood up and said, "Excuse me. I have to get ready for class."

"There's something I need to tell you," I said.

"Phone me at my office," she answered. "I have to go."

She did. With less drama than Cynthia but with equal attraction.

"What's going on?" Estes asked, bewilderment written on his face.

"*La donna è mobile*," I said. But instead of that sprightly song, my internal orchestra played the pensive "Evening Star" from *Tannhäuser*.

I made my own departure then, leaving Estes bewildered and the two composition specialists in a life-or-death discussion of restrictive and nonrestrictive modifiers.

A new convoy saw me back to my office, where I immediately phoned Mara. "Sergeant Spencer says Mitra Fortier kept a handwritten journal. He says it chronicles a long affair between her and me, beginning several years before my wife died. It never happened, and I told him so. He said he had more and more trouble believing me."

"So do I," Mara said. "What is this supposed to mean to me?"

"I guess it's the basis for Clyde Staggart's accusing you of forming a triangle. I wanted you to know he has physical evidence we have to defeat to clear ourselves."

"All right, you've told me," she said. "Now I have to go to class."

She rang off. I realized I still hadn't told her about Bruno Pinkle trying to get into my computer.

CHAPTER 23

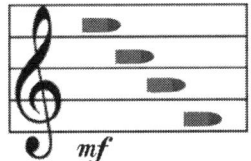

Despite my frustration, I marched myself into the classroom. The class was Western Civ, and I spent the period describing the intellectual developments of King Alfred's reign made possible by the Peace of Wedmore. It must have gone okay, though I could never get my mind fully focused on King Alfred.

Afterwards, I retreated to my office for some serious thinking. There was no mistaking Mara's anger with me, but what was its cause? She might believe I was dallying with Cynthia when I should have been investigating the threat to the faculty's jobs. I hoped, though I had no right, that she was jealous over my response to Cynthia's attentions. I admit I was attracted to Cynthia in a manner not entirely honorable. But I'd been alone for three years, so why shouldn't I get back in the game?

Well, I was jealous, too—over Emory Estes' apparent success with Mara. He wasn't good enough for her, but that was her choice to make. I only hoped she wouldn't regret her choice later. After that bad marriage in her teens, she deserved something better.

That brought me to my unsuccessful questioning of Estes. He'd told me nothing except to mind my own business. Was he only reluctant to talk to a groundling? Or was he hiding something about the aircraft accident? I did not know which, but there was one thing I did know. Estes was a former football player still in fine condition. I wanted no part of tangling with him physically.

That brought me back to Dathan Hormah's opinion about love, which he'd spoken almost immediately after my class on the Imagination. His reductionist view did not accord with my marriage experience with Faith. Continuance of the species may have hovered in the backs of our minds, but the rich and ever-growing harmony of complex personalities far transcended that view. Our imaginations created the wonderful possibilities that Faith and I explored together, but we brought those possibilities to life in the real world.

Actually, Dathan Hormah himself had taken a gigantic leap of Imagination to picture a world limited to physical forces and pre-programmed biological drives. Or was he just whistling past a darkness his philosophy could not penetrate?

Apparently, the Imagination is a force that can create great good or great evil. I wondered how much of our imagined perception of the world actually matched hardcore reality. Was my claim that "I just teach history" grounded in reality, or was it a fantasy I'd formed to shield me from a more complicated life?

I got no further, for Brill Drisko suddenly stood in my door. I noticed again that she moved with restless energy and the balance of a skilled dancer. She wore black tights that emphasized the fullness of her figure, along with a V-neck blouse that was undoubtedly non-nuclear but nevertheless placed her in imminent danger of fallout. I never discovered what kind of shoes she wore.

She marched in without asking and said, "You wouldn't come to me, Professor Barclay, so I came to you. We have things to talk about."

I circled my desk to meet her and said, "Have a chair, and we'll talk about them." My internal musicians swung into a fast-paced two-step.

"I don't have time to sit down," she said, leaving us standing in the middle of the floor. "I'll be honest with you, Professor Barclay: There are things in my life I'd just as soon people around here didn't know about. And the way you've been investigating, they're bound to come out. They would make me a social outcast and might hurt my husband's career."

"I don't gossip," I said.

Her small black eyes focused on mine. "You don't have to gossip for the wrong kind of things to get out. Your poking into it is enough to make people talk."

"I'm not poking into anything," I lied.

"That's not what Emory Estes says. He says at lunch today you put him through a real— what d'you call it—imposition ..."

"Inquisition," I said.

"Whatever it was, he says you put him through it, and he didn't see why you wanted to talk about that airplane crash when some official board had finished with it. He thinks you're out to make trouble."

She moved a step closer, and I took a step back.

I thought it was time to file a disclaimer. "I'm not interested in people's personal lives, Brill. Professor Fortier was a friend of my wife's, and I'm trying to come to grips with her death."

"You say you don't gossip," she said, taking another step closer and holding her gaze on mine. "I think I can trust you, so I'm going to tell you what I'm afraid of."

I took another step back. "Don't tell me anything I might have to repeat if someone put me under oath." She was making no sense at all, and I was beginning to feel like an animal being stalked. I read once that circus lion tamers cracked their whips only for show, that what made the lions back up was the lion tamers' invading their space. It worked as long as the lions were well fed. I didn't consider myself well fed, but Brill's invading my space certainly made me uncomfortable.

She took another step forward. I stepped backward and to the side. She matched the sideward movement and remained confronting me.

"I'm afraid people here will find out I was a showgirl," she said. "They'll leap to all kinds of wrong conclusions. But there's nothing wrong with being a showgirl, is there?"

"It depends on what kind of show," I said. I took another step back and found myself backed up against the desk with no more room to retreat.

"It wasn't *that* kind of show." Brill's gaze bored into mine. "I didn't like showbiz, but Steven took me out of all that. I've made him a good wife, and I don't want anything to spoil it."

"I can understand that," I said. I didn't see how anyone could not know Brill had been a showgirl. But if she wanted to entertain the fantasy that they could, I wasn't going to disillusion her.

"So when you go stirring up trouble," she continued, "it threatens my marriage and my husband's career. Making people angry like you do could be dangerous to you, too. Someone's likely to get mad enough to do something about it."

"Is that someone you, Brill?"

She took a step closer, almost touching me now. Her perfume smelled expensive, but she must have poured it on by the cupful.

"I'd rather be nice to people," she said. "I can be very nice to people who don't threaten my marriage." She put her left hand on my right shoulder and smiled into my face. She was almost my height, which put her face so close to mine that I could see the grains of her makeup. My desk ground into my backside, leaving me no room to retreat.

"I don't want to threaten your marriage," I said.

"That's very nice of you, Press," she said, "so maybe we can be nice together sometime. My husband is away all day at work." With her right hand she reached into the V-neck of her blouse and brought out a small card. She waved it under my nose so I could tell it was perfumed, then deposited it inside my coat in my shirt pocket. Her hand lingered there a bit, then moved to my left shoulder. We stood there a few moments with her hands on my shoulders and her gaze boring into mine.

"That card has my phone number," she said. "We could be very nice together."

It occurred to me that she gave a new definition to "being nice." I preferred the old one.

High heels sounded in the hallway, but Brill ignored them. The heel-clicks stopped and Mara Thorn stood in the doorway, an angry expression on her face. Brill did not turn. Mara's lips tightened, and she moved away up the hall. The click of her heels faded quickly.

I put my hands on Brill's shoulders and gently prevented her advance while I escaped to the side. She dropped her hands and turned to face me but made no attempt to follow.

"Being nice is all very fine," I said, "but several things are threatening my job. That's why I have to look into them."

"It's looking into them that may threaten your job," she said. "My husband is a trustee." The small black eyes stayed focused on mine, and I wondered if she ever had to blink.

"Where did you work as a showgirl, Brill?" I asked.

"Find that out at your peril." The black eyes flashed as she turned toward the door. "It's dangerous to keep making people mad at you."

My musicians abandoned the two-step and launched into a can-can.

Brill left me wondering about her intentions. Nothing she said made sense. She claimed to be worried about people finding out she'd been in show business, but her manner of dress would force that conclusion on them. She claimed to value her marriage, yet she'd used seduction as a bribe to make me stop asking questions. And her ambiguous threats made me wonder if they only pertained to my job or involved physical harm.

I didn't wonder long, for a herd of heavy steps sounded in the hallway and Captain Clyde Staggart barged into my office, followed by Bruno Pinkle and the Keats-quoting detective I'd always called Dogface. I remembered Mara's saying his name was Duggan Hahn, and that he'd looked pained at some of Staggart's methods.

Staggart started to speak, but then sniffed a couple of times. "Phew!" he said. "Press, you smell like a French hotel. I didn't know you used perfume."

"It's for my double life as a can-can girl," I said, thankful for once for my mental musicians' prompt. Now that Staggart mentioned it, I realized that I reeked. Brill must have perfumed her hands as well as that card.

"That's not the double life we're interested in," Staggart snarled. "We have your dean's permission to search your office."

He nodded to Pinkle, who made a beeline for the desk drawer where he'd planted that CD.

"Search away," I said. "You won't find any drugs or automatic weapons." I was glad I'd moved the fingerprint recognition device to my car. I wanted to switch on my voice recorder, but Dogface held me constantly in his baleful gaze.

Pinkle looked up with a puzzled expression, then held my three well-labeled CDs up for Staggart's inspection.

Staggart blinked, but recovered quickly. "Search the rest of the office," he ordered.

"It will save time if you tell me what you're looking for," I said.

Staggart scowled. "Never mind. Just open up that computer."

"I've forgotten how," I said. "These new-fangled gadgets like doorbells and computers keep me confused."

He turned to Dogface ... uh ... Duggan Hahn ... and ordered, "Take his hard drive."

Hahn greeted the order with a scowl but moved to comply. I again tried to switch on my recorder, but now Staggart was watching me too closely. Detective Hahn crawled under my desk, disconnected the computer and lifted it onto the desk. He proceeded to open it and remove the hard drive. Meanwhile, Pinkle busied himself removing books from the shelves and looking behind them. He re-shelved the books haphazardly.

"Of what heinous crime am I suspected?" I asked.

Staggart's lips drew back in a snarl. "Your affair with Mitra Fortier makes you a person of interest in her murder."

"There was no affair," I said.

Staggart laughed. "We have evidence to the contrary. I don't doubt that you lead a double life, Press boy, but not as innocent as a can-can girl."

"I insist on the can-can," I said.

Fortunately, Staggart did not request my dance steps, which in fact were nonexistent. He was too taken up with Pinkle's ending his search with a shrug and another confused expression. About that time, the reluctant Dogface/Hahn held up my computer's hard drive for his inspection. Staggart nodded and jerked his thumb toward the door. Both of his subordinates exited.

"That's all for now, Press," Staggart said, "but we'll be back." He concluded with his characteristic charge, "Keep your nose clean."

I answered with my stock reply. "I always do. I thought you'd remember that."

As their heavy steps retreated down the hall, I surveyed the mess they'd left behind. I put the three CDs back in my desk drawer, shoved the now-useless computer back under the desk, and postponed straightening the sloppily re-shelved books until later.

Outside, the early winter night had fallen. I straggled down the narrow walkway to my home with the wind from the plains gnawing at my neck and ears while I reviewed the disastrous events of the day. I'd alienated Freda Broyles to the point of receiving veiled threats. I'd received not-so-veiled threats from Brill Drisko. And Clyde Staggart and his henchmen were trying to frame me with heaven only knew what. I still had no way to refute the false accusation of an affair with Mitra Fortier. Worst of all, I'd twice offended Mara Thorn, my only real friend on campus. And my class on Imagination had me wondering how much of my own life was real and how much was fantasy. I didn't see how things could get worse.

At home, I opened the front door and carefully checked the hallway before I entered. It was empty except for a piece of paper on the floor.

I turned on the light and picked up the paper. It was a computer-printed note:

STOP THE INVESTIGATION BEFORE IT'S TOO LATE.

CHAPTER 24

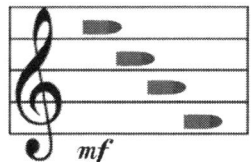

A familiar chill ran through me as I read the warning note. I had no way of guessing who left it: Everyone I'd talked to lately had warned me to quit asking questions. But someone had no trouble breaking into my house.

I chewed on the question while I chewed my way through a ham sandwich and decided I'd better find out a lot more information a lot faster than I'd been doing. I'd started out only to combat a threat to my job, and then to disprove the allegation I'd had an affair with Mitra. But the more questions I asked toward those ends, the more I got tangled up with her death. Everyone thought I was investigating that anyway, so I might as well do it.

The best source of what happened on campus at night would be the night watchman, Elmo Koonz, but he would not come on duty until later. I'd have time for prayer meeting and could catch him afterward.

I drove to St. Mark's Grace Church because I badly needed its prayer meeting. For a long time, I'd felt that my prayers simply bounced back at me off the ceiling. I hoped for a better result if I kept trying. The quiet of the sanctuary and the solemnity of the introductory hymns restored my sense that here things were actually *right*—that the values we'd struggled to maintain during the week were not imaginary, that the struggle was worth the toil and pain.

Nothing on earth is perfect, though. I felt a pang that Mara was not present. Was she angry over my encounters with Cynthia and Brill, or was there a more ominous reason? I pushed these thoughts from my mind and surrendered to the solemnity of the music.

Then Cynthia Starlington entered and sat beside me. Very close.

"I hoped I'd find you here, Press," she whispered. "I need to talk to you."

"Later," I said and shushed her with a finger over my lips. I refused to give up this hard-found sense of rightness.

She made a show of pouting, but she did comply.

After an opening prayer, Pastor Tammons read Christ's statement from the Gospel of John. "My Father is working until now, and I Myself am working." God's active work in this world does not cease, the pastor said, but to see its results we must think not year-to-year or even century-to-century. We must think in units no shorter than five hundred years. For it took a full five hundred years for the Church to halfway civilize our ancestors, the Northern European barbarians.

For thousands of years, he continued, slavery was a standard practice throughout the entire world. And it is only in the past few centuries, even then only in the nations with a Christian heritage, that God's light has convinced us that slavery is evil. In this and in many other things, we can see the work of the hand of God ...

My mind raced ahead of him then. As I'd said, I had no doubt that God directs the great tides of history. But does He control the individual waves? And how about those waves that lash out at each other?

The pastor's theme reminded me of my recent studies in popular Renaissance emblem books like those of Andrea Alciato and Claude Paradin. Each emblem used visual art and writing to illustrate fundamental truths or beliefs, usually derived from biblical or classical origins. The emblem that stung me now was called "Truth, the Daughter of Time." It held that, given time, truth would always find its way through falsehood. As one of Shakespeare's characters put it, "in the end truth will out."

I wanted badly to believe it. But even if truth did win out in the end, and I was proved innocent of an affair with Mitra Fortier, would I still have a job when the end came?

The piano's introduction to the closing hymn jarred me from my brooding. I became conscious of Cynthia's shoulder leaning against mine. It moved away briefly as we stood for the hymn, then closed in again during the second stanza. I admit I enjoyed it.

After the benediction, she turned to face me. "Let's go some place where we can talk, Press."

"Has something new happened?" I asked.

"Not really." She looked suddenly demure. "We'd just talk about things in general. Maybe at Goolock's."

An age-old battle raged inside me. Heaven knows I was attracted to her. And heaven also knows my intentions were not altogether honorable. I knew I didn't love her. But if it made her happy to love me, why shouldn't I play along? That's what one part of me said. Another part demanded that I hold back.

I made the reticent part prevail, if only for tonight. "I can't do it tonight, Cynthia. Remember that thing you wanted me to look into? I have to talk to someone I can't catch at any other time."

"Let me go with you," she said. "I always wanted to be part of an investigation."

I grimaced. "The problem is that you're already part of it. Your presence would skew what people say one way or the other. I'm sorry, but to get a straight story, I have to do it alone."

Her voice hardened. "Your historian's demand for accuracy, I suppose. All right, then. Another time."

Suddenly soft again, she touched a finger to my cheek, pivoted, and was gone. Only then did I see that we had an audience. When I glanced up, they quickly looked away. Now I was glad Mara wasn't there. Strange that I worried about what she'd think even when she wasn't there.

The drive home passed unremarkably except that a dark car seemed to be shadowing me. I didn't try to shake it off, but drove directly home and parked in my usual place in the driveway. The dark car continued and turned off two blocks farther down. I hoped I was wrong about the shadowing, but if someone was trying to frighten me, he was doing a good job of it.

I didn't go inside, but trudged through the winter night back up to the college to find Elmo Koonz. I found him in the janitor's room in the basement of the Liberal Arts Center, his usual hangout on cold nights.

At fifty-five, Elmo was only five years my senior. But he looked closer to seventy. His hair was iron gray, and he sported a ragged beard to match. He stood about five-feet-eight, but hunching under a stiff back made him look shorter. Whatever work he'd done in his life must have left him unsatisfied, for he accepted any attention paid him the way a hungry man accepts crumbs.

"Hello, Professor Barclay," he said as I entered his domain. "I been wondering when you'd come talk to me."

He occupied the only chair, so I perched on a drum of cleaning fluid.

"I'm sorry it took so long," I said. "Things have been pretty hectic."

He showed a yellow-toothed grin through his beard. "I guess they have, what with all the stories about you going 'round. Not that I believe any of it, you understand. 'Specially them stories about you and Professor Thorn." He slapped his knee. "Now there is one sweet little lady. Do you know one Sunday morning last fall she brought me donuts and coffee? We sat and talked together for more than a hour, I guess."

"She's a very fine woman," I said. I didn't tell him that Mara's assignment that day was to keep him occupied while I studied the personnel files of suspects for Laila Sloan's murder

"I knew you'd come see me sooner or later," he continued, "'cause you'd want to know what I told the police about the night Professor Fortier got killed."

"You guessed right," I said. "I would like to know."

Elmo clasped his hands on his fat abdomen. "Well-l-l-l, I told 'em what I saw, up to a point." He paused and studied my reaction. "Early in the evening I saw the usual students milling around here and there—on these winter nights they go straight from one warm building to another. And I didn't see none of them go in the science building."

"And later on," I prompted, "after the reception broke up?"

"By that time, the students had pretty much settled down to wherever they were going to be for the night … "

I did not ask for details.

"… and the faculty folks from the reception mostly went places off the campus."

He paused again to watch my reaction. I made none.

"From the corner windows on the third floor," he said, "I can see the whole campus circle without freezing my whatzis. If I leave the lights off, no one can see me."

I made a note to remember that if I made any more nocturnal excursions on campus.

"That's where I was after the reception," he said. "Like I told the police, it was maybe ten o'clock when I saw three guys go into the science building."

"What kind of guys?" I asked.

Elmo scratched his head. "They wore coats and hats, and at that distance I couldn't see faces. But they sure was chummy—close together with their arms locked. Well, they went in the front door of the building and that was the last I saw of 'em."

I wanted clarification. "You said 'three guys.' Does that mean all three were men?"

He continued scratching his head, and I wondered if he had psoriasis. "Couldn't say either way. They was wearing heavy coats, and I don't know if they wore pants or skirts. Not that that would prove anything these days."

"Did you see them come out?"

"No. I heard some noise over toward the Executive Center, so I went and checked … Turned out to be just a truck engine on the street beyond, and I nearly froze my whatzis finding that out. So since I was frizzen anyway, I might as well loop by the science building before I come back here to get warm. That's when I saw one person come out."

"Out of the Science Center? Only one person?"

"Only one person. She didn't see me, 'cause she was in a big hurry to get somewheres else."

"You said 'she'?"

"Yep, it was that new woman professor they hired this year."

A vision of Mara leaped into my mind. What would she be doing there that time of night? Why hadn't she told me about it? My imagination leaped ahead of the facts, and I wondered if she had a guilty reason.

Then my rational faculty caught up. "Which woman professor was that?"

"I don't 'member her name—that pretty one with the brown hair, used to be a student here. She replaced the guy what killed Laila Sloan."

"That would be Cynthia Starlington."

Elmo nodded. "Yeah, I think that's her name. I recognized her first by the long dark hair, and then I saw her face under one of the lights."

"And you've told the police all this?" No wonder they were questioning Cynthia!

"Naw, not quite." The yellow-toothed grin showed again. "I didn't tell 'em about that lady ... didn't want to make trouble for a pretty little girl like that."

The police really *would* have questioned her if they'd had that information. My temper began a low simmer deep inside—here was another case where Cynthia hadn't told me the complete truth.

I stood up, hoping the drum of cleaning fluid hadn't branded my derriere. "Can you think of anything else out of the ordinary that night?"

He shook his head. "Not a thing. I hope you catch him."

"Catch who?"

"The guy what killed her, of course. Ain't that what you're after?"

"We all are," I said. "Thanks for your help."

The night had grown colder, with frigid gusts whipping in off the plains. I snugged my overcoat collar closer around my neck as I hurried down the walkway from the campus and hoped I wouldn't freeze *my* whatzis. Cold or not, though, I approached my house with caution. I opened the door and surveyed the entryway before stepping into it. But caution ended there, for the phone was ringing.

Cindy sounded like she'd been crying. "Daddy, things didn't go well at the hearing today. Mark and I have been suspended."

My anger surged, but I needed facts. "Suspended for how long and under what conditions?"

"The ... the suspension is indefinite. But we can petition for reinstatement if we do several things ..."

I knew what kind of things, but I waited for her to tell me.

"We have to write a public apology confessing that we engaged in hate speech and that our demonstration incited violence and endangered the safety of students and faculty ..."

I saw more red than Lenin and Stalin put together, but I waited for the rest of it. I'd been around long enough to know much more would come.

"Beyond that, we have to go through sensitivity training and perform twenty hours of community service. If we complete all that 'satisfactorily,' we can petition for reinstatement."

"That will take weeks," I said. "What happens to your studies in the meantime?"

Cindy sighed. "They didn't say anything about that. I guess it doesn't matter to them."

"Were others besides you and Mark involved?"

Cindy exhaled sharply. "Three others, but they got off with sensitivity training. They've accepted it because it lets them stay in school."

"The go-along-and-get-along response?"

"That's it. Mark called them cowards, but they just looked at the floor and kind of slunk out. He and I are in it alone."

"I can't tell you how angry I am about this," I said, my voice suddenly hoarse with emotion. "What will you do now?"

"You told us about that organization ... the Council for Individual Rights on Campus. Mark has already phoned them, and they're interested. Tomorrow we're going to talk to them some more."

"That's the best you can do, Cindy. Do you need to come home?"

"No, Daddy." Her voice grew stronger. "They're not going to run me out of here. I'm going to fight."

My heart swelled with pride. "That's the spirit. Call me if there's any way I can help."

"I will, Daddy."

We said we loved each other, and she rang off. I would have been glad for her to stay there and fight the unjust decision in any case, but I was doubly glad because my affairs were in such a mess here. Cindy didn't need my troubles piled on top of her own.

The phone rang again. I heard Dr. Sheldon's great voice, now trembling with its own anger.

"Press, where have you been? I've tried to reach you all evening."

So much for my refusal to buy an answering machine.

Dr. Sheldon breathed hard into the phone. "Mara has been arrested. They've found child pornography on her computer."

CHAPTER 25

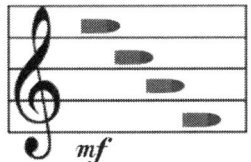

The news hit like a thunderbolt. Like thunder in a violent storm, it echoed back and forth among my clouded memories of recent events like Bruno Pinkle trying to get into my computer. But dealing with the echoes could wait. What I needed now was facts.

"How did it happen?" I asked.

Dr. Sheldon snorted. "Your friend Captain Staggart and Patrolman Pinkle made the arrest at her office late this afternoon. They handcuffed her and marched her out to their car and took her to the police station. She says the TV cameras were waiting for them there—trust Staggart to arrange that. They read Mara her Miranda rights and she took the Fifth. She used her phone call to tell me what happened, and I sent a lawyer down to spring her."

"Brice Funderburk again?" He'd gotten her a habeas corpus last fall, but the way he looked at her left no doubt whose corpus he wanted to habeas.

Dr. Sheldon grunted. "Like him or not, he got her released on her own recognizance. She just called me from home. She's pretty much in shock and doesn't know how that stuff got in her computer.

"I have an idea about that," I said. "I'll have to check it out, but then I'll give Mara a call. Meanwhile, can you warm up your computer for more research?"

"What's the subject?"

I could almost hear the old lion lick his chops.

"Steven Drisko," I said. "His wife tried to bribe or scare me off the case today. See what you can find out about their marriage. Where and when it happened, anything you can find on her background. I don't know if it's pertinent, but it might be."

"Consider it done," he said. "Anything else?"

"Well, I keep running into Gordon Samstag and Emory Estes. It wouldn't hurt to know something about them, too."

He agreed and hung up, obviously invigorated at the thought of more research.

I punched in the number of Richmond Seagrave, my colleague from Army days and the computer security expert who'd given Mara and me those fingerprint readers for our campus computers.

"What kind of trouble are you in now, Press?" he asked. "You never call except when you're in trouble."

Music and female laughter in the background indicated he had a party going. I envied him.

"I think someone has planted illegal material on Mara's computer," I said. "Is there any way to get around those fingerprint readers?"

"Are you sure someone planted it there, or is your blonde Wiccan leading a secret life?"

"*Former* Wiccan," I said. "Besides, I'm pretty sure our mutual friend on the Overton City police force tried to put some bad stuff in my computer."

"Just a minute," he said, and then, away from the phone, "Hey, you guys hold down the noise."

A female voice in the background said, "I'm not a guy, honey. Didn't you know?"

But the noise did quiet down, and Seagrave continued, "How come they couldn't get it in your computer and did get it in hers?"

"I don't know. Maybe because I hide my fingerprint reader in my bookshelf, and maybe she leaves hers on her desk. Is there a way to bypass it?"

"It can be done. You have to have a fingerprint to work with. Given that, all you have to do is lift it onto transparent tape and put the tape over the fingerprint reader. Your culprit has to be either the police or someone who knows how to work fingerprints."

"I'll bet on the police," I said. "A friendly cop told me Staggart has assigned someone to frame me for any kind of felony he could, so maybe he's after Mara, too."

Seagrave laughed. "You have nice policemen down there. They make the Mafia look like Boy Scouts."

"It's not quite that bad," I said. I thanked him and rang off.

Next I tried to call Sergeant Ron Spencer, but I again got his wife.

"He's not here," she said, irritation in her voice.

"Do you know when he'll be back?"

"He didn't say where he was going or when he'd be back," she said, her voice on the edge of anger. "If you see him, tell him to call home."

I said I would and hung up.

I wanted to call Mara then, but it was time for the ten o'clock news. I turned on the TV just in time to catch the obligatory nuclear explosion and bell-ring before Francie LaBouche came on in her chorus-girl costume and grease paint. Tonight her makeup department must have seen some ads for Caribbean vacations. Francie's fair complexion had metamorphosed into the color of a corkboard.

"There's shocking news tonight," she said with the intonation of one about to tell an off-color joke and expecting everyone to enjoy it. "A woman professor at Overton University, a Christian denominational institution, was found with child pornography on her college computer. Professor Mara Thorn, who joined the faculty last fall as a Wiccan and later claimed conversion to Christianity, was led in handcuffs to the city jail this afternoon."

The visual presentation shifted to Mara getting out of the police car, her hands cuffed behind her. Her escort, Bruno Pinkle, attempted to grasp her arm to lead her into the station. That was his mistake. She bumped him away with her shoulder and followed that with a sharp elbow that happened to hit his funny bone. He recoiled and grasped his arm while Mara marched proudly into the station without his assistance.

My heart went out to her. She'd been fighting one thing or another all her life, and now, faced with public disgrace, she met it with head held high. But I knew the heartbreak beneath that brave front.

While that pageant was acted out, Francie LaBouche's voiceover continued—"The discovery of pornography happened as a byproduct of the police's continuing investigation into the murder of Professor Mitra Fortier." She drew a deep breath. "As we revealed previously here on station KLYE, Professor Fortier was reportedly having an affair of long standing with a male member of the faculty. Then, last fall, a new woman who joined the faculty gave Professor Fortier a rival for her lover's affections, and the resulting triangle led to angry confrontations and threats of personal harm. A few days later, Professor Fortier was found dead."

The visual returned to Francie. "KLYE has now learned that the male faculty member involved was Professor Preston Barclay, and the newcomer was none other than the star of tonight's show, Professor Mara Thorn, both of whom were involved with the Laila Sloan murder last fall. A police spokesperson confirmed that they are persons of interest in this continuing homicide investigation. Now the investigation widens as Professor Thorn is charged with possession of child pornography so vile that we can't describe it on the air."

She paused for another breath. "Authorities at Overton University refused comment except to say that appropriate action would be taken."

That meant Mara and I faced another meeting with President Cantwell. If we were lucky. If he was out fishing somewhere, Dean-Dean would be happy to fill in.

Trust Francie and her scriptwriters to put the worst possible face on things. Now, thanks to Francie and her TV crew, the Blatant Beast would have a gluttonous feast. If Truth was going to be The Daughter of Time in this case, Time had better move fast.

"In other news," Francie intoned, "government investigation continues into that rocket failure earlier this week. Authorities have traced the failure to a guidance component provided by Pegasus Electronics. In an unusual move, the corporation's chairman of the board, Gordon Samstag, announced that an internal investigation is being conducted. He promises to get to the bottom of what happened."

At that point I hit the "off" switch. I can take just so much TV news, and tonight I'd heard much too much. So now I did what I should have done earlier. I phoned Mara Thorn.

"I suppose you've heard the news of my life in crime," she said, her voice hard and metallic. "So much for our efforts to avoid scandal. The Beast is loose."

"On TV, they've named both of us in that supposed love triangle with Mitra," I said, "so we can expect another meeting with the president or dean, probably first thing in the morning."

"We have so much to look forward to," she said.

"We can either sit and wait for things to happen, or we can use the old Army procedure—'attack immediately with troops available.'"

"We don't have any troops, and we don't have an objective to attack," she said. But her tone changed. "What did you have in mind?"

"We'll talk about it if you'll go jogging with me." I didn't know if the phones were bugged, so I used a reference only she would understand. Jogging had been the cover for certain activities we couldn't discuss openly.

"I could use a good run," she said, her voice now clear and eager. "Where and when?"

I named a park about four blocks from Mitra Fortier's house and the time as midnight.

She agreed, and we rang off.

I would have liked to give her some reassurance about her computer, but the possibility of bugged phones precluded it. Some of the local judges are overly compliant with requests for bugs and search warrants. I didn't know if we'd find anything in Mitra

Fortier's house that would justify our burglary, but it was the only place I could think of to begin.

Shortly before midnight, I changed into my jogging suit, added a dark toboggan cap and scarf against the winter cold, and made sure the pockets still held my latex surgical gloves. My everyday gloves were dark enough, so I wore them. I sneaked out my back door and followed the darkest shadows around to the front, pausing in one of them to make sure no one was watching. Then I climbed into my old Honda and drove to the rendezvous.

Mitra's house was located about half a mile from mine, the park I'd named four blocks beyond. The deserted park lay in darkness except for the lighted parking area. I arrived early so Mara wouldn't have to wait there alone, and pretty soon her Buick cruised by, circled the block, and returned to park beside my Honda. Mara herself emerged in her dark blue warm-up, her blonde hair concealed under a dark toboggan cap.

"As it says in the poem," she said, "'lead and I follow.'"

"You've been reading Tennyson again," I said, "but I'm not Gareth, and you're not Lynette."

She showed a tense smile. "I noticed you aren't wearing your armor."

"It was too heavy for jogging. Let's go."

She fell in beside me, and we set an easy pace toward Mitra's house. The screwdriver and chisel I had in my pocket kept banging against my leg, but aside from that it was a good jog. Mara asked no questions when I turned into the garbage-truck alley behind Mitra's house, which was located in the middle of the block. Fortunately, all of the houses had the usual six-foot wooden privacy fences. That gave us cover for our approach to Mitra's gate. We opened it and slipped up to the house's back door.

With my surgical gloves on, I tried the door once. It did not open, so I took out my screwdriver and chisel.

"Let me try it," Mara whispered. "You keep lookout."

I gave way and looked toward the gate while she did whatever it was she did.

"*Voila*," she whispered and held the door open for me to enter.

"How did you do that?" I asked.

"I used my 'feminine wiles.' That's what you called them last fall when you told me to use them on Elmo Koonz."

"Then this must have been a male doorknob," I said.

The dark shapes of her hands flew to her hips. "You're coloring outside the lines again."

I was never much good at coloring, so I preceded her into the house.

"What are we looking for?" she asked.

"Anything that would suggest why Mitra was murdered, why she thought our jobs were in jeopardy, or how that confounded journal about an affair came into being."

Mitra's house had a small living room/dining room, a kitchenette, a hallway, a master bedroom, two smaller bedrooms, and two baths. In the living room, Venetian blinds stood open on the single window that looked toward the street. I closed them before turning on my penlight, which I again had covered with red cellophane. Mara also had brought a red-filtered penlight.

We shined our lights around the living room and found it was simply furnished—a divan, an easy chair, and one of the old CRT televisions with rabbit-ears antennae. I'd bet she never watched anything but news and weather.

Mara rifled the bureau drawers and checked the closets in the master bedroom while I looked over the two baths.

"Nothing odd there," she reported. "Simple, business-like wardrobe. Nothing fancy in the cosmetics. She seems to have lived a very plain existence."

"Same with the baths," I said.

One of the other two bedrooms had been converted into a study, the most likely place for us to find anything helpful. Mara tackled the desk while I examined the contents of three well-stocked bookshelves. Most of the books were scientific texts—physics, advanced mathematics, chemistry, and biology. As a just-the-facts lady, Mitra had plenty of facts to play with.

The other books seemed of more recent vintage. Most of these concerned accounting and business, but there was a pamphlet on aircraft safety certification.

"Nothing of interest here," Mara said. "Paid receipts, stationery, pens, and pencils. That's it. Did you find anything?"

"Nothing conclusive," I said. "The books on accounting confirm what Freda Broyles told us, but the pamphlet on aircraft certification suggests she was looking into Jerry Vaughan's crash."

Mara sniffed. "Emory Estes didn't want to talk about that when you questioned him."

"Are you suspecting him? I thought you two were friends."

I could not see her eyes, but I felt them scorching me. "That's a subject for another occasion. Let's get on with the search before we get caught."

"Yes, ma'am," I said.

In the last bedroom, I had only enough time for an impression of many shelved books before I heard a car stopping in front of the house. Mara and I dashed to the living room and saw, around the closed blinds, red and blue flashing lights. We hurried to the back door, but another police car with flashing lights occupied the alley by the back gate.

We were trapped.

CHAPTER 26

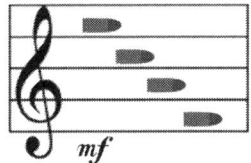

For a few seconds we stood frozen in place, certain we were lost. I cursed myself for getting Mara involved. With all the other strikes against us, we wouldn't stand a chance in court.

"Come on," Mara whispered. "They may not check the closets."

She seized my arm and pulled me down the hallway. Even in those straits, I remembered her abhorrence of being touched. In a strange way, I felt honored.

Heavy steps sounded outside, and someone fumbled with the front door. At the end of the hall I turned toward the master bedroom and its large closet.

Mara seized my arm again. "That's the first place they'll look." She pulled me into the third bedroom and into the tiny closet in its most remote corner. There wasn't enough room for one person in there, much less two. I backed up against one wall. Mara, as near as I could tell in the pitch black, did the same against the other wall with the door on her right. That left only an inch or two of space between us.

I'm not tall, but my five-feet-ten made me stoop to fit under the shelf. I wondered how long I could hold that position.

The sound of the front door opening came clearly, and we heard two sets of heavy footsteps inside.

"Don't sneeze," Mara whispered.

"I hadn't planned to," I whispered back. Then I felt her finger laid across my lips in the age-old motion to command silence. I tried to answer with a nod, but that made her finger poke my nose, which proceeded to itch. She withdrew the finger, and I could hear her soft breathing an inch or two in front of my face.

Footsteps moved about in the house, accompanied by voices whose words we couldn't identify. The steps and voices came closer down the hall, and one said, "Check the closet." I think my heart would have stopped if my nose had not kept itching and threatening the forbidden sneeze. I needed all the heartbeats I could muster to support the finger I pressed at the base of my nose to prevent the sneeze.

There are times of heightened perception when one is aware of many things at once. My primary attention was given to the pain of my cramped position and my efforts to forestall the sneeze, but I was also aware of Mara's soft femininity only inches away. She smelled of cleanliness and soap, and I remembered the feel of my consoling hand on her back that night when she'd wept uncontrollably. Now, as then, desire welled up in me as it had not done since Faith's death. This was a desire far beyond the physical attraction I'd felt with Cynthia Starlington. This desire called for complete merging of body and soul. I knew that Mara had the intellect, the emotional force and, yes, the *Imagination* for that total companionship.

But she abhorred being touched, and I needed to sneeze.

Through the rear wall of the closet, I could hear the policemen searching the study. My legs and shoulders ached from the stooped position, and my nose felt like it had been overdosed with itching powder, but the pressure of my finger still held back the sneeze.

Footsteps entered the room that hosted our closet. A reflection of light became visible under the closet door, and presently the flashlight's white beam shone directly under the door. I held my breath and clamped my finger harder on my nose.

Then the light withdrew and full darkness returned. "Nothing here," a voice muttered from the hallway, and another said something about "nervous old woman ..." Footsteps retreated, and presently we heard a door close.

"Not yet," Mara whispered.

I couldn't answer because I was too busy preventing the sneeze.

A car engine started out front and receded as the vehicle withdrew. We stood in silence and waited. I don't know what Mara was thinking, but I was thinking of my cramping muscles and wondering when I could sneeze. I was also increasingly aware of Mara's closeness and my desire to embrace her.

She exhaled. "It's all right now, Cupcake. They've gone."

She opened the door and stepped silently out into the room, then moved soundlessly up the hallway. I unfolded myself from my constrained position and tried to stretch the kinks out of my muscles. As soon as I removed the finger's pressure from my nose, the long-suppressed sneeze asserted itself with an explosion. In the silent house, it sounded like a ten kiloton nuclear blast. Francie LaBouche could have used the sound to enhance the ersatz mushroom cloud that announced her advent on the news program.

Mara stood beside me. "The one in back has gone, too," she said. "It's a good thing. That sneeze must have waked half the neighborhood as well as spreading enough germs for a biological warfare attack on China."

"We'd better get out of here," I said.

Her chin tilted upward. "Not until we've searched this room."

"There's nothing here but books," I said. It was true. The room held nothing except bookcases on three walls.

"But what kind of books?" Mara illuminated one bookcase with her filtered penlight. I cast my light on another bookcase. It was filled with Regency romances by Georgiana Lowe. I already knew Freda Broyles had lied to me when she claimed to be a fan of Georgiana Lowe, and I suspected she'd lied about removing the Regency-style dresses from Mitra's house. Now these paperbacks suggested that Mitra, not Freda, was the romance reader. Did she also own the dresses Freda took from the house? And if so, what kind of discovery was Freda trying to shield Mitra from?

"Press, I don't believe this," Mara whispered. "You said Professor Fortier was a just-the-facts scientific type. But here she has a whole shelf of bodice-ripper romances." She paused, then asked, "What's in your bookcase?"

"Paperback romances, but more tasteful ones. Georgiana Lowe."

"Hers are good—accurate representation of speech and people's concerns from the Regency period."

Score more points for Mara's erudition. She'd read all the classics and period romances to boot.

We converged on the center bookcase and found that it contained romances whose content lay about halfway between the clean romances of Georgiana Lowe and the raunchy ones Mara had found.

"Well, we've searched the house," Mara said, "and the only thing we've found out of line is this roomful of romances. What do you make of it?"

I couldn't make anything, so I said, "I make of it that we'd better get out of here before the cops decide on an encore."

"One thing first." She moved to the living room windows and pulled the Venetian blind a tiny bit aside.

"What do you see?" I asked.

"Someone peeking out a window in the house across the street. I saw the curtains move."

"That's Freda Broyles' house," I said. "We have a lot more to question her about."

Mara nodded, and we moved without speaking out the back door and into the alley. The night had grown colder, and our breaths made steam clouds in the frigid air. At the mouth of the alley, we began jogging. In the park we walked for our cooldown and called it sufficient when we stood beside our cars.

"You're really great, Mara," I said. "You're threatened with jail time, yet tonight you've been as poised as if you'd been serving afternoon tea."

"More poised," she said. "I wouldn't know what to do at a tea, and at least we're doing something. What next?"

"We grab the time we have left before someone else preempts. Given tonight's news, the administration will have us on the carpet before classes tomorrow ... uh ... later this morning. I need to talk to Freda Broyles about why she lied to me, and I need to find out if Weldon Combes actually made a play for Mitra after her boyfriend was killed. And I wonder why he came back to the campus the night we found the body."

She sniffed. "You can't get that done before our glorious meeting with the administration, and you may not have freedom to do it afterward. Why don't I take Freda Broyles? Will she get to work before eight?"

"By seven-thirty usually."

I briefed Mara on the lies Freda had told me and the questions I would ask. "Use a woman-to-woman approach and work on her conscience," I said. "Now we'd better head home before the police check the park. Do you need a convoy?"

Mara's chin lifted again. "I can handle it. Go home and get some sleep."

I cranked up the Honda, but I didn't put it in gear until Mara's Buick cleared the park. A sudden loneliness descended on me, the same loneliness I'd felt last fall when we parted company after working together.

No one followed me home this time, so maybe organized crime types kept union working hours. Once in bed, I fell dead asleep and knew nothing until the alarm clock woke me at six-thirty. If it hadn't waked me, Dean-Dean's phone call would have at seven. His scratchy voice was pitched several tones higher than normal.

"Professor Barclay, I heard the news last night ..." He made the mistake of pausing for dramatic effect.

"So did I," I said. "There isn't a word of truth in it, but Francie LaBouche *is* kind of cute, isn't she?"

He stammered a few incoherent sounds. "That's beside the point. The point is your personal conduct. See me in my office at eight."

"A.M. or P.M.?" I asked.

"A.M., of course," he fumed. "Be there."

He hung up before I could answer.

I knew what was coming. I'd either be suspended or summarily fired. Maybe Emory Estes Experienced Autos could use another salesman.

Seven-thirty found me waiting outside Weldon Combes' office, and the incumbent himself arrived shortly after. He stopped when he saw me, consternation on his face.

"I didn't expect to see you here, Press. Not after last night's news. What's the occasion?"

"Unresolved questions," I said. "Do we talk here or in your office?"

He unlocked the door, and we entered. He closed it after us and retreated behind his desk. I took one of the chairs along the wall. Sweat showed on his bald pate in spite of the cold day. I held his gaze and let him stew.

"What kind of questions?" he asked.

"Tell me about the play you made for Mitra Fortier after her boyfriend got killed."

A long scarecrow arm wiped his forehead with a handkerchief. "I don't know what you're talking about."

"Yes, you do," I said. "You can answer me now or answer under oath in court."

That was pure bluff, but it worked.

"I ... there wasn't much to it," he said. "I felt sorry for Mitra ... We worked closely in the department, and I kept going by her office to see how she was doing ..."

"Go on," I said.

"She was an attractive woman, and the wife and I weren't getting along too well right then." He threw me another defensive glance. "I made a few comments that I shouldn't have."

"What did she say to those?"

"Nothing ... She just looked at me."

"This happened several times?"

Combes looked at the floor. "Three, to be exact."

"So what did you do then?"

"Well, I saw it wasn't going to happen and decided to make the best of it."

"But that isn't what makes you so nervous today, is it?"

I stood and advanced on his desk and leaned on it with both hands. He looked up at me the way a bird looks at a snake.

"Now tell me the real reason you came back to the office the night we found Mitra's body."

His face whitened, "Press, I've never seen you like this …"

I showed him the glower I used to use on sticky occasions in Special Forces. "You'd better hope you never see me like this again. Now, you can answer the question to me or to the judge. Which will it be?"

I hoped he didn't know I was bluffing.

"All right." He put his head in his hands. "I found her body before you did."

That rocked me back on my heels. I'd known he was hiding something, though I had no idea it was that big. But I mastered the shock and bored in again.

"How did that happen?"

His head remained in his hands. "I meant to catch her at the reception—something about a student adding one of her classes after the deadline. But whenever I looked, she was busy with someone else. I started for home, then decided to come back and leave her a note. But I found her dead behind the desk."

"Wasn't the office locked?"

"It's a two-person department. Each of us had a key to the other's office."

"What did you do when you found her body?"

"I panicked. I did check to see if CPR would do any good, but she was already too far gone. I was afraid my … my advances toward her would come out, and I ran. I was late enough that no one saw me leave."

That must have been while Elmo Koonz was checking out that car's backfire. If he'd been unfreezing his whatzis in his lookout post, he'd have seen Combes leave.

"So you left the body for Professor Thorn and me to find," I said.

He looked up, more defensive than ever. "I didn't know who would find her. I just knew it couldn't be me."

"Did you remove anything from her office or rearrange anything?"

"Not a thing. I got out of there and locked the door behind me."

"Why did you come back later?"

"I ... I couldn't leave her there all night. But when I got there you'd already—"

"Did Mitra ever say anything to you about a number of faculty going to lose their jobs?"

"No." His face looked blank as well as white. "She never said anything like that ... Press, I won't have to tell this in court, will I? My wife ..."

I backed toward the door. "I don't know, but if I were you, I'd have a witness for everything I did the night she was murdered."

"Press ..." He stood and leaned on the desk. "I wonder about something else ... I locked her door when I left. But you say you found it unlocked when you got there. That could mean that someone else ... Well, I've been wondering ..."

I grinned at him. "Now I'm wondering, too."

That was probably a low blow, but my anger had been building ever since he admitted finding Mitra's body. If he'd acted like a man instead of running away, then Mara and I wouldn't have been involved. We'd still be in trouble, but we'd have one less thing to worry about.

And speaking of trouble—I trudged through the winter cold toward my meeting with Dean-Dean.

CHAPTER 27

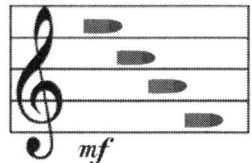

Mara hailed me, and I turned to see her emerge from the Science Center. The chilling wind put a pleasant glow on her ivory complexion.

"I'll brief you about Freda when we get through with Dean-Dean," she said.

"He called you, too?" You'd think Dean-Dean would have learned better than to take on both of us at once.

"It's not going to be pleasant."

"We'll survive," I said. I hoped.

In the Executive Center we found Mrs. Dunwiddie fiddling with things on her desk. When Dean-Dean opened his door, she said, "The Vice President will see you now."

I flicked on my pocket voice recorder.

The setup was much like our last encounter—two hardwood chairs facing his desk with Dathan Hormah seated behind us. In addition, Mrs. Dunwiddie sat back there to take notes. My internal bassoon sounded its recognition of Dean-Dean's presence.

Dean-Dean's face was red with agitation. "I'm sure you both know why you're here," he blustered.

"I was hoping you'd tell us," I said.

He blinked but otherwise ignored me. "The last time you were here, I told you I was drawing a line in the sandpile—"

"Sand*box*," I said.

Dean-Dean's mouth worked, but no sound came out. He swallowed once and began again. "As intelligent people, you know that when a person reaches the point that they can no longer perform effectively in a given position, that it's best to move on. A time to cut one's losses. A time to throw up the towel—"

"Throw *in* the towel," I said.

Dean-Dean sputtered before regaining his voice. "What I'm leading up to is that it's time for you to resign."

He paused, and I said, "I've done nothing to justify either resignation or any unfavorable personnel action."

"Nor have I," Mara said.

Dean-Dean turned to Mara. "Professor Thorn, you've been arrested for having child pornography on your office computer. That is a disgrace to the college—"

"*University*," I corrected. Anything to blunt his attack on Mara.

"You keep out of this," he said to me.

"You're the one who ordered me to come here," I said.

Mara torched him with her gaze and said, "I demand to see President Cantwell."

Dean-Dean showed a malevolent grin. "That is impossible. President Cantwell was taken to the hospital on emergency last night with pneumonia. Given his past reactions to antibiotics, he won't be out anytime soon. In his absence, I am in charge."

Visions of the sorcerer's apprentice floated through my mind, but now the apprentice wore the black hood of an executioner.

"Now, Professor Thorn," Dean-Dean continued, apparently aware that the news of President Cantwell had shocked Mara and me into silence, "why did you think you could use a ... uh ... *university* computer for an illegal purpose?"

Mara's chin rose that eloquent fraction of an inch. "I stand upon my constitutional right to remain silent. Any statements will be made through my counsel."

"That may be well enough for the legal system," Dean-Dean said, "but this is a purely administrative inquiry in which fine points of law do not apply."

I interrupted again. "Are you saying that because she's a member of this faculty she has no constitutional rights? If you act on that you'll get the college sued for every cent it's worth."

Behind me, Dathan Hormah cleared his throat. Dean-Dean looked at him and blinked. Neither corrected my calling the university a college.

"Be that as it may," Dean-Dean said, "I'm told the police have documentary evidence of illicit conduct by both of you. It's been all over the news. This institution cannot tolerate that kind of bad publicity. We are on the monthly budgets of more than one hundred churches."

I interrupted again. "You'll get publicity worse than that if you authorize coed dorms."

"That's beside the point," Dean-Dean flared. "We're speaking of your personal conduct. The police have evidence that you, Professor Barclay, had a long-standing affair with Professor Fortier, and that the two of you were carrying on even before your wife died—"

"That information is completely false," I said. "No one who knew Professor Fortier will believe it, and no one who knew Faith will believe she would tolerate it."

"Nevertheless," Dean-Dean said, "your conduct in that affair has brought disgrace to this institution—"

This time Mara interrupted. "'He that answereth a matter before he heareth it is folly and shame to him.'" She turned to Dathan Hormah. "In case you don't recognize the quotation, sir, it's from the Book of Proverbs."

That turned Dean-Dean's attention back to her. "The evidence shows that you gave Professor Fortier cause for jealousy, and that resulted in a confrontation with threats of violence."

"That never happened." Mara's face flushed with anger. "Neither the cause nor the confrontation."

"In view of these actions," Dean-Dean said, "you are both placed on suspension from the faculty pending action by the Faculty Hearing Committee."

"You know what happened last time," I said, reminding him that his false accusations last fall had blown up in his face when the students held a mass demonstration for Mara and the chairman of the Faculty Hearing Committee was indicted for murder.

"Nevertheless," Dean-Dean said, "you are both placed on suspension. You will be notified later when the hearing will take place."

"Okay," I said, and rose to leave.

Mara followed my example.

"Before you go," Dathan Hormah said to Mara, "I need to know what to do about your classes."

Mara's face flushed full red. "I can't help you, Professor Hormah. That is a faculty action, and I've been suspended." She spun on her heel and strode out of the office.

As I followed, Dathan Hormah said to Dean-Dean, "You forgot to bar them from the campus."

I don't know what Dean-Dean said then because I slammed the door behind me. Mara and I grabbed our coats and hurried outside before anyone could say anything further.

"I have things to tell you, Press," Mara said, suddenly calm. "Someone left a warning note under my office door this morning."

"I found one of those in my house. And I think a car followed me home the other night."

Mara frowned. "I think someone followed me, too. We have a lot to talk about. At Dr. Sheldon's?"

I nodded. "He'll love it. Maybe he has results from his research."

"I'll see you there," she said.

"One other thing," I said. "I think there may be hope for your ... uh ... computer problem. I'll explain at Dr. Sheldon's."

Her eyes flashed. "I won't even hope until you explain."

We headed out in different directions. The thought that both of us had been followed worried me. That suggested organized crime involvement, but nothing in the Mitra Fortier murder or Clyde Staggart's slanders could account for that. Our student convoys had apparently moved the stalkers off-campus, but someone still had put that note under Mara's office door.

As I descended the walkway to my home, I used my cell phone to call Ron Spencer about the CD Bruno Pinkle had planted in my desk. His wife answered again.

"I still haven't seen him," she said. "I called the police station, but all they knew was that someone saw him yesterday afternoon talking to Steven Drisko's wife."

"Brill Drisko?" I asked.

"Yes," she said, "and while I was on the phone, some guy laughed in the background like he'd heard a dirty joke. So I asked for Duggan Hahn, one of the detectives Ron had worked with before, but they said he'd gone on emergency leave." She gave something close to a sob. "Ron's going off and leaving me and the children—it isn't like the man I married. Professor Barclay, I don't know what to think anymore."

"I don't know, either," I said. "If I see Ron, I'll tell him to call home."

She thanked me, and we hung up.

My heart sank deeper in despair. My suspension cut me off from teaching history, which I'd long ago declared the only life left to me, and I had no idea how to combat the forces aligned against me. Mara's plight seemed even worse. She could do prison time as well as lose her job.

There seemed to be no substance to that Renaissance emblem's claim that Truth was The Daughter of Time. The more time passed, the deeper we became buried under falsehoods.

I didn't go inside my house but climbed into my Honda for the cross-city ride to Dr. Sheldon's. The car cranked instantly despite the cold morning, and I silently thanked Manny Clampett for keeping it dependable despite its age. I promised myself again that I'd replace it a year or two after Cindy graduated.

If she graduated. Her suspension hung like a lead coating on my heart. My anger rose again that anyone so young and sincere had to battle a powerful and corrupt system that masked its tyranny under the façade of virtue.

By this time, I was spinning along through Overton City on one of the main streets that had few traffic lights and a speed limit of forty-five miles per hour. There was a sizeable dump truck ahead of me, but it moved along smartly.

Things went well until the truck slowed in anticipation of a red light. When I slowed in response, my brakes felt a little mushy. Then the traffic light changed to red and the truck's brake light glowed full bright. I slammed on my own brakes. They began to take, but then my foot carried the brake pedal to the floor.

Complete brake failure.

My Honda sped onward, and the rear of the truck loomed huge before me.

It's strange how much detail can be compressed into a few split-seconds. The body of the truck was high enough that my Honda's hood would pass under it. The truck's first impact would be against my windshield. Its second impact would be against my head. I couldn't dodge to the left because of oncoming traffic nor to the right because of a car paralleling me on that side.

Without thinking, I seized the parking brake handle between the Honda's front seats and yanked as hard as I could. Maybe the knowledge resided somewhere in my mind that the parking brake had a mechanical linkage rather than hydraulic. I only know that I reacted that way. But even as those brakes took hold, I knew it was too late. The truck grew greater before me, and I watched the Honda's hood pass underneath it. I threw my body flat across the parking brake and the passenger seat.

My last impression of the collision was the sound of the truck's body crashing into the Honda's windshield and a tremendous jolt that shot pain through my entire body.

My cerebral pianist responded with a mechanical performance of Schumann's "The Happy Farmer."

CHAPTER 28

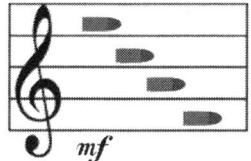

Pain flared through my body, so intense I wanted to scream. Then came a deadening sense of deep bodily violation. For a few moments, I lay there trying to decide which parts of me were broken. Dully, moving only my head, I looked around to see about getting out of the wreck.

It wasn't going to be easy. Though I was lying on my side with the hand brake handle gouging my ribs, my feet remained under the steering wheel. I'd slipped out of the shoulder strap of the seat belt, but the lap belt still held. And the truck bed had penetrated the windshield and bent the steering wheel down over my hips.

As the babble of bystanders increased outside, I got a hand under my body and released the seat belt. The door handle on the passenger door didn't work. The door itself had been bent too much to open. I felt along the door-side of the passenger seat and searched for the seat controls while my internal pianist kept banging away at "The Happy Farmer." If Schumann had been present, I would have committed mayhem. But then he also suffered musical hallucinations, so maybe that should have earned him amnesty.

I pulled the lever that lowered the seat back, but nothing happened. I put my other hand on it and pulled as hard as I could. With a slapping noise, the seat back collapsed. I managed to wriggle out from under the steering wheel and over the flattened passenger seat to the rear door. Miraculously, that door handle worked. The door opened, and I tumbled out into the street.

While I brushed fragments of shattered glass off my suit and the crowd of onlookers gabbled, the truck driver made uncomplimentary remarks about my probable origins. To the best of my knowledge, he was misinformed.

He ended his diatribe with a reasonable question. "Where'ja learn to drive?"

I knew the answer but found it safer to say, "*Ich spreche keine English.*"

He looked puzzled. "What are you? Some kind of furriner?"

I said, "*Je ne parle pas l'anglais.*"

At that point, a policeman took me aside and asked if I wanted transportation to a hospital. When I said I didn't, he jerked his head toward the accident scene, and said, "Okay, you hit him from behind. What's yer excuse?"

"My brakes failed," I said.

He gave me a look normally reserved for Iranian used car salesmen. "I've heard that one before."

"I imagine people's brakes have failed before," I said.

"I'll bet you was yappin' on a cell phone," he said.

"I'm not a 'phoney,'" I said.

His facial expression filed a nonconcurrence, but he said nothing. Instead, he wrote a citation for following too closely and failure to maintain my vehicle.

When he asked where I wanted the vehicle towed, I told him Manny Clampett's garage.

He waved to one wrecker among the flock that converged on the scene like buzzards. The wrecker driver winched what was left of my Honda up onto the flatbed of his wrecker. I knew the car was totaled. I'd been lucky to escape with bruises and wrenched joints.

The truck driver left after donating a few more dirty looks. His truck appeared no worse for the encounter. The crowd also drifted away. I leaned against a lamppost and felt in my pocket for my cell phone. It wasn't there.

The policeman looked up from writing his report and spoke in a softer voice. "Lose yer phone? I'll give ya one local call. What's the number?"

I gave Dr. Sheldon's number. The policeman punched it in and handed me the phone. He kept an eye on me so I couldn't steal it.

When Dr. Sheldon answered, I explained what happened and asked if Mara would pick me up. He spoke a few words away from the phone, then said Mara was on her way.

Perhaps ten minutes later, she picked me up in her Buick and asked if I was hurt.

"Bruises only," I said. "The luck of the Irish, I guess."

She raised an eyebrow. "You're not Irish."

"I stole the luck," I said.

Mara made no reply but drove grim-faced. She let me borrow her phone, and I called Manny Clampett to tell him the car was coming. He was as surprised as I was at the brake failure. He knew that I'm a fanatic about tires, brakes, and oil changes. That and Manny's mechanical skills were the reasons my Honda had remained operational in spite of being old enough to vote. I gave him Mara's cell number if he needed to call back.

In Dr. Sheldon's room, the old lion greeted me with an anxious look. "Children," he said, "President Cantwell is in serious condition in the hospital. He may not make it."

I took a moment for silent prayer. Our president really wants to do right by the college, but too many people are pulling him in too many directions. He hasn't yet learned to set a course and lead others to follow.

When I opened my eyes, I saw Mara's lips form a silent "Amen."

Dr. Sheldon launched into business. "Press, I don't know what you've gotten into, but it looks dangerous. What can we do to help?"

I sank into the room's one easy chair. "The answer to both questions is that I don't know. The only thing certain is that I've made several people awfully mad."

He laughed. "You have a talent for that. The question is who they are and how you've made them mad."

I named Gordon Samstag, Steven and Brill Drisko, Emery Estes, Malcolm Combes, and Freda Broyles. "All by asking questions," I said. "Every one of them has warned me off. What I really don't understand is the harassment by tough characters that look like mob operatives."

Mara was perched on a straight-back chair. "You've said all of those except Brill were in on that trip to Las Vegas several years ago. Maybe one of them got tangled up with the mob like last semester's murderer did."

"But which one?" I asked. "I can't find enough evidence to justify suspicion."

Dr. Sheldon harrumphed. "Let's begin by listing the problems we're trying to solve. The most pressing is Mara's being charged with child pornography. Next is that journal claiming an illicit affair and a love triangle. That leads to the third, the unsolved problem of Mitra's death."

"I can see how the journal and the death could be related," Mara said, "but I don't have a clue how that stuff got on my computer. I always use that fingerprint security device Richmond Seagrave gave me."

"I called Seagrave about that," I said, and told them how a lifted fingerprint could fool the device. I also told how Bruno Pinkle tried to get into my computer and, when he couldn't, left a strange CD in my desk drawer.

"What was on the CD?" Dr. Sheldon asked.

"I don't know," I said, and explained about persuading Ron Spencer to fingerprint it. "But Ron has disappeared. His own wife doesn't know where he is."

"That's a great help," Mara said.

I couldn't think of any way to paint a rosy picture, but I wanted to leave her with a pleasant thought. "I still think there's hope, Mara. Staggart and Pinkle tried to plant something on my computer, and they came back and took the hard drive. That time they brought Dogface with them."

"That poor man." Mara shook her head. "He looks like everything Staggart does hurts him, but he has to go along if he wants to keep his job." She looked a question before she asked it. "Why could they get into my computer when they couldn't get into yours?"

"I hide my fingerprint reader in a bookcase," I said. "Where do you keep yours?"

Her face showed disgust. "On my desk. I didn't know it could be bypassed."

"Neither did I until Seagrave told me," I said. "I just didn't want the net administrator to know I had one."

We hit a dead end with that, so we went on to other things. I briefed them on Elmo Koonz's seeing "three guys" enter the Science Center the night Mitra was killed. And I repeated Malcolm Combes' shocking admission of finding Mitra's body. Dr. Sheldon exclaimed, "That yellow rat," thus revealing that he'd been watching old gangster movies on TV.

"Now tell me what you learned from Freda Broyles," I said to Mara.

She torched me with a blue glance. "Not until you tell me what Brill Drisko wanted with you."

"Children, let us not squabble," Dr. Sheldon said.

"All right," I said. "Brill phoned and wanted me to come out to her house and talk." Mara looked skeptical, so I added, "At least, that's what she said. I told her I had to keep office hours, and she showed up there. She claimed she wanted me to 'stop the investigation,' and I told her I wasn't investigating anything. She came back at me with my questioning Emory Estes about Jerry Vaughan's crash. That was at lunch, so someone told her about it in a hurry. She said she didn't want people to find out she'd been a showgirl, that it would ruin her marriage if they knew …"

"As if they didn't already," Mara said.

"My thought exactly," I said, and ignored Mara's raised eyebrow. "She said if I kept poking into things, I'd make somebody mad enough to do something about it. Then she stalked me and tried to bribe me with seduction …"

"And you protected your virtue by running away," Mara said.

"I backed away until I ran out of space," I said.

"Children, let us not quarrel," said Dr. Sheldon.

Mara would not be diverted. "When I saw you, she had her hands on your shoulders, and you were gazing into each other's eyes."

"You ought to commend me that I looked at her eyes," I said.

"Children—" said Dr. Sheldon.

"You've been in that pose before—with your baby brunette," Mara said.

It suddenly occurred to me that I hadn't told them Elmo Koonz had seen Cynthia Starlington come out of the Science Center on the fatal night. But I said, "Don't change the subject. I kind of pushed Brill back and said I had to ask questions because something was threatening my job. She said my asking questions threatened my job, that her husband was a trustee, and I shouldn't keep making people mad. Then she left. I don't know whether the bribe or the threat was dominant."

Mara turned to Dr. Sheldon. "What do *you* think of Brill Drisko?"

Dr. Sheldon's eyes twinkled. "I think there's a lot of her."

Mara made a face and spoke one eloquent word—"Men!"

Still twinkling, Dr. Sheldon said, "You don't think Brill radiates intellectual brain waves?"

Mara sniffed. "The only brain wave she ever had was waving good-bye."

"Don't underrate her," I said. "There's a lot of cunning behind that showgirl exterior."

Mara lapsed into iceberg silence, but Dr. Sheldon mused, "It sounds like Brill got spooked by Press' questions about Jerry Vaughan's crash. That means we have to keep looking into the crash, too." He pursed his lips, then added, "I've tried researching Brill, but I haven't found anything yet."

"Start with Las Vegas," I said. "We know Drisko picked her up somewhere out West, and we know he went to Vegas with the faculty group. It's a guess, but it's a start."

Dr. Sheldon rubbed his hands together. "I'll get on it."

We both looked at Mara, who returned from her Arctic journey. "When I visited Freda Broyles, it wasn't clear who was going to ask the questions. She called the police last night because someone was breaking into Mitra Fortier's house, and she asked if it was Press and me. I told her I never heard of such a thing, which was true to the best of my recollection. I don't recall that we *discussed* breaking into her house—we only *did* it. Then Freda launched into a tirade about how she felt obligated to protect Mitra's reputation against the slanders that were going around."

Mara turned to Dr. Sheldon. "Freda asked me straight out if I'd had an affair with Press and a confrontation with Mitra. I answered 'no' to both counts. Then she got emotional and started rambling about how 'that policeman' kept coming around and bugging her."

A lock of Mara's blonde hair slipped onto her forehead and she brushed it back—a reminder of the femininity that lay behind her fortress façade.

She continued, "Freda said Mitra became like a younger sister to her. That was after Faith died. The point is that they—Freda and Mitra—confided in each other. And when Jerry Vaughan died in that crash, Freda grieved along with Mitra. Later, Mitra said she didn't believe the crash was an accident. She never said why."

Mara flipped her unruly lock back with a toss of her head—another remarkably feminine gesture. I enjoyed watching it as she continued her story.

"Freda does know that Mitra met several times with Robert Lee, who is a CPA like Jerry was. Freda thinks Mitra was onto something phooey—her word—about Samstag or Drisko. And about two weeks ago, Mitra told her she'd found a lead about the accident. She only needed a few more bits of information, and then she was going to 'shake down the rafters.' But she never said whose rafters."

Mara gave up the battle against her unruly lock and let it brush freely on her forehead. "When Freda didn't know any more on that subject, I asked about the dresses she took from Mitra's house. She gave me the same story about their belonging to her and her being a collector of Regency costumes. I asked her point blank what she knew about that alleged journal, and she said she'd never heard of it until it was mentioned on the news …"

"But it wasn't mentioned on the news," I said. "The news cited unnamed 'police sources.' I only know about the journal because Ron Spencer told me."

"I threw that at her, too, and she said she must have heard it through the campus rumor mill. I couldn't pin her down about it."

Mara's exasperation showed. "So I made a strong pitch that Mitra's reputation wasn't the only one involved—that you and I were still alive and having to live with slander. She looked away and said we'd have to live with the consequences of whatever we'd done. Then she stood up and said she had to go to class, which was a lie because classes don't start on the half hour. Then she kind of walked me out the door. The last thing she said was something about letting sleeping dogs lie or we might wind up like Mitra."

"Wow," I said.

Dr. Sheldon stroked his chin. "So we end up with more mystery than we started with. And no new leads."

"One." Mara's eyes blazed. "Freda denied knowing anything about Mitra's ex-husband, but she did say Mitra was raised by an aunt—I have her name—who's now in a nursing home in Cloverdale. I checked the phone directory, and there's only one nursing home there."

She gave me a scorching glance. "Press, do you think you can tear yourself away from Brill Drisko and your baby brunette long enough to join me in asking questions?"

I deadpanned my response. "Professor Thorn, you know that is a loaded question, which as a matter of principle I decline to answer. However, I will be happy to join your question-asking expedition. There is also one co-owner of the fatal aircraft who lives in Cloverdale."

Dr. Sheldon laughed. "Nothing stuffier than a professor on his high horse. You two have fun, but be careful. There's a lot that we don't understand."

Mara checked her watch. "Shall we catch a quick lunch at Goolock's and then go?"

I nodded, and we rose to go. At least, she rose. I strained up into a standing position with every bone and muscle protesting. It took three steps before my legs responded reliably to commands. And as I straggled out to Mara's car, a mood of foreboding dominated my mind.

I didn't know what we would find in Cloverdale, but it had better be good if we were going to salvage our reputations.

CHAPTER 29

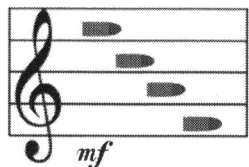

As I dragged my aching carcass in at Goolock's, Mrs. Lee gave me a worried look but said nothing. Mara ordered her customary Reuben and Coke. For variety, I ordered a ham and cheese sandwich with my coffee. We'd hardly settled in before Mara's cell phone rang. She listened briefly and said, "Thank you. You're very kind." She rang off.

"That was Pastor Tammons," she explained. "He said he didn't believe a word of the things being said about us, and he offered to be a character witness for us."

"There are still good people around," I said. "Unfortunately, they're not in a position to help us."

That optimistic comment ended conversation. Robert Sun Lee came directly to our table as we were finishing.

"There's something I think you ought to know," he said. "Those toughs that the police stopped here the other night ... I think they were here because of you, so I think you should know how it ended."

"I never thought to ask," I said.

Lee frowned. "They and the patrolmen were still arguing when that captain of homicide arrived—"

"Staggart?" I asked.

"That's the one. He gave orders to the patrolmen, and they packed up and left. Then he jerked a thumb at the toughs, and they headed out in a different direction."

I mused aloud, "Why was a captain of homicide giving orders to patrolmen who don't answer to him?"

"Where's your Army training?" Mara asked. "A captain is a captain, and that's that."

"I suppose that dog-faced sidekick of his was with him," I said.

"He was alone," Lee said. "And he was alone when I saw him today. He had a police car pulled driver-to-driver beside an unmarked car. The other driver was one of the bad guys from the other night—the one that kept looking daggers at you."

That was a shocker. I knew Staggart was corrupt, but I never thought he'd be connected to organized crime. Or was I wrong in thinking the mugs harassing Mara and me were from the mob? Could Staggart have deployed an undercover police unit for such a trivial purpose?

"So maybe you're in more trouble than you know," Lee said. "People say you're trying to find out who killed Professor Fortier."

"That's the least of my worries right now," I said. "We're trying to clear our names of that story about an affair and a lovers' triangle."

"And that stupid pornography charge," Mara put in, her eyes blazing.

"That may be true," Lee said, "but it also matters what people *think* you are doing. Is there anything about the pornography or the affair that would provoke those men into following you?"

Mara and I exchanged glances. We had no answers.

"If you have any ideas," Mara said to Lee, "I wish you'd tell us."

"My only idea is to stay out of trouble," Lee said, nodding toward the counter where his mother held forth. "My parents depend on me, and I'm putting my sister through college. I can't help any of them if I'm dead."

"What is threatening you?" Mara asked.

Lee looked away. "Nothing if I'm not involved. Some things I don't know and don't want to know. But I gave information to two people, and both of them are dead."

"Jerry Vaughan and Mitra Fortier?" I asked.

Lee nodded.

"And the information you gave them?"

"Are you sure you want to know?"

"I have to know," I said. "I'm in this thing too far to start playing safe."

Mara answered with a nod.

"A week before Jerry Vaughan crashed, we were talking CPA stuff. I told him I was changing jobs from Steven Drisko's Overton Technologies to one of Gordon Samstag's companies. He said his firm was auditing both companies in the next few weeks. I told him to look at their accounts with an El Paso subcontractor named Dustin Industries, Incorporated. He asked why, and I said that was all I could tell him. A week later he was dead."

Mara fixed her blue gaze on him. "Are you saying there's a connection between your telling him that and his dying in the crash?"

Lee showed no expression. "I'm saying that a week later he was dead. I do know that he sent word to both companies that he was interested in Dustin Industries. I only began to wonder about it last week when Professor Fortier came around asking questions."

"What kind of questions?"

"Accounting questions about Drisko's and Samstag's corporations, and anything I'd told Jerry about them before his crash. I told her what I'd said about Dustin Industries, and she said she'd have to look into that. Three days later, she was dead."

Mara was the first with a follow-up question. "What was it about Dustin Industries that got you interested?"

Lee showed a sad smile. "As I said, I have family responsibilities. And there is a lady I hope to marry next year after my sister graduates. These things I can do only if I remain alive. You will have to find out about Dustin Industries for yourselves."

He turned abruptly and disappeared behind the serving counter.

Noon had passed, so Mara and I left quickly, too quick even for Mrs. Lee to wish us Goo' lock.

"What do you make of Lee's story?" Mara asked as she turned her car's ignition. "Could the word on that card Sally Finhatter showed you be 'Dustin' instead of 'Ruskin'?"

"It's worth looking into," I said, "and I know how to start if you'll run me by my house and let me check a phone number."

"I'd rather run you by the emergency room and get you checked over. If you'll pardon my saying so, you don't look so good."

I grunted, whether from pain or disgust, I don't know. "I don't need the emergency room. And I will not pardon your saying I don't look good."

Her blue eyes sparkled. "With or without pardon, you still don't look good. So we'll use a field expedient."

I was wondering about her military jargon when she pulled into a strip center and parked in front of a health food market. She made a show of removing the ignition keys as she went inside, presumably so I couldn't steal her car and proceed on my own. It's nice to be trusted. A few minutes later, she emerged carrying a sack that obviously contained a bottle. She drove on without comment until we pulled into the driveway at my house.

"This is liniment," she said, handing me the sack and the bottle. "While you're in there, rub yourself down with it from head to foot. It will keep your muscles from knotting up."

I took it silently but with gratitude. I already felt like The Wreck of the Hesperus.

Inside, I searched through my desk and finally found the number I wanted. Then I stripped down and rubbed Mara's liniment into my protesting muscles. I couldn't decide whether it smelled more like a rendering plant or a feed lot on a rainy day. It burned like acid, but it brought immediate relief from the worst of my aches. My blue suit hadn't fared well in the wreck, so I changed to the brown one and rejoined Mara in her car.

She beamed at me. "I can smell ... uh ... *tell* that you used the liniment, Cupcake. You'll feel a lot better by sundown."

"If I don't incinerate first," I said.

"Actual combustion is rare," she said.

I didn't answer. I was afraid to open my mouth for fear of a flameout.

The threatened conflagration did not happen, though, and when we were established on the two-lane highway to Cloverdale, Mara broached another thought. "Have you noticed that no one is following us today?"

"I have noticed," I said. "I'm thankful for small favors."

She threw me an apprehensive glance. "But what does it mean? I can't believe those yahoos have given up."

"Change of tactics, maybe," I said. "But I can't imagine what."

With that dead end, she changed subjects. "What's that phone number you had to find?"

"An Army friend," I said. "May I use your phone again?"

She handed me the phone, and I dialed.

Unlike Richmond Seagrave and me, Leonard Morley had made the Army a career. After twenty-odd years' service, including work in procurement, he'd retired as a Colonel and established himself in Dallas as a business consultant.

His receptionist treated my request to speak with Len as if he were the pope. "Whom shall I say is calling?" she asked.

I resurrected my Special Forces voice. "Tell him it's Preston Barclay with a Code Red."

Len's hearty voice came on a moment later. "Press, you old hump on a mangy camel, how come you're scaring my receptionist with that Code Red nonsense?"

"I wanted to talk to you and not her," I said. "She isn't that cute."

He laughed. "Don't judge by the voice, son. Come down here and have a look."

"I have faith in your good taste," I said, "but I need some business info in a hurry."

He humphed into the phone. "If you'd leave that academic fairyland of yours and come into business with me, you wouldn't have to ask."

"I'd rather ask," I said. "I find business as boring as a lingerie ad without models."

Mara scorched me with a coloring-outside-the-lines glance, and Len said, "Same old Press," so I described the problem without further byplay.

At the mention of murder, Len grew serious. He knew of Overton Technologies and Gordon Samstag's companies, but he'd never heard of Dustin Industries, Incorporated. He said he'd look it up and call me back.

"One other thing," I said. "Could you have someone look at Dustin's physical facilities?"

"Look at it?" His voice exploded into the phone. "Press, do you have any idea how far El Paso is from Dallas?"

"It's just a thought," I said.

"Then you'd better think again about Texas distances," he said, and rang off.

Mara gave me a sly glance. "Winning more popularity contests, I see."

"He has a flair for the dramatic," I said.

"Speaking of popularity," she said, "Emory Estes called to break our dinner date for tonight. I gather my TV appearance wasn't good for his business."

"The Blatant Beast bites again," I said, "but Estes wasn't good enough for you anyway."

She sighed. "We broke about even. He used me as window dressing, and I used him to fight the rumors about you and me."

Relief flooded through me. I had no claim on Mara, yet I felt relief that no one else had.

"It would never have worked out," I said.

"You don't seem to have any trouble with companionship," Mara said, her voice hard and metallic. "You have one brunette and one corkscrew-haired blonde chasing after you."

"Brill doesn't count," I said. "She had an axe to grind, and she might use it to chop my head off."

"And the baby brunette?"

"A former student," I said. "She majored in history." That was the best I could think of. My conscience stabbed me for fantasizing about returning Cynthia's love. But then I remembered the two critical lies she'd told me ...

"Do all your former students rub circles on your back in public and leave lipstick on your teeth?"

"Not all," I said, my temper rising. "Some of my students are men."

Now Mara's temper was up. "Did she tell you she'd been married?"

"Cynthia? Married?" A thunderbolt crashed into my mind.

"Married and divorced. I found it in her personnel records the night you and I raided the Executive Center. Everyone on campus knew she'd thrown a fit at Mitra Fortier, but I guess it never occurred to you to look at her records."

I didn't answer. It hadn't occurred to me to check her records, and now other words from Cynthia echoed through my mind—*I'm glad I waited for you, Press* and my all-too-accurate thought, *She'd been practicing while she waited.* I spent several minutes kicking myself for imagining a love affair with her. My Renaissance lecture on the Imagination returned with a vengeance, and I heard my voice reciting Shakespeare's description of lovers, as frantic as lunatics, seeing ultimate beauty in ugly women.

Cynthia had true beauty, externally, but the waiting-for-you bit made the third important lie she'd told me. No amount of physical beauty could compensate for that.

"I didn't know," I said after a while.

We drove on in cold silence that matched the winter chill outside.

Cynthia also hadn't told me she'd visited the Science Center the night Mitra was murdered, but I didn't see how she alone could have killed Mitra. There were no signs of a struggle, and Mitra wouldn't have let Cynthia get close enough to use the chloroform.

My morale hit absolute bottom. The only pleasant thing I could think of was that the stench of Mara's liniment had dissipated. Either that or I'd gotten used to smelling it.

I forced my mind onto immediate problems. I needed to disprove the alleged affair with Mitra, and Mara needed to disprove the love triangle story and the pornography on her computer. Somehow those problems kept getting tangled up with Mitra's murder and Jerry Vaughan's death. All we could do about any of these was to keep asking questions. And some unknown person thought our asking questions constituted a danger to him. Or her. Otherwise, why the warnings and harassment by thugs? Who had ordered that harassment, and why? And was its cessation a cease-fire or only a change of tactics?

None of these things made sense. All we knew for sure was that we were driving to Cloverdale to interview Mitra's aunt—and Ralph Dornberg, if we could find him.

Mara's cell phone rang. I was still holding it, so I answered. Manny Clampett's voice came through. "Press, your brake lines was cut clean through and bound up with duct tape. They'd hold just long enough to get you into traffic, and they'd give way first time you braked in earnest."

That seemed to answer our question about a change of tactics.

CHAPTER 30

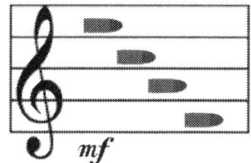

Storm clouds gathered overhead as we parked in front of Pleasant Meadow Residences in Cloverdale. The town had changed since my last visit several years ago. It then was a moderately prosperous agricultural town with a population of about ten thousand. Its architectural distinctions were a downtown area of red-brick two-story buildings and a periphery of grain elevators.

Since then, its population had increased by half as workers moved in to man high-tech industries that now served as the town's commercial mainstay. The buildings housing those industries radiated newness and vigor. The older parts of town were sliding into a gentle seediness appropriate for a way of life once *de rigueur*, now becoming *de rigueur mortis*. The Pleasant Meadow facility lay in the fading section of town.

The front desk attendant cast a suspicious eye on me but passed us through on Mara's statement that we were friends of Reva Cranewood's recently deceased niece. We found Reva in a private room with her hospital bed raised to a sitting position. She had a well-lined face with silvery-gray hair, and she wore an old-fashioned cotton gown with a bed jacket that looked like it came off the rack in Wal-Mart. She hit the mute button on her TV as we entered. The room seemed overly hot, even after Mara and I shed our overcoats. She handed me hers, and I stood back as she became our official spokesman.

"Mrs. Cranewood," she began, "we're friends of Mitra Fortier from Overton University. Could we visit about her for a few minutes?"

"Call me Reva," the older lady said, "and shut that door to the hall. Arrrgh! That smell! The wind must be blowing from that place outside the city limits where they burn old tires."

Apparently, the liniment still reeked, and I'd only gotten used to it.

I shut the door and said, "The law ought to make the wind blow in the other direction."

Mara scorched me with her ocular blow torch, and I shut up. Reva didn't even glance in my direction, and I noticed that she didn't look around when she spoke, but kept her gaze pointed at the TV.

"Reva ... " Mara kept her voice soft. "Reva, we were wondering if you could tell us something about Mitra's growing up. We only knew her as an adult."

I reached in my pocket to switch on my voice recorder. It wasn't there. Here was a conversation I desperately needed to record, and I'd lost my recorder. Where? Maybe in the wreck with my phone. To make matters worse, my internal musicians swung into a Louis Armstrong instrumental of 'I'll Be Glad When You're Dead, You Rascal You.'"

Mara's hand moved slightly in her pocket, doubtless setting her cell phone to record. I breathed a sigh of relief.

"The very idea of burning tires right here in town!" Reva said. "But that's not what you came for. Mitra was seven years old when her mother died, and Mitra came to live with me. Her mother—my sister—married a real ring-tailed no-good. Sissy knew he drank when she married him, but he got worse. They had angry shouting matches, and then he'd go get drunk, and Sissy would dread his coming home. She used to hide Mitra in a closet so Rafe couldn't beat up on her."

"I'm sure she was better off with you," Mara said.

Reva snorted. "You'd better believe it. That was no home for a child, and Mitra lived with it for seven years. Then Sissy died. Rafe was happy enough for me to take the child, and then he went downhill fast. Finally went to prison for burglary. We never heard from him again." She kept gazing at the silent television, or maybe through it.

"How long did it take Mitra to get past all that?" Mara asked.

"She never did. Oh, she finally came around to trusting me—even shared confidences with me at times. Like last week, she came down to visit. Worried, she was, and needed to talk. You know she lost her fiancé in that airplane crash? Well, last week she told me Jerry's death wasn't no accident, but she didn't know how to prove it."

We waited, afraid to prompt and afraid not to.

"She said Jerry was about to uncover some kind of scandal. She knew the college's trustees were mixed up in it, but she wasn't sure which ones. Or maybe only one. But she'd bust her gullet if she didn't find out and make him pay. Or them."

Reva gave a bitter laugh. "Looks like she was the one who paid." For the first time, she looked straight at Mara. "Other folks are paying, too. I don't see much, you know—they call it 'immaculate degeneration' or some such—but I hear pretty well, and I listen to TV. So I know who you are and why you're here."

We waited again, uncertain where Reva's tale would go next.

She sighed and changed course, her half-seeing eyes back on the muted TV. "Mitra always did well in her studies, all the way through school. She dated some boys in high school, but every boy would disappear after two or three dates. Then late in college, she met that Cochran fellow, a really bright one. So they got married, and I guess they were happy for a year or two before the divorce. The poor fellow couldn't take it and started drinking—like Mitra's father did, except he was a crying drunk instead of a cursing drunk."

"So she divorced him?" Mara's voice grew husky with emotion. Memories of her own bad marriage, I guess.

"No, he divorced her." Reva shook her head. "Like I said, he couldn't take it."

"Couldn't take what?" My own voice surprised me. Mara rewarded me with another scorch.

Reva went on as if she hadn't heard. "By the time she came to me, it'd become a habit she never broke. Her home life was too awful to think about, so you can't blame her if she played 'let's pretend.' But her pretend world got to be more real to her than the one she wanted to forget."

Reva sighed again. "At first, it was just playing dress-up with her as Sleeping Beauty and a handsome prince to come kiss her and take her away. Then in junior high she started writing stories, instead. She'd breeze through her homework. Then she'd shut herself in her room and write in those books—stories about herself and one-or-another man that loved her. Sometimes it was a movie star and sometimes just an upperclassman that caught her eye, but she always built him up into an ideal no man could live up to. That's why her dates went somewhere else. She never told them, of course, but they all somehow realized they couldn't match what she expected."

Mara spoke in a whisper. "You read her journals, of course."

"Her stories? Of course I did." Reva spoke in full voice. "I read those romance books of hers, too—some of 'em scandalous. I had to know what she was doing, so while she was in school, I read what she wrote. They was just love and romance, perfect like it could never be in real life. Better she did that than hang around the pool hall, and a fantasy never got anyone pregnant. Before she went off to college, I talked to her about her stories. She was mad at first, but then she seemed glad to share with someone.

"Mitra said it couldn't hurt as long as she knew the difference between the real world and the make-believe world. And she did keep them separate. No one could complain about her schoolwork. Brilliant she was. But every now and then she'd get to feeling low and let everything slide. It'd only last a few days, and then she'd be herself again—catch up her schoolwork and everything else."

That rang a bell with me. A couple of times a year, Mitra had gone through periods of depression. Faith would spend evenings with her until things got better.

Reva's voice saddened. "When she got married, I thought everything would work out. But her husband caught on that he wasn't measuring up, so he started drinking. The crux came when he found one of her storybooks where she'd imagined an affair with a friend of theirs. He grabbed a handful of her books, moved out, and filed for divorce. He was decent about it—just called it incompatibility and didn't try to embarrass her. But he kept the books."

"Where is he now?" Mara asked, her voice still a whisper.

"Lord knows," Reva said. "Maybe ten years ago he had a job here in town. But his drinking kept putting him in and out of rehab, and I lost track of him."

Mara still spoke in a whisper. "Do you still have any of her storybooks?"

Reva's eyes squinted as if she could still see. "I burned them all when she went off to college. If I'd died of a heart attack or something, some stranger would have poked through those and poor Mitra never would have lived it down. I couldn't let that happen to her."

Mara spoke now in a normal voice. "One of her storybooks has gotten some people in trouble, accused of things they didn't do. Would you be willing to tell their employer what you've just told us?"

Reva turned her face to the wall and said nothing. The silence grew, as did my apprehension that my job and my future might hang on the slender thread of her decision.

She spoke more to herself than to us. "That policeman came around asking questions, but I didn't tell him anything. I couldn't do that to Mitra."

"What did the policeman look like?" I asked.

"You're asking *me* for a description?" she said, turning back from the wall. "With my half-blind eyes? All I can tell you is that he was a big fellow with a voice to match."

"A harsh voice?" I asked. That could be Staggart.

"A strong voice," she said. "A big man with a strong voice."

There was no use pursuing that further. I threw Mara a shrug, and she took over again. Recording or no recording, we both knew our reputations and our futures might hang on Reva's decision. Dean-Dean would undoubtedly claim this recording was faked. But neither he nor anyone could deny Reva's direct personal testimony.

Mara's soft voice repeated, "Mitra's stories have fallen into the wrong hands and hurt some people. Would you be willing to tell their employer what you've told us?"

Reva turned her face back to the wall. "I couldn't do that to Mitra. I couldn't spoil her memory like that."

A slight edge crept into Mara's voice. "You'd let Mitra's make-believe world ruin the lives of real people in the real world?"

"Make-believe is make-believe," Reva murmured. "People ought to know that. I'm tired now, you'll have to go. And will you please tell those people to stop burning those stinking tires?"

Mara and I looked at each other in despair. We'd learned the secret of Mitra's journal, but we'd been denied Reva's testimony. Proving our innocence now depended on Dean-Dean's crediting Mara's recording. We gathered our overcoats and headed back down the hall.

Outside, my anxiety took over, and I asked, "Did you actually record all that?"

"I think so." Mara took the phone from her pocket. "Oh, no!" Consternation possessed her face. "My phone is dead. I don't think I got any of it."

We looked at each other in horror.

From somewhere in the Northwest came the rumble of distant thunder.

CHAPTER 31

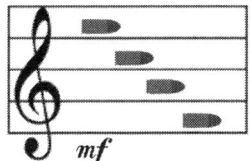

Rain fell steadily as we parked in front of Ralph Dornberg's office. A gusty wind drove it in small whiplashes across the puddled pavement. The weather formed the perfect mirror for our dampened spirits. I kept cursing myself for losing my voice recorder. I knew Mara was beating herself up for letting her battery go dead and for not bringing her recharge equipment for the car. But we weren't interviewing Dornberg about Mitra's journals, so recording him didn't seem to matter.

The corner unit of the little strip center that hosted Dornberg's office sported a faded "For Lease" sign that looked old enough to draw Social Security. Next door stood a pizza place manned by a lone teenager playing a video game. A sign on the third unit proclaimed "Ralph Dornberg, Financial Consultant." Its display windows were covered inside with aluminum foil up to about six inches from the top. Lights showed through the uncovered strip. The fourth unit bore a sign that read "Oncology Clinic: J. Carson Oma, M.D." The final unit flaunted a neon sign blinking out the word "Nails."

"Maybe I won't have to sell used cars," I said. "I could open a hammer shop."

"A *what*?" Mara gave me a querulous look.

"A hammer shop," I repeated. "Every place I go, I find a shop advertising nails. If they're that much in demand, there ought to be a market for hammers."

Mara's voice remained soft. "Press, you idiot, they're talking about *finger*nails."

"We learn something every day," I said.

Heaven knows we needed that levity. I especially needed it, for my body kept reminding me of the beating it had taken in the wreck.

"Come on, Cupcake," Mara said. "Let's get this over with."

She opened her door and skipped through the rain onto the relatively dry sidewalk beneath an overhang. I tried to follow suit, but my aching joints slowed me down, and I got a good sprinkling of rain on my hat and overcoat. As I looked back at the rain, a familiar-looking dark car cruised by on the street. Without knocking, we opened Dornberg's door and went in.

We'd seen the teener next door playing a video game. Dornberg reflected a generational difference by propping his feet on his desk and reading a magazine. I caught a glimpse of a half-clad female on the cover before he dropped it out of sight. He was a bit slower getting his feet off the desk. The furniture consisted of that desk and chair plus three hardwood straight chairs, all looking like relics from a furniture rental.

Dornberg's appearance contrasted sharply with his drab office. Well into his sixties, he showed a carefully-combed head of gray hair above a ruddy complexion. He wore a multi-colored silk shirt with a healthy crop of gray chest hair showing at the collar. An overcoat hanging on a nearby coat rack must have cost more than five hundred.

He greeted us with light blue eyes that glittered. "Welcome to Dornberg's Consulting Services," he said. "How can I help you?"

"We wanted to talk to you about aviation," I said.

The blue eyes flickered. "Airline stocks aren't doing well right now. You'd do well to put your money elsewhere." He made a face. "Phew! Till you opened the door I didn't realize how bad it smelled outside. I thought they'd closed that feed lot."

Apparently I still carried my olfactory halo.

"Actually," Mara put in, "we want to talk to you about one particular airplane—the one that Jerry Vaughan crashed in."

Dornberg's eyes held steady. "He cashed in, all right. Wing came off when he pulled out of a loop."

Mara didn't acknowledge the pun. "Mr. Dornberg, we're interested in *why* the wing came off."

That should have drawn some kind of reaction, but Dornberg answered as if reading from a script.

"The accident board said the wing was improperly installed," he said. "No matter how careful you are in aviation, you're still a fugitive from the law of averages."

I tried another tack. "Have you always been a financial consultant?"

Another scripted answer. "I owned several businesses around here, but they were getting to be too much work. A couple of years ago I sold them all and started this financial consulting business. It keeps me busy and out of trouble."

Busy reading girly magazines, I thought. But I said, "How long had you and the others been building your own airplanes?"

He stretched and leaned back. "Oh, this was our third. We'd had good luck with the other two. Eventually, someone would make us an offer too good to refuse. We liked this one better than the others, and I doubt we'd have parted with it for any price." He gave a half-laugh. "Maybe we should have."

"Do you remember who put the wings on it?" I asked.

He wrinkled his nose. "They ought to close that feed lot. It stinks up the whole town. Well, we all had a hand in putting the wings on—under Jerry's supervision, of course. He was the one with the background in aeronautical engineering."

I refused to let go. "Could anyone have tampered with the wings after they were installed?"

"It's possible." Dornberg's tone gave nothing away. "The accident board looked into that. Any one of us could have sabotaged the aircraft. But if it was sabotaged, they couldn't tell when it was done. We'd all flown the aircraft in the last couple of weeks. I flew it myself the day before the crash."

"But you didn't do aerobatics," Mara said.

Dornberg squinted. "Only Jerry did aerobatics. But what's your interest in this? Are you friends of Jerry's?"

"Of Mitra Fortier," I said. "We're following up where she left off."

Dornberg nodded. "She talked to me a couple of weeks ago. I told her the same things I'm telling you. Nice lady. I was sorry to learn of her death."

I changed tactics again. "Do you have any connection to an El Paso company named Dustin Industries, Incorporated?"

He shook his head. "I never heard of it."

"Do you own stock in Overton Technologies or any of Gordon Samstag's companies?"

"I used to, but I unloaded." Dornberg grinned. "Overton was flying higher than the hard facts would justify. I had a few hundred shares in Samstag's Pegasus Electronics, but I dumped them when that rocket failed. Good thing, too. That stock's down thirty percent or more."

He stood up, indicating the interview was over. "If you want to know more about that airplane, go talk to Cocky Joe. He's the night watchman at the airport."

"Night watchman?" Mara asked. "I thought an airport would have more security than that."

"It's a small airport," Dornberg said. "Nobody much but crop dusters used it till the new industries moved in. They lengthened one runway to accept corporate jets, but they bring their own security when they're here. I guess Cocky Joe would call the police if anything ever happened, but it never has."

"Is he there all the time?" I asked.

"He lives in a little room in the hangar." Dornberg began moving us toward the door. "Joe is paid to watch at night, but he gets off at eight in the morning. By then, some of the regulars have arrived and started work. The regulars all know each other and would ask questions if a stranger monkeyed with one of the aircraft."

"What is Cocky Joe's full name?" I asked

Dornberg shrugged one shoulder. "I never heard anything but 'Cocky Joe.'"

By this time we were at the door.

"Thank you for the information, Mr. Dornberg," Mara said.

He showed her a hearty grin. "Don't mention it." The grin vanished. "Look, if somebody did sabotage Jerry's airplane, it's not safe for you two to go poking into it."

"Who do you think would make us unsafe?" I asked.

"Whoever killed Jerry," he said. "*If* anyone did."

"Thanks for the warning," I said.

The grin returned. "No extra charge. Maybe you should save talking to Cocky Joe for another day. Bad weather's coming in, and you'd be smart to get home before it hits Overton City."

Hand on the door, he sniffed and turned up his nose. "We really have to do something about that feed lot."

He shut the door, effectively pushing us out onto the windswept sidewalk. The door closed on more than his office. It closed on another avenue of inquiry without our learning anything helpful.

CHAPTER 32

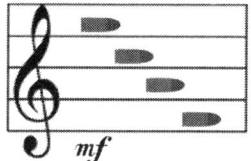

The rain continued its steady fall with the wind whipping it across the puddles. Our gray afternoon subsided into night without benefit of sunset. The temperature plummeted, presaging an overnight freeze. I shivered once in spite of overcoat and gloves.

We made it into the car without taking too much rain in with us.

Mara cranked the engine and turned the heater to high. "Well," she said, "we can scoot back to Overton City before the roads ice over, or we can see what 'Cocky Joe' has to say."

"Find Cocky Joe," I said. "We couldn't accomplish anything in Overton City."

Mara gave me a straight look. "Then we'll have to stay overnight. You know what the Blatant Beast will do with that."

"We're already bitten," I said. "What more can they accuse us of?"

Her lips quirked into a half smile. "They'll think of something. Meanwhile, let's find some food."

We bypassed the fast food places on the main highway and found an old-style café downtown. We parked beside two pickup trucks and scrambled up under the café's awning without getting drenched. A dark car drove by but did not stop. Inside, two middle-aged men wearing tractor caps sat at a counter and jollied with a brassy waitress of equal age. Mara and I took a table on the opposite side of the room.

"Be on your good behavior, Cupcake," Mara said. "You remember what happened in Insburg."

That was where I'd wised off to a waitress who named me Cupcake.

The waitress delivered menus, then looked at me and sniffed. "Are you one of them workers out at the rendering plant? I thought they only burned carcasses on Saturdays."

"We're ahead of schedule this week," I said.

Mara gave me a cold-steel glance.

The waitress was not to be denied. "Or maybe you're one of them illegal aliens they brung in from Canada or Mexico."

"I'm actually a space alien from the planet Pluto," I said.

The waitress placed one hand on her hip. "There ain't no human life out there any further than Mars."

"Sometimes I exaggerate," I said.

Mara forestalled further byplay by ordering a cheeseburger and Coke. I dittoed the cheeseburger but took a chance on the coffee.

"You'll be lucky if she doesn't poison you," Mara said when the waitress had departed.

"Don't prompt her," I said.

Our cheeseburgers proved to be old-fashioned delicious. Apparently, the diet police hadn't penetrated this far into the hinterlands. Silently, I awarded a posthumous decoration to the cow.

"What do you make of Reva's story?" Mara asked.

"It's hard to match that with the Mitra Fortier I knew," I said.

Mara frowned. "But aren't there cases where people invented fantasies to create a part of life that the world of fact didn't satisfy?"

"Some," I said. "In Victorian England, Lady Harriet Mordaunt told her husband she'd committed adultery with the Prince of Wales. The scandal never made it to divorce court because she was declared insane. She'd imagined the whole thing."

"Do you think Mitra was insane?"

"A week ago, I'd have said completely sane. But now I remember those periods of depression. After them, she'd be as right as ever."

"It sounds like a double life," Mara said. "As if she worked efficiently in public and then went home to those fantasies about being loved."

"Sometimes I think the Renaissance people were on target," I said. "They thought the faculty called Imagination colored our perception of the real world so that we never got anything exactly right, that our ideas of reality always had some element of fantasy in them."

Mara showed a wistful smile. "How about us? I wasted years in the fantasy world of Wicca until last fall when I faced up to the reality of evil."

I could have mentioned the idea she still held, that she could fight everything through on her own. But I thought better of it.

"And how about you?" she asked. "You keep saying you 'just teach history,' but you know very well you're capable of more than that."

"Like what?"

Her eyes sparkled. "Like burglary, for one thing." The light faded from her eyes. "And that wasn't exactly history you were teaching Brill Drisko and Cynthia Starlington."

"I thought they were teaching me," I said.

She arched one eyebrow. "Any old fantasy will do ..."

"Let's go find Cocky Joe," I said.

The waitress must have briefed the men in tractor caps on my interplanetary origins, for they took in every detail as I paid the check.

"Cash or credit?" she asked, studying me as if I had two heads.

"Credit." I handed her my card. "If you run it through backwards, will the café pay me?"

"It don't work that way here," she said.

"It does on Mars," I said. "Try it next time you visit."

We completed the transaction in silence.

In the car, Mara said, "Cupcake, someday someone is going to take your measure but good."

Then she laughed, and I joined her. We laughed with the spontaneous, uncontrolled laughter we'd shared after we defeated Dean-Dean's petty plot about our contracts. The laughter purged the tension from our systems.

"Let's go find Cocky Joe," Mara said. "Since we're only talking about the aircraft thing, I don't guess it matters that we can't record."

A pair of headlights followed us but went straight past when we turned onto the airfield road. We parked beside the lone hangar and made a dash through the lone doorway. Under the dim interior lights we viewed six small aircraft parked facing great closed doors that in better weather would open onto a taxiway.

A scratchy male voice hailed us. "What's your business here?"

The speaker was a small, unshaven man with unkempt dirty-blond hair. He wore blue jeans and a high-collared olive-drab jacket that emphasized the slump of his shoulders. As he advanced with a shuffling gait, I realized he was the stranger I'd seen at Mitra's memorial service.

"What do you want here?" the scratchy voice repeated.

"We're looking for Cocky Joe," I said. "Ralph Dornberg told us to look him up."

"I'm him," he said. "The name's Joe Cochran, but they call me Cocky Joe."

Mitra's married name had been Cochran, but I bit back questions. Our first job was to get the man talking.

Mara took the initiative. "We're interested in Jerry Vaughan's crash—especially the maintenance of the airplane beforehand."

"I told all that to those government people. What's your interest?"

"I was Mitra Fortier's friend." Mara's smile would have melted a diamond. "She was looking into this and didn't live to finish the job."

It occurred to me that Mara was getting to be as good a liar as I was.

Joe's eyes narrowed. "Why d'ya think I'd be interested in Mitra Fortier?"

I clamped my teeth shut, but Mara answered without hesitation.

"If you'd known Mitra, you'd want to help. She was murdered while she was trying to find out if Jerry Vaughan was murdered. We're picking up where she left off."

He gave half a shrug. "What d'ya want to know?"

Mara spoke earnestly. "We need to know if anyone had access to his airplane long enough to sabotage it."

Joe squinted one eye. "Well, I don't know how long that would take. I don't know much about airplanes."

"Then tell us who came here in the nights before the crash."

"As I told the accident board, all the owners came by in those last two nights. Ralph Dornberg; that car dealer, Emory Estes, and those guys Drisko and Samstag. And the afternoon before the crash, Drisko and Samstag came at different times and made a few takeoffs and landings."

"But no aerobatics?" I asked.

"I wouldn't know about that."

Mara took over again. "When was the last time Dornberg and Estes flew the airplane?"

"I wouldn't know that, either." Joe looked bored. "I sleep in most mornings and don't go on duty till five in the evening. I just happened to be wandering around that Friday afternoon."

Mara smiled but bored in again. "But there's a lot of activity out here in the afternoon? People would see if someone did something unusual?"

Joe repeated his half-shrug. "I suppose."

"So if the airplane was sabotaged, it would have to be done at night."

Joe bristled. "I'd have seen it and called the cops. That's what I told those accident investigators, and that's what I'm telling you."

Mara's eyes narrowed. "And you were here on the job every night."

Joe said, "I was." But his gaze drifted off toward the ground.

I jumped in again. "What about the time you weren't here?"

"How'd you know about that?" Consternation gripped Joe's face.

"You'd be surprised what I know," I said. He would have been more surprised by what I didn't know, but I had no intention of telling him. "Let's hear your side of it."

He squinted both eyes. "I could lose my job."

"Not if you play ball with us," I said. "Tell us about it and don't skip any details."

Joe's shoulders slumped lower. "It was that Wednesday afternoon around five, and I got this phone call. The voice said it was Mr. Dornberg, but it didn't sound like him. He said get a taxi and come see him. I said I couldn't afford a taxi, but he said he'd pay for it, so I called one and started out."

"What did he want?" Mara asked.

Joe pursed his lips. "When I talked to him later, he said he never called me."

"So what happened?" Mara's voice was soft.

"Just outside the airfield, a car full of guys ran us off the road. Then four big guys piled out of that car and beat us up good and left us laying on the sidewalk. They jumped in another car and got clean away. Turned out later their first car was stolen."

Joe took a deep breath.

"We just laid there a while," he said, "but somebody'd called an ambulance. In the emergency room they said our ribs was bruised but not busted. The taxi driver got one of his buddies to bring me back here, free. But it must have been midnight before I got back."

Mara's voice was sympathetic. "And you didn't tell anyone about this? Not even the accident board?"

Joe's eyes hardened. "Not a word. I have to keep my job."

I jumped in again. "What about the police? They must have investigated the accident."

Joe gave a sly grin. "They did, but I gave 'em another name. Same thing in the ER. So nobody ever asked me about it."

There we had it—six hours when anyone could have sabotaged Jerry's plane. The plot that provided those six hours smacked of more mob action. But Joe Cochran, if he were indeed Mitra's ex-husband, would have had a perfect motive to dispose of her new boyfriend. I made a quick test.

"I've never understood much about these airplanes, either," I said. "I always wondered how they could get enough air pressure beneath the wings to push them up off the ground."

Mara threw me a what-on-earth-are-you-doing look.

But Joe grinned. "I've wondered about that, too. I guess when they get up speed and raise the nose, the air under the wings kind of pushes 'em up."

"I used to know a guy that repaired propellers," I said. "When some pilot made a gear-up landing and bent the propeller blades back double, he'd heat them up on a forge and have them back in shape in nothing flat."

"Sounds like good work if you can get it," Joe said.

Those answers told me what I needed to know, so I decided to drop the bomb.

"You've helped us a lot on that subject, Joe," I said. "Now tell us about your marriage to Mitra Fortier."

CHAPTER 33

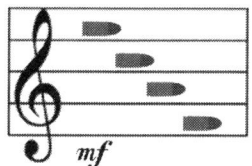

Joe's eyes widened, then narrowed. "What marriage? I never heard of that woman."

I resurrected my Special Forces voice. "Don't hand me that, Joe. You attended her memorial service in Overton City, and her personnel records say she was married to a man named Cochran. You'd better tell us the whole story."

He looked down and muttered, "I don't know what you're talking about."

I kept pressing in. "If you don't tell us, we'll tell Ralph Dornberg you were AWOL from the job."

His eyes burned with a deep fire, and I feared he might remain defiant. But sudden tears doused the fire, his shoulders slumped, and he said, "You have me over a barrel."

His face took on a faraway look. "We met in college. She was pretty. And, boy, was she smart. I was kind of slow in the science classes, but she tutored me, and I passed the exams. And somewhere in all that we got interested in each other."

He paused, apparently in thought. "After we got married, we graduated together and found good jobs. We were happy for maybe a year. Then she started spending time by herself, and she made it clear I wasn't welcome in that part of her life. When I watched TV, she'd take one of those romance books and close herself up in the bedroom."

"That couldn't have been very pleasant for you," Mara said.

"Pleasant?" Joe grimaced. "It was pure hell wondering what I'd done to deserve that. She spent more time by herself and less with me until I had a gullet full. So one night, I burst into that closed bedroom and found her writing in some kind of notebook. She slammed it shut. I asked what was in it, and she said that was none of my business. We started yelling back and forth at each other. But she wouldn't tell me what she was doing, and I wouldn't stop demanding that she tell. It came out a draw, and that night we slept with a lot of empty space between us in the bed—a wonder we didn't fall out on opposite sides."

"That's terrible," Mara said, her tone sympathetic.

He warmed to his story. "Well, our marriage had gotten cold anyway, and I thought maybe she'd been carrying on with someone else. I waited for things to calm down. Then I called in sick at work and shadowed her around for a whole week. Nothing. Not one thing suspicious. So instead of following her, I went home and searched through her books. She had six notebooks, all hidden behind the romance books in her bookcase."

Mara whispered, "What was in them, Joe?"

His face showed the saddest expression I've ever seen on a human being. "They were full of details of her romantic adventures—all with male friends we'd had, and all of them married. So at first I got real mad. But in one notebook, she'd written about being involved on specific dates and places with a guy named Murray Whitfield. But I'd run into Murray's wife a few weeks before, and she told me Murray had spent a week in the hospital with knee surgery. I hadn't mentioned that to Mitra. And she'd written the hottest parts of her romance with Murray while he was laid up in the hospital."

Mara whispered again. "So she'd made it all up?"

Joe nodded. "That's it on the button. So I had it out with her again, and she admitted everything. She said she'd had that ... uh ... 'fantasy life,' she called it, ever since she could remember. She said it was what kept her going in a world where 'most everything was bad.' So I said, 'What about *us*?' And she said something about 'I like you, Joe, and you'll always be a good friend.'"

He continued, tears in his eyes. "I said that wasn't enough for me, and I filed for divorce. She couldn't contest it because I had her notebooks and could use them as evidence if she wanted to get nasty. She didn't, so the judge gave us the divorce for incompatibility."

"Have you seen her since?" Mara asked.

Joe shook his head. "I never went back. But other things weren't so clean. My calling in sick when I wasn't cost me my job, and I started drinking. I couldn't live with the idea that she had to imagine love affairs to make up for what I couldn't give her. And I hit bottom. In and out of rehab, couldn't hold a job, sometimes living on the street. I ended up here—a place to sleep and sixty dollars a week the pilots give me to look after their airplanes. And I let 'em down on that. I don't know who set me up, but I know somebody or other got in here and ... and did *something* to Jerry Vaughan's airplane."

"You couldn't help it," Mara said, ignoring his failure to give essential evidence. "Do you still have Mitra's journals?"

He looked away. "I burned them all long ago."

"We couldn't know all you've been through," she said, "but we do understand part of it. The police have one of Mitra's journals that says she had a long affair with Press here. It says I was her competition and that we had a shouting quarrel about it. Press and I have lost our jobs because of that journal." She gave him a searching glance. "To undo some of that damage, would you tell the police what you've just told us?"

Joe recoiled as if she'd handed him a cobra. "The past is dead, and it's going to stay that way."

Her voice became a whisper. "You'd let innocent people suffer for things they didn't do?"

Joe clamped his jaw shut. "I won't put myself through that shame, and I won't put her memory through it. I've fooled around with you too long. Now go away."

He turned and slouched off toward the far end of the hangar.

Mara and I exchanged looks of despair, and I cursed myself again for losing my voice recorder. She must have been doing the same for letting her phone go dead. Without speaking, we went back to her car, getting a little more wet this time because the rain came harder.

"Tell me," Mara said, "what was that business about propellers and air pushing up under wings?"

"I wanted to know if Joe knew as little about airplanes as he claimed," I said. "Jealousy of Jerry Vaughan would have been a perfect motive for murder, but whoever did it had sophisticated knowledge of aircraft. Joe swallowed both my lies about airplanes, so he knows less about them than most high school kids."

She looked at me narrowly, so I explained. "Most lift forms above the wings, not below. And no one could ever restore the balance on a propeller that's been bent." Silently, I awarded myself points for finding a subject she hadn't mastered.

As we headed back to the main highway, the car skidded on the first turn. Mara handled it perfectly, steering into the skid and accelerating so that the front-wheel drive stabilized the car.

"The worst of all weather conditions," she said, slowing to a creep. "There's warm air up above where the rain is forming, but it's falling into cold air and freezing when it hits. We'd never make it back to Overton City."

"That's not the worst of our troubles. Did you see that dark-colored car parked where we turned out from the airport?"

She threw me an alarmed glance. "I didn't notice. I had my hands full of skid." She returned her gaze to the road and concentrated on driving.

"It's following us about a block back," I said. "I've seen it several times today, always near but never too near. There were two guys in it, but I couldn't make out any details."

She frowned, gaze still fixed on the road. "I don't understand. At the airport, they could have taken us out with no one to stop them."

"I don't know, either," I said. "We've been warned to stop investigating. Maybe it's surveillance to see if we heeded the warnings."

On the main highway, we found two motels facing each other on opposite sides of the highway. Mara pulled into the parking lot of one and stopped to look it over.

"Exterior corridors," she said. "Not good with those fellows following us."

The other motel, across the highway, proved to have interior corridors.

"Let's hope they have vacancies," she said as she stopped under the motel's overhead. "At least we won't get rained on going in."

The lobby was empty except for a well-dressed man with graying temples behind the registration desk and a wide-screen TV where a young floozie in boots and a leather bikini stomped around in something she thought was a dance. The desk man sniffed a couple of times but elected to remain silent about my aroma. At our request, he assigned us rooms on different floors. The separate-floor assignments were feeble precautions against the Blatant Beast—not that he ever let facts come between him and a good bite.

Mara let me go out and park her car. As I entered again, I spotted the dark car idling near the edge of the parking lot.

"I don't mean to make trouble," I said to the desk man, "but a couple of guys in a dark car are hanging around out there. I thought you ought to know."

"Thanks," he said. "We were robbed last month, and since then the police have been most helpful."

Mara handed me her cell phone. "No one ever calls me on that phone," she said, "and you're expecting a call back from that guy in Dallas."

When I protested that the battery was dead, she took the charging cord from her purse and handed it to me.

"I sometimes charge it in my office," she explained, "but I never thought I'd need to charge it in the car."

With that, we headed to our respective rooms, mine on the second floor and hers on the third. In my room, I left the lights off and watched from a window overlooking the parking lot. Five minutes later, a police car eased up beside the dark car and turned on its flashers. The policeman got out and spoke briefly with the dark car's driver. Pretty soon the dark car drove out onto the highway and turned in the direction away from Overton City. The policeman waited a few minutes and drove away.

With that problem settled, I stripped down and hand-washed the liniment smell out of my undergarments and hung them on the shower rod. Then I applied a whopping fresh dose of Mara's liniment to my aching body. It burned like battery acid and smelled like concentrate of *eau de polecat*, but it brought immediate relief. As my muscles relaxed, deep fatigue from the event-packed day seeped in. In a near daze, I remembered that all the information we'd gathered seemed to provide no help for either our suspensions or Mara's arrest.

So if Truth was really The Daughter of Time, it looked like Time had a runaway in the family.

When I recalled Joe Cochran's sad story, my internal musicians featured a trombone playing "None but the Lonely Heart." The soloist must have been a baseball player because he kept sliding into the third.

I was just sliding into sleep when Mara's cell phone rang.

It was Leonard Morley. "Press," he said, "you've got the proverbial tiger by the tail with Dustin Industries."

"How's that?" I asked.

"You remember that you wanted me to take a look at it, and I gave you the short course about distances in Texas? Well, I have a friend in El Paso who owed me a favor, and he checked out the address where that company is supposed to be."

"What did he find?" I asked.

"He found a lawyer's office."

"Does that mean Dustin Industries doesn't exist?"

"It exists, all right," he said. "It's legally incorporated, but it exists only in a file cabinet in some lawyer's office. I think you've found a dummy corporation that someone uses to scam government contracts."

CHAPTER 34

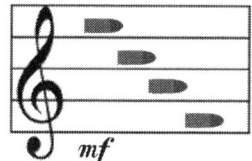

That brought a possible motive for the murder of two people. Jerry was the CPA who said he was looking into Dustin Industries and paid for it with his life. Robert Sun Lee had told Mitra about Jerry and Dustin shortly before her death. But what could I do with the information?

"Press, are you still there?" Morley's question jolted me out of reflection.

"Uh ... yes. Just wondering where to go from here. I don't suppose you know who owns the corporation?"

"Not yet," he said. "I've traced the ownership to the Cayman Islands. It'll take me a while to find the real owners. Do you have any ideas?"

"Only suspicions. Mainly Gordon Samstag and Steven Drisko. But I suppose Ralph Dornberg and Emory Estes could be in on it."

"I've heard of Samstag and Drisko," he said, "but who are the other two?"

"Local businessmen in or around Overton City."

"I'll keep checking," Morley said. "Meanwhile, Press, take care of yourself. People involved with dirty money play rough."

After we rang off, I sat there wondering what to do next. Then Mara's cell phone rang again.

Cindy's voice came through as sweet as ever but tinged with worry. "Daddy, I had to call and check on you. I've been worried."

"I'm okay, Cindy," I said, "but how did you know to call me on Professor Thorn's phone?"

Her voice had steel in it. "I got no answers on your landline and only voice mail on your cell phone. So I called your next-door neighbor." She sucked in her breath. "He said he saw you drive off with a blonde, so I tried Professor Thorn's number."

"How did you get that?" I asked. "She only gives that to friends."

"She gave it to me last Christmas when we all had dinner together. She said we both were fighting Establishments, so I should call if I needed advice."

"I've been worried about your situation," I said, eager to change the subject. "How's that going?"

"You don't get off that easy, Daddy." Her voice rang with resolution. "The TV is saying awful things about you and Professor Fortier and that Professor Thorn. I don't believe a word of it, but I had to call and see how you're doing."

Her tone said she had to know if I'd cheated on her mother.

"I swear to you, Cindy, there's not a word of truth in it. But trying to disprove it is something else again. We're working on it, but we haven't gotten very far."

Cindy's voice stiffened. "Who is that 'we,' Daddy? You and Professor Thorn?"

"That's right," I said. "We're the two people who've been lied about, so we've joined forces to try to disprove the lies."

"And where are you now, Daddy? I know you're not at home."

"I'm in a motel in Cloverdale."

"And where is Professor Thorn?"

"She's in the same motel. She's on the third floor, and I'm on the second, so turn off the suspicions."

Cindy's voice half-sobbed. "I have to believe you, Daddy. I have to believe none of that ... that awful stuff is true."

"Look, sweetness," I said, "you know how I loved your mother, and I hope you know how I love you. I could never betray either one of you."

Even as I said it, my conscience stabbed me for imagining a fling with Cynthia Starlington.

"All right, Daddy." Cindy's voice softened. "You know that I trust you."

"You may have to, honey," I said. "I don't know if we can disprove those stories. But how is your situation?"

She gave a sad laugh. "We're in limbo, but that beats being convicted without hope. The Council for Individual Rights on Campus has threatened the university with a lawsuit on our behalf. Mark Weston says if it goes to court, the university will be the laughing stock of all academia. But so far there's been no response. All we can do is wait."

I thought Mark was too optimistic. Time and time again, universities have proved shameless in enforcing political correctness. They no sooner lose in court than they figure some other way to deny the same basic rights to students or faculty who don't have the approved politics.

But all I said was, "We'll hope the administration does the right thing."

We said we loved each other and rang off.

My heart went out to Cindy. In spite of the scripture Pastor Tammons cited, at times like these, I find it hard to believe God is actually working in the world. Nevertheless, I suppressed my skepticism and prayed for Cindy. This time, my prayers didn't bounce back from the ceiling.

I woke next morning to gray overcast skies and winds that whistled in the electric wires outside my window. I showered and shaved.

Afterwards, Mara and I returned to the café where we'd eaten the night before. The middle-aged waitress had been replaced by a tall, thin woman equipped with a voice like a buzz saw. Mara ordered eggs, bacon, and toast while I splurged with an order of two eggs, bacon, and a full stack of pancakes.

The waitress cranked up her whangy voice. "Grits?"

"Half a dozen," I said.

She squinted one eye. "You don't count 'em, Sonny. You gets three spoonfuls on yer plate. Don't you know nothin' about civilization?"

"I'm culturally deprived," I said.

The waitress continued honking. "You must be that man from Mars what Hildegarde was telling me about last night." She sniffed twice. "You don't smell like him, though. She said he smelt like he hadn't took a bath since the planet was formed, but you smell almost human."

"Thanks for the endorsement," I said.

Mara intervened. "Could you put in our order please? We have to go to work."

The waitress departed, muttering something about "not from Mars, no matter what she says."

Mara graciously avoided comment until our food arrived. The food itself was delicious, further proof that the diet police had not yet destroyed the cuisine of Cloverdale.

Mara seized the check and settled it, probably to preclude any further byplay between me and the waitress. As we left, the waitress muttered something about "... no man from Mars."

I suppose you can't satisfy everyone.

We crept back to Overton City on roads that were icy but drivable.

In late morning, Mara's cell phone rang. I answered, and Dr. Sheldon's great voice boomed in my ear. "Press, have you heard anything from Freda Broyles? She seems to have disappeared."

"No contact for a couple of days," I said. "Mara visited with her yesterday morning. What's going on?"

His voice showed concern. "We don't know. Weldon Combes called me and asked if you or I knew anything about her. He had to be desperate to call me. How should I know where she is? She didn't show up for classes this morning. She wasn't at home, and he couldn't find anyone who'd seen her since noon yesterday. He's worried she might have suffered the same fate as Mitra Fortier."

"I'm sorry," I said. "I don't know anything about it."

He sighed. "All right. But there's good news, too. President Cantwell is out of danger. He'll be weak as fleas on a field mouse, but he'll pull through. And I found some information on that research project. When can we get together?"

I thought a minute. "How about tonight? This afternoon I have to rent a car and pacify my insurance company."

"Tonight's fine," he said, "but not here. This confounded place is driving me nuts. How about your house?"

"Okay by me, but maybe you should talk to Mara about it." I handed her the phone. Her past avoidance of my house had bordered on phobia.

She said yes and handed the phone back to me. "The rumors can't get any worse," she said, "and, at least, we have a chaperone."

I asked if she knew anything about Freda Broyles' alleged disappearance.

She frowned. "Nothing. I leaned on her conscience for letting Mitra's fantasies ruin our reputations—that was before Dean-Dean suspended us—but it didn't seem to make a dent in her."

I considered Freda's horned-toad physique. "If you did make a dent in her, would it show?"

Mara's chin raised that eloquent fraction of an inch. "That is a most unkind remark, Preston Barclay. What if she's tried to complete Mitra's investigation and gotten herself ... into real trouble?"

"I sit corrected," I said. The customary cliché was "stand corrected," but Mara had corrected me for using it while sitting the night we raided the executive center.

Her eyes never left the road, but she showed the flicker of a smile.

She dropped me at my place around noon and headed out toward hers. But instead of calling the insurance company, I called my list of suspects. Ralph Dornberg had denied knowing anything about Dustin Industries, so I began with Emory Estes.

Before he could try to sell me a car, I asked, "What can you tell me about Dustin Industries, Incorporated?"

"About what?" He sounded surprised. "I never heard of it."

"Don't you own stocks?" I asked.

He grew wary. "They're my business and not yours. Press, you're already in trouble. You could get hurt worse than you are now."

Before I could reply he said, "I hear you smashed your car. I can make you a real good deal on a replacement."

I said I'd think about it and hung up.

Next I called Steven Drisko and asked the same question. "What do you know about a company called Dustin Industries?"

He answered without hesitation. "Not a thing, Professor Barclay. Or maybe I should say *former* Professor Barclay."

"Thanks for the optimism," I said. "You know nothing about Dustin Industries?"

His voice remained even. "Nothing at all. But I'll have some of my people look into it. Call me tomorrow afternoon, and I'll tell you what they found. Meanwhile, take care of yourself. I hear you had an accident."

He broke the connection. Thus far I was getting nowhere, but out of sheer stubbornness, I placed a long-distance call to Gordon Samstag and asked the same question.

Samstag said he was sorry about my accident and it wouldn't be proper to discuss my suspension before the administration acted on it, but he would be in Overton City tomorrow and we could talk about Dustin Industries then.

"Could you tell me something now?" I asked.

"Better we talk about it in person," he said. "One-thirty in my Overton City office?"

"That's fine," I said.

"However," he added, "you'd be much wiser to let this rest."

"I'll see you at one-thirty," I said and hung up.

Then the doorbell rang. I dragged over to answer it and found Manny Clampett on my doorstep. I invited him in, but he said he had to get home to Mama if he wanted to keep peace in the family. Then he added, "I thought you might need these things from your car."

He handed me the papers from the glove compartment, the fingerprint reader I'd also stashed there, and my voice recorder he'd found on the floor—the recorder I'd needed so badly in Cloverdale. He also handed me my cell phone, smashed beyond use.

Sic transit gloria technicae, I thought. But I said, "Thank you, Manny. You've really gone the Second Mile."

"No, I ain't," he said. "Your place is only half a mile off my route home."

Okay, so Manny doesn't register on allusions. He's a great mechanic, and I'm grateful to him for keeping my Honda running ten years past its forecast demise.

"We got good pictures of what was done to your brake lines," he added. "Call me when you needs 'em."

I thanked him, and he departed on his connubial peacekeeping mission.

I spent the next hour wrangling with my insurance company. The claims adjuster showed no interest in someone's tampering with my brakes. The upshot was that because I carried no collision insurance for my antiquated Honda, the only settlement would be medical expenses, of which I had none unless I put in a claim for Mara's bottle of liniment.

"Thanks," I said.

"For what?" Puzzlement showed in his voice.

"You're the first person I've talked to in three days that hasn't asked me about Mitra Fortier."

He began, "Say, I wondered about that—"

I hung up on him.

I tried to call Sergeant Ron Spencer about the CD Bruno Pinkle planted in my desk, but I again got his distraught wife. She hadn't seen or heard from him in three days.

I told her that if I saw him I'd tell him to call home. Then I worried about Ron. He'd been a good friend, and I hoped my giving him that CD hadn't gotten him into trouble. But there was nothing I could do about that now.

Next, I called a car rental to arrange for temporary wheels. By then, the winter night was descending and the rental agent, like Manny Clampett, wanted to go home to Mama. So he told me to call back in the morning. Where I wanted him to go had nothing to do with Mama, but with admirable restraint I refrained from advising him of that preference.

That done, I contemplated a change into my blue suit. It was too dirty from the wreck, so I stayed in the brown one. It was disreputably wrinkled by now, but it would have to do.

Somewhere in there, I realized my internal orchestra had been shut down for several hours—a welcome relief from distraction.

Afterwards, I dined on the customary ham sandwich and coffee while trying to make sense of all that was happening. As a historian, my stock in trade was sifting through reams of data until I found a pattern. But in this case I had reams of data with no apparent pattern. There were incomplete sub-patterns, of course. The most serious was Jerry Vaughan's and Mitra's interest in Dustin Industries just before their murders. Yes, murders. I agreed with the police about Mitra's death, and after hearing Joe Cochran's story, I had no doubt about Jerry's. The missing links in that pattern had to wait until Leonard Morley learned more about Dustin Industries. My interim hypothesis was that Gordon Samstag, Steven Drisko, or both were deeply involved. I had no evidence to involve Ralph Dornberg and Emory Estes.

Mitra's journal presented a more pressing problem. It was flagrantly untrue, but completely damning for Mara and me. We now knew about Mitra's fantasy life, but our two witnesses—three counting Freda—refused to come forward. Because this was not a court case, we could not subpoena them and compel their testimony.

So as the temperature fell in the Midwestern winter night, I could only hope Leonard Morley would find the key to Dustin Industries or that Dr. Sheldon's research on Brill Drisko would turn up something helpful on the two murders.

On the problem of the journal, I had no hope at all.

CHAPTER 35

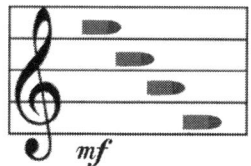

Mara and Dr. Sheldon parked in front of my house at six-thirty. He again showed his fierce independence by wheeling himself up the walk to the front door. There he turned himself around with a triumphant flourish. While Mara held the door, I wheeled him backwards up the one step and across the threshold into the entryway. Mara hung his hat and their topcoats beside mine on the coat rack, and we proceeded into the dinette with Dr. Sheldon leading the way.

The dinette had originally been a full-size dining room, but they had to expand the living room to make room for Faith's Steinway. The living room received the outside wall and windows, and the dining room became the dinette, an interior nook between the living room and the old-fashioned spacious kitchen. It was a cozy fit for tonight's business session.

When we were seated on three sides of the table, Dr. Sheldon said, "Mara told me about your trip. I'm sorry you found no help on the suspensions."

"What about Freda Broyles?" I asked.

"I've told all I know. She didn't show up for class this morning and wasn't at home, so Malcolm Combes phoned around and found that no one had seen her since noon yesterday." He rubbed his palms together. "Your suggestion to check on Brill Drisko in Las Vegas has borne fruit."

"Don't keep us in suspense," Mara said. "What about her?"

Dr. Sheldon showed the smile he uses when he's posed a question no one can answer. "None of the current entertainment websites proved helpful."

"Brill has lived in Overton City for more than two years," I said. "For Las Vegas, you'd have to find a historical site or an archive."

The leonine brow furrowed. "That is precisely what I did, child. It's called 'Vegas Historical Review,' but it did not immediately solve the problem because I did not know the lady's maiden name."

"If she ever qualified for one," Mara said, looking at me.

Dr. Sheldon ignored her comment. "But I did know the lady's husband's name. So I searched under his name and ...Voila!" He waved his hands like a stage magician. "I found he'd married one Brill Kramersdorf about three months after that faculty trip to Sin City."

"So that gave you the lead you needed?" Mara asked.

He frowned. "Unfortunately, no." He brightened again. "But I returned to the Vegas Historical Review site and found they had archives in depth. Drisko must have met the lady during the faculty trip, so I chose that week and perused photographs of the various shows."

He shook his head. "That site dealt in more flesh than the Fort Worth stockyards, and I looked through most of it without finding what we were after."

"I'm sure that pained you deeply," Mara said, "but you did find Brill?"

"That I did." Dr. Sheldon showed a self-satisfied grin. "The photo showed her as the star of what I would euphemistically call a burlesque show. There was no mistaking her with those tight peroxide curls. But you'll never guess her stage name ..."

"I won't even try," Mara said.

"You have to understand the pictorial presentation," Dr. Sheldon continued, careful to build suspense. "With one hand she held some kind of fan that covered the essentials, more or less.

With the other hand she pointed a forefinger at the camera and her viewers. And she glowered as if she were daring her viewers to do I-don't-know-what. The photo showed her stage name—Ruby Conn."

I groaned. "That's terrible."

Dr. Sheldon smiled in satisfaction. "If you think that's terrible, just wait: The caption under the photo said, 'Don't cross me, Caesar.'"

I groaned again. "That's the worst pun I ever heard."

"Almost as bad as some of yours," Mara said.

"Let us stay focused on our research, children," Dr. Sheldon said. "So now we know Brill Drisko is a former burlesque queen. The place where she performed was owned by a gentleman named Guido Stefano, who is reputed to be involved in various illegal activities in Vegas. And there were a few hints that before she became a star, Brill had a second job in an escort service."

"No wonder she didn't want me looking into her past," I said. "It seems Steven Drisko bought himself a bundle of trouble. At last week's reception, she had quite a time with younger trustees who hadn't brought their wives."

Mara wrinkled her nose. "You saw that, too? I thought I must be the only one who noticed."

"Children, you have much to learn," Dr. Sheldon said. "Many faculty members would notice Brill's antics, but they wouldn't gossip about the wife of a rich trustee."

"Okay," I said, "what happened in Vegas didn't stay in Vegas. So we know Brill was an exotic dancer and probably a call girl before she married Drisko. Where does that get us?"

The doorbell rang.

Dr. Sheldon ignored it and said, "Nowhere in particular, I'm afraid. You said you made some phone calls this afternoon?"

The doorbell rang again.

"I called several people about Dustin Industries," I said. "The first—"

The doorbell rang a third time.

Mara arose with an exasperated expression. "Since you two are so busily engaged, I suppose I'll have to answer the door." It occurred to me that this was a radical change from her desire not to be seen in my house.

"The first call was to Emory Estes," I said. "He says he never heard of Dustin. The next call was to Drisko—"

"I might have known I'd find *you* here." The angry feminine voice came from the front door. "Where is Press?"

Mara didn't answer. High heels clicked on the hardwood floor, and Cynthia Starlington marched into the dinette. My internal musicians returned with a vengeance. No soft clarinet this time but the hoarse wail of a jazz saxophone.

"Where have you been, Preston Barclay?" Cynthia demanded. "I've been trying to phone you for two days, and you didn't answer. This afternoon your line was always busy. And you don't even have voice mail. That's not only rude, it's ... it's *Neanderthal*."

I hadn't seen this side of Cynthia before, but it matched with the temper fit she'd pitched at Mitra Fortier.

"I plead guilty on both counts," I said. "I've been out of town."

"I don't have to ask who you were with." Cynthia threw an angry glance at Mara, who quietly slid into the chair she'd occupied before. Cynthia's left hand held something hidden behind her.

"So it's true," Cynthia said, blinking away tears and gesturing with her free hand. "Everything they've been saying about you is true."

"What's true, Cynthia?" I asked. I knew what she meant, but I wasn't about to admit it.

Her eyes blazed dark fire. "Those stories about you and Professor Fortier and this ... this blonde *Wiccan*."

"*Former* Wiccan," I said. "There's no truth—"

"How *could* you?" Cynthia stamped her high-heeled foot and waved the free hand again, the other still hidden behind her. "How *could* you make those promises to me while you were carrying on with those other two women?"

My mouth hung open. "What promises? All I promised was that I'd look into Mitra's death. *Look into it*, not—"

"I started calling you yesterday before I heard about those ... those disgraceful affairs. All I wanted was to give you this." The left hand came out from behind her back and threw a soft object onto the table.

It was a long-sleeved shirt, the kind to be worn with the collar open. It was ornate with orange palm fronds on a background of deep blue, a far more expensive garment than I'd ever worn. It fit my personality like a boxing glove fits an earthworm.

Cynthia's voice became an angry sob. "I wanted to get you out of those grubby old suits so you could relax and not be so *stodgy*. I wanted to bring you into the twenty-first century—nobody teaches in a coat and tie anymore."

All three of us sat staring at her. I think my mouth still hung open, but I'm not sure.

Cynthia stamped her foot again. "I wanted to do so much for you, Press. You could have retired from teaching and devoted yourself to scholarship. You could have become anything we wanted you to. And I told you ... *confidences* ... things I wouldn't share with anyone else ... because I *believed* in you. And all the time you were playing me double with this ..."

She gestured toward Mara. "With this—"

I will never know what her next word would have been.

For that was when the house blew up.

CHAPTER 36

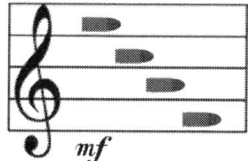

An explosion shook the house. Two more followed. Cynthia put her hands to her head and screamed. Even in the midst of shock, the old Special Forces part of me knew they were incendiaries, not high explosive. At the rear of the house, fire blazed into instant inferno. But I'd heard three explosions, one on each side plus one in the rear. That left the front as our only way out. The walls of our interior dinette would shield us momentarily, but we had only seconds to escape.

My Special Forces training took over in earnest. I seized the screaming Cynthia by the shoulders, aimed her at the front door, and shouted, "Run!"

She did not move. Flames leaped toward us from the back of the house. Heat closed in on either side like an oven in hell.

I pushed Cynthia toward the front door and applied a resounding slap to her derriere.

That time it took. She ran screaming for the front door. I turned to Dr. Sheldon, knowing too well that the flames would soon suck all the oxygen out of the air.

"Hold your breath," I shouted.

"Get Mara out of here," he commanded. "Don't waste time on me."

Even in this crisis, I remembered he was more accustomed to giving orders than to following them.

Mara stood beside him with his computer tucked under her arm, watching me for a signal. I scooped the protesting Dr. Sheldon up from his wheelchair and ran for the front door. The moment we moved into the blazing living room, heat attacked viciously from all sides. I held my breath and ran, wondering how I'd open the front doors with my arms full of Dr. Sheldon. Smoke filled my eyes with tears. Through the blur I saw Faith's Steinway burst into flames. I stumbled on something, kicked it aside, and saw it was a high-heeled shoe, evidence that Cynthia had fled in total panic.

I need not have worried about the doors. The main door stood wide open where Cynthia had left it, and the storm door had locked where she must have flung it into the full open position. I charged through and instantly felt relief on my face and sides, for now the heat burned only the back of my ears and neck. I ran for Mara's car, which was still parked at the curb. As I neared it, the door locks released with a click. Dr. Sheldon reached down and opened the car door, and I deposited him in the passenger seat.

I had a fleeting impression of Cynthia's Lexus disappearing two blocks down the street, but I had no time to think about it. We had to get Mara's car away before the fire spread to it.

Dr. Sheldon pointed behind me and shouted one word, "Mara."

I turned, ready to dash back into the house for her but dreading the near-certain death I would suffer. Then Dr. Sheldon's wheelchair catapulted into my shins. Mara came close behind, car keys in hand and her arms full of topcoats and Dr. Sheldon's computer. I should have known it was she who unlocked the car. I opened the car's rear door. Mara threw the coats on the back seat and eased the computer in under them, then ran to the driver's door. As she did, I folded the wheelchair and plopped it onto the floor behind Dr. Sheldon's seat. I slammed the door shut as Mara drove the car out of harm's way.

The heat at my back had grown intolerable. I sprinted away from my house, now all ablaze except for the front wall. Only when the heat grew less did I stop and look back. My neighbors were already in the street, those from next door in obvious distress for their own homes.

One neighbor ran up to me and said, "I called the fire department, Press. What on earth did you do to set that off?"

"Someone firebombed it," I said.

He ran back into the crowd as if he thought my body itself might erupt in flames. Sirens and horns of fire trucks sounded in the distance.

"Make way here!" Dr. Sheldon's booming voice announced his return. The crowd made way for his wheelchair.

Mara followed close behind. "Here," she said, handing me my topcoat.

For the first time, I realized the midwinter cold was freezing my back while the fire still threatened to scorch the front. Mara and Dr. Sheldon had donned their coats. But none of us had hats or gloves.

Thus far I'd been acting on reflex, but now my mind began to awaken. We'd been firebombed on three sides, but not on the fourth. Only now I remembered an old guerrilla trick—confront the enemy on three sides but leave an apparent escape route on the fourth. Then shoot him down as he attempted to flee. The arsonist's obvious intent had been to kill us, yet we hadn't been shot as we escaped. Something about this didn't ring true. I searched for it in vain.

The first fire truck roared onto the scene, horn blaring. As it did, the thought I'd been searching for clicked into place. I ran to meet the truck and seized the first fireman as he dismounted.

"Firebombs on three sides of the house," I shouted, "but none in the front. There has to be a fourth."

His face showed his unbelief. He pointed toward the crowd and ordered, "Get back over there."

Even as he spoke, the fourth firebomb exploded. Flames leaped up to engulf the front wall of the house. The skepticism on the fireman's face dissolved into surprise, quickly replaced by a grim set of jaw. He gave me a push toward the crowd, then directed his crew toward preventing the fire's spread to neighboring houses. Mine was obviously lost.

From that point, the evening grew jumbled. I remember sitting on the curb several doors down from the fire, Mara beside me and Dr. Sheldon in his chair nearby as I watched twenty years of memories go up in flames. Only then did deep sorrow strike home. That house held everything I had left of my life with Faith and with Cindy's growing-up years. All I had now were the clothes on my back and (thanks to Manny Clampett) the little voice recorder in my pocket.

I remember being glad Cindy had moved most of her things to her apartment near the university. I dreaded having to tell her why our home had gone up in flames: Once too often, I'd stepped on the wrong toes.

Emergency medical personnel arrived and checked the three of us for possible injuries. They only found the equivalent of moderate sunburn, so they gave us a useless referral for psychological counseling and retreated to the vicinity of the fire trucks.

The head fireman questioned us separately about how the fire started. We must have told the same story because his only follow-up question was why anyone would want to kill me. I could only shrug. I didn't understand it myself. All I knew was that I'd made someone very, very angry. But I was no closer to knowing who that someone was than I'd been a week ago.

When the fireman finished with me, I returned to my place on the curb by Mara and Dr. Sheldon. Mara surprised me by slipping her arm in mine. Apparently, sympathy overrode her abhorrence of touching.

My neighbors stood in groups, muttering and casting disapproving glances in my direction. Apparently, I would become the neighborhood pariah as well as the campus pariah. The firemen had saved the homes adjacent to mine, though paint on both houses had blistered.

From my position on the curb, I watched walls and roof collapse into the house that had been my home for more than twenty years. Their collapse brought deeper depression than I had ever felt, aggravated by the bitterness of failure. I had made no significant progress toward solving Mitra's and Jerry's murders, I'd found no usable evidence toward disproving the false rumors about me or the false accusation against Mara, and I had no idea how to go about saving my job. It looked like everything I valued in life had come to an end.

As if to taunt me, my internal pianist played that haunting melody from the movie *Enchantment*—the one that distracted me during the faculty meeting. As before, the piano began softly, high on the keyboard, and I recognized Faith's inimitable touch on the Steinway that no longer existed. In memory I relived the intimate times she'd sent that melody to call me for an embrace. My internal orchestra picked up the theme with strings and flutes, and it seemed I could hear Faith's voice singing her version of the words:

I'll live for a soldier
And follow my love.

As suddenly as it began, the music stopped and left me sitting on the curb staring at the smoldering ruins of our house, the ashes of Faith's Steinway among them, now forever silent. The winter wind off the plains chilled my ears and my hatless head. I pulled my coat collar closer about my neck and put my gloveless hands in the pockets.

Then I remembered the only other time a theme from a movie had possessed me in a faculty meeting. It happened last fall and repeated itself later when Mara and I were in desperate straits. That repetition had triggered my memory of a single sentence I'd heard in the faculty meeting, and that sentence proved the key to solving the Laila Sloan murder. Since then I'd often wondered if the memory trigger was a gift of Providence.

Hopeful now, I searched my memory for the first thing I'd heard after this present melody possessed me during the faculty meeting.

I came up empty.

I remembered words and phrases from the meeting but nothing I could connect to anything learned in my investigation. My prime suspects were trustees who were not present at that meeting, so how could that melody point toward one of them?

My hopes dissolved into the atmosphere like smoke from the smoldering ruins of my house, and my depression grew more bitter. If, as Pastor Tammons said, God was continuously working in this world, He must be working somewhere else. I was not angry with God. Only skeptical. Then as I stared at the ashes, anger came. But not with God. I felt a deep, burning anger against my unseen enemies. But I had no idea who those enemies were. So my anger soured into frustration and then into even deeper despair.

"Come with me, Press," Mara said, her voice resonant with the soft melody of her Kentucky upbringing. "I have to take Dr. Sheldon home. Then we have to find you a place to stay, and we have to get you a hat and gloves before you catch pneumonia."

I said nothing. I was too busy drowning in despair. Mara's arm linked in mine and the touch of her shoulder should have brought reassurance, but in my despair I was hardly conscious of them.

Mara tugged on my arm. "We have to get moving, Press."

I tugged back. "It's no use. I'll just stay here." How dare she interrupt my despair! Everything meaningful in my life was ended.

Then her cell phone rang.

Mara answered, but her words flowed past me like unknown words in a foreign tongue. Then she shook my shoulder and handed me the phone.

"Take the call, Press. It's Leonard Morley."

I took the phone and muttered a dull hello.

"I'm sorry about your house," Len said, "but the fact that someone firebombed it means you've got your teeth into something big. I think I know what it is."

"Then tell the police," I said. "I'm beaten."

"All right. Then quit." Len's voice reverted to his Infantry colonel days. "You're within sight of the finish line, but quit if you want to. There doesn't seem to be much of Special Forces left in you."

My anger boiled up, but curiosity also stirred. "What's this 'finish line' bit? What have you learned?"

"That's more like it," Len said. "I've finished tracing the Dustin Industries outfit. I thought the Caymans ownership was a dead end, but I pulled some strings and found out the Caymans company is owned by an outfit in Toronto."

"How does that help?" I asked.

Len ignored the question. "Here's what I think is happening. Some corporation—call it Company A—lands a juicy cost-plus contract from the Defense Department. So Company A puts out bids for subcontracts. Company B submits the low bid on one of them, but it doesn't win. Dustin Industries wins that subcontract with a substantially higher bid. Then Dustin turns around and subcontracts the job *in toto* to that same Company B for its original low bid. So for doing nothing but paperwork, Dustin makes a handsome profit at the expense of American taxpayers."

My interest quickened. "Wouldn't Company B blow the whistle?"

Len sputtered a few times, then said, "Some companies would and some wouldn't. But there are plenty who'd just shrug and take the money."

"So who is the 'Company A' that's getting the original contracts?"

"I'd have to see the contracts to be sure, but tracing the ownership to that company in Toronto gives me a pretty good idea."

"How is that?" I asked.

Len chuckled. "The company in Toronto is owned by two men. One of them I never heard of, a guy named Guido Stefano."

I'd heard that name recently, but I couldn't place it. "And the other man?"

"You know him well."

Len actually laughed.

"It's your good friend Steven Drisko."

CHAPTER 37

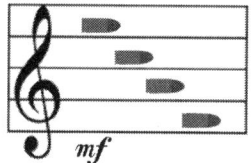

I rang off and sat staring into space, trying to work out what that information meant. As the flames of my home dwindled into smoldering embers, the winter cold gave my ears and back of my neck a burning sensation.

Mara shook my shoulder and gave me an anxious glance. "What was it, Press?"

"Later," I said. "Right now, we have to get Dr. Sheldon out of the cold." I'd just seen him shiver. One side of his face looked like a good case of sunburn, and it must have felt as sensitive as my ears. We got off easy. If that fourth bomb had gone off on time we'd have been too well-done for a starving cannibal to stomach.

We wheeled Dr. Sheldon around the corner to Mara's car. We settled him into the passenger seat while I took the back. Mara turned the heater on. Strange contrasts—running out of the burning house, I'd have traded both ears and one eye for the winter cold. But with the wind off the plains gnawing at my flesh, I'd have done the same for more heat. Mara's car heater provided a comfortable compromise.

"All right, Press." Dr. Sheldon turned in the passenger seat and spoke to me. "What did you learn?"

Before I could answer, Mara's cell phone rang again. Without taking her eyes from the road, she handed the phone to me in the backseat.

When I answered, Cindy's voice bubbled with excitement. "Wonderful news, Daddy, you won't believe it, and I hardly do though I know it's true, but I've had the hardest time getting hold of you. I rang the house and kept getting a recording that your line was out of service, and it took me forever to remember where I'd put your Professor Thorn's cell phone number ..."

"Cindy, there's something I have to tell you—"

"And I have something wonderful to tell *you*, Daddy." There was no stopping her as she gushed on. "It's about our suspension. You remember that CIRCA was looking into it? Well, they ended up defending us and told the university they'd take it to court for violating our constitutional rights to free speech and due process, and you know what happened?"

I tried again. "Cindy, I have to—"

Her verbal express train raced through all warning signals. "The administration gave up. They wiped out our suspensions and reprimands and gave us full reinstatement. And that's not all. They're giving us protection while our papers are distributed, and they're going to talk with CIRCA about the illegal parts of the university 'speech code.'"

I gave in. "That's wonderful, Cindy. I'm proud of you for standing by your guns, and I'm proud of you for winning. But I have some bad news. Our house burned down tonight."

She sucked in her breath and the phone grew silent.

I wondered if she'd fainted. "Cindy?"

"Yes, Daddy?" Her voice was weak. "Are ... are you all right?"

"I'm fine," I said, ignoring the still-burning sensation on the backs of my hands and ears. "Dr. Sheldon and Mara Thorn were with me, and we all got out okay. But the house and everything in it is lost. Total loss." I didn't remember until later that I hadn't mentioned Cynthia Starlington's being there.

Another silence while Cindy digested that information. Then she said, "I'm glad you're okay, Daddy. How did it happen?"

"We're not entirely sure," I said, assuaging my conscience with that weasel word *entirely*. "One moment everything was fine and the next moment fire was everywhere. All we could do was run." That much was true, at any rate.

"We lost everything..." Her voice began softly, then strengthened with resolution. "But *you're* all right. That's the important thing..." She paused a moment. "And about your pictures of Mother—I'll have mine copied for you..."

She was so much like Faith, then, thinking of someone else first.

"Thank you, Cindy," I said. "You're most thoughtful."

"But Daddy, what about those awful rumors on TV? Do you have any news?"

The question stabbed at my heart. "I'm afraid not, Cindy. We're working on them, but we don't have anything concrete."

"You don't have to prove anything to me, Daddy. I won't *ever* believe a word of them."

My heart melted. "Thank you, sweetie. That's all that matters. I'm really glad about your good news. You enjoy that, and I'll take care of things around here."

I spoke brave words, but Cindy's believing in me was far from being all that mattered. My job and my reputation mattered, Mara's job and reputation and her freedom mattered, and it mattered that someone wanted both of us dead. It looked like I was doing a lousy job of taking care of things.

Mara asked, "That was Cindy? How did she take it?"

"Like a champion," I said. "Not a word of regret about her things that burned." Cindy's suspension was a family matter, so I'd never mentioned it to Mara or Dr. Sheldon.

"That other phone call," Dr. Sheldon boomed. "Don't keep us waiting."

In retrospect, I've wondered how all three of us managed to focus on that problem. We'd come very near to being burned alive, and I had lost my home and the accumulated memorabilia from twenty years of a wonderful marriage. In many ways, I was still in shock. But instead of descending into self-pity, we all returned to concentrate on the question of why someone wanted to murder us.

In my case, it had been drilled into me in Special Ops to turn off my emotions, regardless of tragedy, and complete the mission. Mara had much the same training in her military experience, and Dr. Sheldon must have reverted to similar discipline from his Korean War days.

In response to his question, I repeated Leonard Morley's explanation of the Dustin Industries scam, culminating in his naming Steven Drisko and Guido Stefano as co-owners of the parent company in Toronto. I concluded by saying that I wouldn't be surprised to find Gordon Samstag wrapped up in it somewhere.

Mara nodded. "Samstag has his fingers in a lot of pies. Not surprising if some are hot."

"Guido Stefano?" Dr. Sheldon said. "He was Brill Drisko's boss in Vegas."

At long last, the name fell into place in my mind. I knew I'd heard it recently, but I couldn't bring it up until Dr. Sheldon mentioned it.

"Stefano's involvement gives you the tie-in you've been looking for," he continued. "You'd wondered why mob hoodlums would be interested in you, but Stefano is supposed to have mob connections."

Dr. Sheldon put his hand to his brow. His body was tiring, but his mind stayed as determined as ever to fight through to a conclusion. "Samstag and Drisko both have problems. The government is investigating Samstag for that rocket failure, and your friend Morley says Drisko is defrauding the government. That's double trouble for Overton University. It's heavily invested—too heavily invested—in Drisko's company's stock. It has a lot invested in Samstag's companies, too, but there's more variety there. Failure of one of Samstag's companies wouldn't be catastrophic."

He surveyed Mara and me through now-drooping eyelids.

We hung on every word.

"It's different with Drisko," he said. "Five years ago, I was faculty representative to the trustees when they almost came to blows over that. Some said we should buy a little of Drisko's stock but keep the college portfolio diversified. Others said Drisko's management was driving the stock up so fast we'd be foolish not to buy a lot of it and ride it up. In the end, we bought so much that the college would either get rich or go bankrupt."

He sighed. "Last week I'd have said we were rich. Now it looks like we're broke."

Mara frowned. "That must be why Mitra Fortier said we'd all lose our jobs. Robert Lee put her onto the Dustin Industries fraud. She must have been looking for a good way to handle it when she asked Press and me for help."

"There's no good way to handle it," Dr. Sheldon said. "If you blow the whistle, the college goes under, and you all lose your jobs. If you don't, a fraud against the taxpayers goes unpunished."

That silenced us for a while. Mara and I already faced loss of our jobs, but the thought of all our colleagues losing theirs was too terrible to contemplate.

"Maybe it's not an either-or," I said. "If we can buy a little time—say, about three months—maybe the college can sell enough Overton Technologies stock to avoid disaster."

Mara's jaw tightened. "Don't forget our personal disaster. Those people tried to kill us."

"Maybe we can negotiate that, too," I said. "I'm going to talk to Steven Drisko."

"You're out of your mind," Mara said. "That's gambling with our lives."

"I'm only gambling with mine. You two stay clear."

Mara was too kind to point out the flaw in my logic. I'd meant that only I would be at risk when I met with Drisko, but she surely knew that afterwards we'd both remain vulnerable.

Dr. Sheldon's head tilted forward as he dropped into sleep. Mara shifted into "Drive" and headed toward the Assisted Living Center. She said nothing, but her expression showed what she thought of my proposal. That told me I had to get something started before she could argue me out of it. Fortunately, I still had Mara's phone.

I didn't remember Steven Drisko's phone number, but I remembered putting Brill's personal card in my wallet. I found it now and dialed her number. It was past nine o'clock, so Steven Drisko should be at home.

Brill answered in her brusque showgirl's voice.

"This is Preston Barclay," I said, "May I speak—"

Her gasp cut me off.

That should have warned me, but I began again. "This is Preston Barclay. I'd like to speak to Steven if I could."

"He's ... he's not here at the moment." She sounded confused, and I thought she might be inventing the scenario as she went along. "He should be back in about an hour if you'd care to call back." I could hear her breathing as she waited for my response.

"Isn't that kind of late?" I asked.

"Not for us." Her voice gained confidence. "We never turn in before midnight."

"I'll call back," I said and rang off.

"Another tryst?" Mara asked.

"You're trysting my words," I said. Even from the back seat I could see the quirk of her lips that meant she was teasing.

"Don't look now," Mara said, "but that dark car is following us again."

It was all I could do to keep from turning and looking out the back window. Instead, I eased out of my seatbelt and slid into a position where I could look past Mara into the driver's mirror. The car was a full block behind, but definitely trailing us on the nearly deserted streets.

Mara drove as if nothing unusual was happening, and we arrived at the Assisted Living Facility without incident. Dr. Sheldon woke up when the car stopped. I took a quick look around as we got him into his wheelchair, but I didn't see the dark car. Its driver was doing a professional job.

Once in his room, Dr. Sheldon waved us away and said he could manage. We conceded the point and headed back to the car.

"What's this about calling Drisko back?" Mara asked.

"I'm not going to phone," I said. "I'll see him in person if you'll lend me your car."

"I'll drive you," she said as she pulled out of the parking lot. Her chin tilted up the now-familiar fraction of an inch that said argument was useless. "What will you tell Drisko the *Wunderkind* when you find him?"

The truthful answer would have been, "I'll think of something," but that would never pass muster with Mara. So I said, "The first order is our safety. I'll try to bluff him into calling off the dogs—convince him I have documentary proof of his fraud that will be delivered to the FBI if anything happens to you or me."

"And if he's not the one who's putting them onto us?"

"He has to be. He's the only one we know who has mob connections."

"And if someone like Gordon Samstag also has mob connections?"

She had me there. "Then I guess we continue our career as targets. But my other objective is to buy time for the college to sell off its stock in Overton Technologies. With Dr. Sheldon's help, maybe I can convince President Cantwell to make the sale. In any case, we have to act on the information we have instead of sitting on our ... benches and wishing we had more."

She threw me a quick smile. "You almost colored outside the lines then, Cupcake. But don't worry about that now. There's a dark car following us again. A different one this time."

I checked the outside mirror on my side. Our shadow this time was an SUV rather than a sedan. But as I watched, another dark car turned out of a parking lot and struck the driver's-side fender of the SUV. As near as I could tell from the reduced-size image in the mirror, the impact only brought the two vehicles' fenders together. Not the kind of collision that crushed passenger compartments and caused dire injuries, but enough to create a nuisance for both drivers.

A wave of gratitude swept over me, and I thanked Providence. Maybe God *was* working in this world, even if He was a little bit late.

Those drivers' attention would be taken up with themselves, so I turned and watched the scene directly through the rear window.

Occupants piled out of both vehicles to survey the damage. Each vehicle disgorged at least two men, and I couldn't tell where the fifth man came from. Two men, one from each car, gestured vigorously and seemed to be quarreling, while the other three seemed to be watching our departure. That was about all I could see before Mara turned a corner and headed west toward the river.

"Where to now, Sherlock?" she asked.

"Turn left after you cross the river," I said. "We're going to pay Steven Drisko a visit."

CHAPTER 38

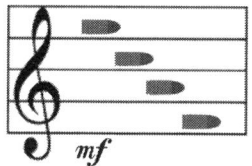

The Drisko estate lay a mile or two southwest of the city proper but within the city limits. Mara's left turn put us on the highway that ran by it. I needn't have worried about finding the right place. Behind the roadside ditch, a white board fence marked off acreage tended with care, though now marked by streaky drifts of snow turned into ice. Soon afterward, red brick gateposts marked a paved and lighted snow-free driveway leading perhaps a hundred yards uphill to an impressive ranch-style house. Light showed from the house in a single window.

"What now, General Barclay?" Mara asked. "Do we go straight in or do you have another plan?"

She stopped the car while I hesitated. Truth to tell, I was having qualms about my plan. "Brill said Drisko would be home in an hour," I said, "and it's only been thirty minutes. I want to be sure he's there. The last thing I want is another brush with Brill."

"Why not?" Mara teased. "She might brush some lipstick onto another tooth."

"She did not leave any lipstick," I said. "She only stunk up my suit collar with her perfume."

"'The lady doth protest too much, methinks,'" Mara quoted. At least she got the "methinks" in the right place, which few people do.

I ignored her. "Pull in over there, and we'll watch for him to return." I pointed to the dark hulk of an abandoned filling station across the road from Drisko's estate. It must have rankled the Wunderkind for that unsightly ruin to mar the view from his house.

It looked like a good place to wait, though it was pitch black beyond our headlight beams. Mara drove carefully through scattered debris around the hulks of abandoned pumps, circled the station, and parked behind it.

"What are you doing?" I asked. "If we can't see the road, we won't know when Drisko comes home."

"Two cars followed us earlier tonight," she explained. "We don't know what happened to one, and the other crew won't let that fender-bender stop them. There's no use taking chances."

She pointed toward the western side of the filling station, the side away from town. "We can watch from over there without getting caught in anyone's headlights."

She switched off the ignition, and sudden darkness hid everything. Then Mara opened her door, and the interior lights came on. I followed her lead and exited my side of the car, shutting the door with as little noise as I could. Darkness closed in like a velvet curtain.

We picked our way carefully around the western side of the station to its front corner. As Mara said, the station would shield us from the lights of cars approaching from town.

It did not protect us from the cold. The temperature held below freezing, aggravated now by what would have been a gentle breeze in warmer seasons. We both snugged the collars of our topcoats close and left our ungloved hands in our pockets. At that moment, I would have traded a fortune for a hat. Mara, standing close beside me in the dark, must have had similar feelings.

She asked instead, "What if Drisko is already home?"

I checked the illuminated dial of my watch. Still twenty-five minutes left in the hour Brill had cited.

"We'll wait twenty-five minutes," I said. "If he hasn't come by then, I'll go in anyway. If he's here, I'll talk to him, and if he isn't, I'll try to jar something out of Brill."

"Or vice versa."

When I didn't reply, she changed the subject. "Press, you don't act like a man whose house has just burned. Most people would sit around moaning about it, but you're charging ahead as if nothing had happened."

"I'm just numb," I said. "I don't feel like any of this is real. Besides, you don't act like a woman who'd barely escaped being burned alive."

"It doesn't seem real to me, either," she said, "but we both keep doing the things that have to be done."

"About the fire," I said, now whispering. "Every second in that house brought greater risk, yet you remembered Dr. Sheldon's computer, and you brought out his wheelchair and our topcoats ... "

"I had time to think while you were ... uh ... motivating Cynthia. I made my own mental checklist—computer, wheelchair, coats."

Admiration flowed through me. "You even thought to have the keys in your hand so you could unlock the car."

"I wasn't all virtuous. I dumped Cynthia's ocelot-collared coat on the floor. May the Lord forgive me."

"She'll never miss it," I said. "She left her shoes behind, too."

Mara laughed softly. "Along with that designer shirt she bought for you. It looked nice and comfortable, Press. And really mod. You'd have enjoyed wearing it."

"Like I'd enjoy a dog collar," I said.

"So you finally realized that," Mara said.

"That brings us back to the fantasy thing," I said. "Maybe Mitra wasn't as different from me as I thought."

"I wish Drisko would hurry," Mara whispered. "It's getting colder."

"Use me for a windbreak," I said.

I squared my back against the drift of frigid air. Mara took a position to the leeward of me and about a foot away.

"That helps," she said. "From now on, I'll keep a scarf in the car, just in case."

By this time, my night vision had fully adapted, and I could see her face as more than just a dark form. My internal orchestra had shut down. Silence enveloped us, sealing us off as if we two were a separate nation. Perhaps a separate planet.

After a few moments, she spoke again. "I suppose we all have fantasies at one time or another."

"That's what Pastor Tammons told us. I confess I had one about Cynthia."

"I've had my own fantasies, too," Mara whispered, "and I've wondered if any of them would ever become real."

The dim form of her face, so very close, looked up into mine. My hands came out of my pockets as if they had minds of their own. They touched the shoulders of her coat, brushed aside her cascade of blonde hair, and stopped with my fingers lightly touching the back of her neck. She stood motionless, her shadowy face still looking into mine, neither inviting nor retreating.

I bent forward and brushed the briefest of kisses on her lips.

She did not move.

I brushed another kiss on one corner of her lips and matched it with one on the other corner, followed by a firm but gentle one fully in the center.

She came into my arms with a rush, returning the kiss with a fervor equaling the one she'd given me last fall. Yet there was a difference. Our kiss last fall had been frantic, an act of desperate comradeship when our fates depended on events of the next few minutes. This one equaled it in intensity, but brought with it a calm certainty that made the threats and vagaries of outside circumstances dissolve into irrelevance.

Even under the spell of its magic I knew, and she must have known, that we had stepped into a new world of unknown quantities we would have to explore together.

After a few moments, she stepped back. Not far, with my hands still touching her shoulders and her face still lifted toward mine. And that enchanted silence continued.

"Is this a fantasy, Press?" she whispered.

"Not for me," I said. "It feels like enchantment, but it's as real as anything can get."

"Then where does it take us? This is uncharted territory for me. If we go on, I'll have to rethink my entire way of living. Where do we go from here?"

"We go into deeper friendship." As I said it, my whole being longed to kiss her again without stopping, and my Imagination leaped ahead with images of intimacy in marriage. Renaissance geniuses would have been proud of me, though, for my Reason intervened before Imagination stampeded me into ruining everything. "We need to spend time together and explore that friendship. We have to take a hard look at the barriers between us—the age difference, our habits, our value systems—and we have to spend a lot of time in prayer. Sooner or later, we'll know if we're supposed to spend the rest of our lives together."

Put into words, it sounded so unromantic I feared it might frighten her off. But I'd forgotten how her mind clamped an iron control on her emotions.

"It's going to be a wonderful time," she said. "Lord willing, a wonderful life."

She came into my arms again and we kissed—long and calm in our newfound certainty of intent. That kiss drove from my mind all thoughts of the Blatant Beast, of losing my job, of the burning of my house, of the mob's attempts on our lives. Everything dissolved into nonexistence before the wonderful reality that was Mara.

I thought we might go on kissing forever.

Then from the Drisko estate came the sound of a pistol shot.

CHAPTER 39

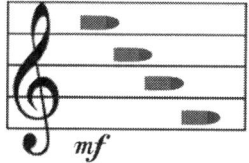

We startled apart, listening. But no further sound came. Not even an echo. I whirled and stared at the Drisko estate. One window had been lighted before, but now the house stood in darkness, contrasting sharply with the long, lighted driveway.

Mara's whisper broke the silence. "Could he have come back, and we missed him?"

"We'd have heard the car approach," I said.

I reached in my topcoat pocket and gave back her cell phone. "Call 911 and report the gunshot."

Then I ran toward the Drisko house. My thought, if indeed I had one, was to give first aid to anyone who might have been injured. I did have qualms about running up a lighted driveway toward a dark house where someone had just fired a gun. Yet, in that moment, my instinctive desire to help overcame all doubts.

Standing on the lighted front stoop, I rang the doorbell. I heard it ring two continents away, somewhere deep in the house. No one answered.

The contrast of light and darkness, the interplay of flickering shadows and silence, brought the same sense of unreality I'd felt the week before at the trustees' reception, but my rational mind stayed locked onto reality.

I rang again, knocked on the door, and called, "Anyone home? Anyone hurt in there?"

Still no answer.

If the pistol had discharged accidentally, someone might be lying there wounded. The door was unlocked, so I eased inside, leaving it open behind me. If I had to retreat, I didn't want the obstacle of a closed door. In the near-darkness of the long hallway I could see shadowy shapes of heavy paintings on the walls. Dark rooms opened up on either side. At the far end stood a single lighted doorway.

My feeling of unreality grew. So did my sense of danger.

But my rational mind still functioned. I dropped my topcoat on the floor and waited. I heard nothing. Was the house deserted?

In the oppressive silence, seconds ticked uselessly away. If someone was hurt, I had to find him quickly. So I walked down the hallway, walked as fearfully as if the contents of that lighted room would determine my fate. Perhaps they would.

I stopped short of the doorway and peeped into the room, half expecting to look into the muzzle of a pistol. There was none.

The room was a den, its walls lined with bookshelves filled with the covers of uniform special editions. The Driskos apparently bought their culture prepackaged in wholesale lots. In one corner stood a leather-upholstered chair with a reading lamp beside it. Seated in the chair with a book in his lap was Steven Drisko.

He was thoroughly dead. The shot that killed him had entered the right temple and exited the left, taking a good bit of matter with it. But it had left enough face for positive identification.

So much for rendering first aid.

Frustration crowded in on my sense of unreality. My whole plan rested on confronting Drisko and forcing a truce long enough to secure Mara's and my safety and give the college time to unload his stock. Now that plan was as dead as Drisko himself.

But was his death suicide or murder? If it was suicide, where was the gun? Drisko's left hand held the book in his lap, but the right hand lay empty. The Persian rug on the right side of his chair also lay empty. Could the gun have fallen to the left of the chair? It seemed impossible, but I checked anyway.

The rug on that side contained only matter that had previously filled Drisko's head.

No pistol. He had not committed suicide. I stood frozen in place, trying to fathom what this murder meant and what I should do next.

Then, as from a distant country, I heard the sound of the front door easing shut. In the silent house, the click of its spring lock echoed as startlingly as another pistol shot. That closed door had cut off my escape route. And that person's stealth meant he intended no good.

I searched frantically for a place to hide, but found none. So I stood waiting with my pulse hammering in my temples as slippered feet slithered softly down the hallway toward the door of this room. Then the statuesque form of Brill Drisko stood in the doorway.

And now I knew exactly where the pistol was.

It was in her hand.

CHAPTER 40

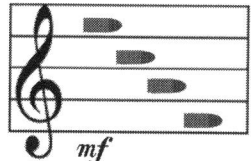

Brill's throaty voice came out as a snarl. "Well, Professor Barclay, you can't say I didn't give you a chance."

I raised my hands while my internal orchestra mocked me with something on a muted trumpet. Brill's eyes blazed with black fire. Her hand held a .32 caliber automatic—enough weapon to do the same job on me it had done on Steven Drisko. And Brill's eyes said she was eager to do just that. I had to stall, somehow, and hope the police heeded Mara's call for help.

"A chance, Brill? I asked. "The same chance you gave your husband?"

"The same chance." Brill's lips twisted into a sarcastic smile. "You and he have a lot in common."

"There's no way," I said. "I'm poor as a church mouse." My comparison was clichéd at best, but under the circumstances I couldn't think of anything better.

Brill wasn't attuned to academic distinctions. "You both had a habit of getting in over your depth."

I didn't like her use of past tense, so I protested. "That's nonsense, Brill. Steven Drisko succeeded at everything he ever tried."

I was kicking myself for not turning on my voice recorder before Brill entered the room. It might have produced evidence of my murder that could be used in court. I'd missed that chance, so I concentrated on mere survival.

Brill bridled at my claim of Drisko's success.

"Successful?" She gave a bitter laugh. "Hardly! He thought he could beat the tables in Vegas the way he beat the competition in business. That trip your hick trustees and faculty made three years ago ... Before they came, we knew what each one of them was worth. We wrote the script, and they followed it to the letter."

She squinted and the gun muzzle wavered. "Except the Fortier woman. She knew her numbers, and we had to get her back on script. The rest were like sheep to the slaughter."

"They all lost?" I asked.

"We let some lose a little and others win a little. The house broke about even on them, but we chose two to lose big."

"Drisko was one of those?"

Brill gave a snort of contempt. "By the time he left Vegas, we owned him. He had to embezzle from his company to pay up. Once he did that, we had him for good."

"Why for good? One annual audit should have found the embezzlement. How did you stretch it out for three years?"

Brill showed a satisfied smile. "For one thing, he got interested in me during that trip. Guido thought if he had a little interest on the side, he wouldn't have his mind on the game. As it worked out, Drisko got more than a little interested and asked me to marry him. I put him off for a while, but Guido thought it was a good idea. That would give him someone to look over Drisko's shoulder full time. So as soon as we knew Drisko had embezzled, we closed the deal, and I married him."

She sighed. "Marriage was no fun, but it was less work than hoofing around the stage every night."

"You were lucky," I said and tried to drive my previous point. "The first competent audit should have shown the embezzlement." Holding my hands up made my arms ache. I began easing them down a little at a time. My internal orchestra lapsed into silence.

"Not just lucky." Brill's confident smile returned. "Guido showed Drisko how to put the money back and make a lot more."

"Dustin Industries?" I asked. "I wondered how that figured in." Leonard Morley had told me, but I needed to keep Brill talking. I had my hands halfway down, but Brill didn't seem to notice.

She talked like one who thought time was on her side. "Drisko would subcontract parts of a defense contract to Dustin at an inflated price. Then Dustin would subcontract it to the original low bidder and make a quick profit. The scam had low overhead, and most of the profits ended up with Guido and Drisko."

I kept listening for the sound of car engines, but none came. The police were taking a terribly long time to respond. I'd gotten my hands all the way down, and Brill hadn't reacted. Now if I could flick the switch on my voice recorder …

I tried another tack. "But Jerry Vaughan got on to you."

"That was his problem." Brill gave another bitter laugh. "It became his last problem. When we learned he was going to check into Dustin Industries, Guido had some of his boys fix the airplane, and that was that."

"But Drisko flew it after they sabotaged it," I said. "He might have been killed."

"He might have been, but he got his orders. It might have been his hide if he flew it, but it *would* have been his hide if he didn't. He came back so white in the face that he looked green—said he never gentled an airplane like that before in his life."

"Gordon Samstag also flew the airplane after it had been sabotaged," I said. "How does he figure into this?"

Brill showed a sadistic grin. "That's for you amateur detectives to figure out."

"We came up blank on that one," I said, and shook my head as cover for moving my hand toward the pocket with the voice recorder.

"Put your hands up again," Brill shouted.

I complied. So much for my attempt to record my murder. The muted trumpet returned to mock me.

I tried another stall. "The crash took care of Jerry, but what about Mitra Fortier?"

"That nosy broad." Brill snorted again. "We knew she was poking into things, so Guido sent us some chemical stuff to take care of her if she got too close. He said to make it look like an overdose. We carried the stuff around in Drisko's car."

"What brought things to a head?"

"That reception. We saw her talking to several people, but the only ones we worried about were you and your blonde Wiccan."

"*Former* Wiccan," I said reflexively. I was getting tired of people's describing Mara that way, but this did not seem like the time to make a great issue of it.

Brill's mouth twisted in disgust. "For all the Fortier woman's smarts with numbers, she was dumb enough to ask Drisko about Dustin Industries. And she was stupid enough to believe him when he said it was confidential, but they could talk in her office. He coaxed her into the front seat of his car, and I rode in the back. Like I said, we kept the stuff from Guido there. So I reached up and chloroformed her good. Then we parked at the edge of the campus circle and carried her standing up between us like she was drunk or something. We used her keys to get into her office, and I gave her the big shot there. Drisko didn't even have the nerve to do that."

"Weren't you afraid someone would see you or notice the light in the office?"

"Someone did see the light. A woman. We heard her high heels stop outside the door, and for a minute I thought we'd have to take care of her, too. But she left, and we knew she hadn't seen us."

Cynthia Starlington would never know how close to death her spite against Mitra had brought her.

Brill laughed again. "We left the Fortier woman on the floor and got out before someone else came."

She would have shown less bravado if she'd known how near they were to getting caught. Elmo Koonz would have seen them leave except that a loud car engine drew him from his third-story lookout. He saw Cynthia leave, but apparently didn't get back to his post until after the Driskos had gone.

Still no sound of a police car. I goaded Brill again.

"But the police found chloroform residue on Mitra's lips ..."

Brill squinted one eye. "I guess I used too much of the stuff. I'd never done that before."

"But you'd done other things."

"Not really. Once in a while, I set up a John so Guido's boys could take care of him. But I never did it myself."

"Until tonight," I said. "Why did you shoot Drisko?"

"Guido's orders. Drisko had gotten greedy in ways we didn't know about."

"I thought you were supposed to keep an eye on him."

Her eyes flashed black fire. "How was I to know he was cheating on quality control? He used substandard parts on his subcontract for that botched rocket, and one of the parts went bust. They'd eventually find out that part came from Drisko, and then they'd look at everything else about him. They'd stumble onto Dustin Industries, and Drisko would buy himself a shorter sentence by squealing on Guido. With the government that close, Guido said it was time for Drisko to commit suicide."

Where were the police? I tried desperately to gain more time. "The cops will never believe it was suicide."

"They would have, but now you've given them a better story. They'll figure that Drisko shot you and then killed himself. That'll keep them scratching their heads till I'm out of the country. Besides, the cops on our payroll will believe anything Guido tells them."

Fireworks went off in my head. "That's why Clyde Staggart was talking to some of your goons?"

Brill nodded. "And that's why he didn't solve that other murder last fall. Guido told him to kick up a lot of dust but let it turn into a cold case. You and your little Wiccan messed that up but good."

With great restraint, I refrained from saying "Former Wiccan." The last thing I wanted was to shunt Brill's train of thought onto a siding.

She continued, "Staggart was supposed to write the Fortier case off as an accidental overdose, but then the lab people found traces of chloroform. After that, Staggart had to call it murder and either hang it on somebody or make a lot of noise and let the case go cold."

A car engine sounded outside. I hoped it was the police, but Brill had other ideas.

"That'll be Guido's boys, come to haul me out of the country. Now all I have to do is take care of you."

I made one more try. "What makes you think they're going to do that, Brill? You know too much. They'll take care of you the same way you took care of Drisko."

She laughed. "Guido looks after the people that look after him."

Her finger tightened on the pistol's trigger. In that split-millisecond I remembered being shot by last fall's murderer, except that Mara had sabotaged the ammunition so that the bullet only stung. I'd have no such luck this time. I stared into the black hole of the pistol's muzzle.

Suddenly from the dark hallway a small white object flew through the air. A light bulb, for heaven's sake! It burst with a loud pop on the floor to Brill's left. As Brill's head jerked in that direction, Mara sprang out of the hallway and knocked Brill's gun hand upward. The gun went flying and caromed across the floor. I dived after it. Out of the corner of my eye, I saw Mara throw Brill to the floor the same way she'd thrown me in the executive center. By the time I grasped the gun, Mara had Brill face down with her arm twisted up behind her shoulder and Mara's knee punching into her kidney.

Brill squirmed and yowled. Mara twisted the arm higher and dug her knee deeper into the kidney area. With her free hand, she bounced Brill's head on the floor a couple of times. Brill grew quiet.

Mara looked up at me with a smile. "You almost bought it that time, Cupcake." The grisly spectacle of Drisko's body didn't seem to bother her.

"How long had you been there?" Last fall, she and Sergeant Ron Spencer had listened to the murderer's confession too long, and he'd shot me with that sabotaged bullet.

"I just got here," Mara said. "It took me a while to get in."

Another thought occurred to me. "How did you get in? Brill locked the door."

"You have to hand it to Drisko: He bought top quality locks." A half-smile graced her lips. "One summer in college, I worked for a locksmith."

"That proves the value of higher education," I said, "but what about the police? Did you call 911?"

"They said they'd send a car," she said. "But when they weren't prompt about showing up, I thought I'd better see what was going on."

"I heard a car," I said. "But is it police or Guido Stefano's goons?"

As if in answer to my question, someone pounded on the front door.

Mara was keeping Brill subdued, so I had to answer the door. I wouldn't open to anyone but police, but first I had to make a positive identification. As I walked up the hall, Brill's pistol in hand, my heart practiced percussion on my ribs, and a Dixieland band counterpointed my wah-wah muted trumpet.

What would I do if the newcomers were mobsters? If I fired the first shot, I'd be a murderer. If I let them fire it, I'd be dead. Or, if it were police at the door, why hadn't they identified themselves? I would have given anything to hear that one word, "Police."

Then the pounding came again, and a deep voice called, "Police. Open up."

My heart sank. Those were the words I'd hoped to hear. But the voice was the mellifluous voice of Duggan Hahn, the dog-faced detective who always accompanied Captain Clyde Staggart.

CHAPTER 41

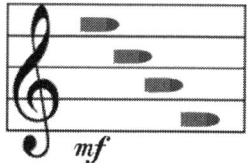

The voice called again. "Police. Open up."

I found the light switch, and light flooded the hallway. Darkness retreated into the adjacent rooms.

I retreated, too, about ten feet back down the hall and laid Brill's pistol on the floor. I wouldn't let Dogface see it in my hand. Some cops take a liberal view of "imminent threat."

"Preston Barclay here," I called. "The house is secure." I unlocked the door and opened it, stepping back with my hands raised.

Dogface stood there a moment, gun in hand, as his eyes searched the hall behind me. Behind him I could see the shoulder of another plainclothesman, but I couldn't see the man's face. I hoped it wasn't Staggart.

"Against the wall, Press," Dogface commanded.

I spread-eagled myself against the wall and said, "The only weapon here is the one on the floor."

No one answered. Rough hands searched me and handcuffed my hands behind my back. My internal orchestra responded with a minuet.

"Who else is here?" Dogface demanded.

"Mara Thorn, Brill Drisko, and the body of Steven Drisko," I said. "Brill says she shot him."

Hands pushed me away from the wall and turned me down the hallway.

"Take me there." Dogface gave me a push in that direction.

I still hadn't seen who the second policeman was, and I didn't dare turn around to look. I'd made a good show of outward bravado, but it only masked my inward despair. I'd escaped death in the holocaust of my home, and I'd learned who murdered Mitra Fortier and Jerry Vaughan, only to find myself—and Mara—at the mercy of two rogue cops, with Guido Stefano's hoods not far behind.

Dogface stopped me at the door into the den.

"Police, coming in," he shouted. Then he pushed me ahead of him into the room.

He obviously thought that if someone inside wanted to shoot a policeman, I'd get shot instead. In present circumstances it did not seem practical to file a nonconcurrence, particularly since that violent shove propelled me several steps into the room before I caught my balance.

"Mara," I called, "for heaven's sake don't throw Brill at this poor policeman."

I heard Dogface and his companion enter behind me, but I wasn't about to turn around until someone told me to. No one did.

"What's going on?" Dogface demanded.

Brill shouted, "They broke in and killed my husband and they're kidnapping me ... Ugh!"

The accusation ended in a grunt as Mara used her free hand to push Brill's face into the floor. When Brill looked up, her cheek had a smudge of dirt on it. If she walked free, some poor housekeeper was going to catch what-for.

A different pair of hands pushed me over against the wall, and I lost sight of Mara and Brill. Mara released Brill at Dogface's command, and the two women apparently received the same search for weapons that I'd received.

Mara spoke in a calm voice. "When I came in, Brill was holding Press at gunpoint. Drisko was already dead. I took her down, and Press grabbed the gun. I think you'll find only one shot has been fired. That's the one I reported, and Press and I were together when we heard it."

"She's lying," Brill screamed. "They broke in and murdered my husband."

Dogface spoke again. "If they killed him, Mrs. Drisko, why did they call 911?"

Until then, I'd assumed that Dogface was in the mob's pay along with Staggart. Now he acted like a detective who only wanted to know the facts.

Brill made no answer to his question.

"Careful," I said. "She says some mob types are coming to take her out of the country."

Someone joined me facing the wall. Out of the corner of my eye I saw it was Mara. The sound of other movements suggested Brill was being placed somewhere else.

"Didn't you hear me?" I asked. "Brill said some of Guido Stefano's goons are coming to take her out of the country."

If Dogface didn't react to that, he was probably in the mob's pay after all. My heart jackhammered my ribs again.

"Turn around," Dogface ordered.

I turned. He had no weapon in his hand. He did have a grin on his face. So did the other policeman, Sergeant Ron Spencer.

"You wife wants you to call home," I told him.

He blushed but said nothing.

Dogface spoke again. "Stefano's boys had a slight collision. They were carrying illegal weapons, so they're now in the city jail."

"That only takes care of one crew," I said. "There was a second car—a dark sedan with two men in it. It followed us for several days, part of it down in Cloverdale."

Dogface and Spencer exchanged knowing looks. Spencer asked, "Shall we tell them?"

At that point, though, four uniformed patrolmen arrived as backup.

Dogface nodded toward Brill. "Book her on aggravated assault and suspicion of murder. Don't let her wash her hands and set her up for a paraffin test."

Two patrolmen led her out as she protested that she wanted a lawyer.

Sergeant Spencer took off my handcuffs. I rubbed my wrists to get circulation going again.

"You two also get paraffin tests," Dogface said to Mara and me. "We have to know who's fired a weapon and who hasn't."

At his nod, Spencer began the explanation. "Professor Barclay, you gave me a classic hot potato with the CD Bruno Pinkle put in your desk. I couldn't handle it alone, and I only knew one man I could trust." He nodded toward Dogface. "Detective Duggan Hahn."

"Detective Hahn did the fingerprints himself," Spencer said. "He walked them through the experts without saying what they were for. They all belonged to Bruno Pinkle."

"I'd suspected a lot of things," Dogface said, "but those fingerprints brought the first concrete evidence. Meanwhile, Pinkle found child pornography on Professor Thorn's hard drive, and Captain Staggart had me take the hard drive from your computer. All that was a little much for me, so after I looked through the Barclay hard drive, I copied it and put the copy in the evidence room. When Captain Staggart said there was child pornography on it, I knew he'd planted it there. That's when Sergeant Spencer and I went to the chief."

"With him," Spencer said, "we checked the photos on both hard drives and the CD Bruno Pinkle put in your desk. They were identical."

"Pinkle confessed to fabricating the evidence," Dogface said. "And he implicated Captain Staggart."

Mara started up. "Does that mean …?"

Dogface smiled. "It means your arrest will be expunged from your record."

"And Captain Staggart?" I asked.

"I guess you two didn't watch the TV news tonight …"

"We were too busy being cremated," I said.

Dogface ignored the comment. "The public announcement was that Captain Staggart is suspended pending investigation of alleged irregularities with evidence."

"Staggart also accepted bribes from Guido Stefano," I said. "Brill told me that while she was getting ready to shoot me."

"That's being investigated, too."

"That's good news," I said, "but the second car following us might still be trouble."

"That car was us," Spencer said. "The chief said make some excuse for emergency leave and see what we could find. The quickest way was to follow you two and maybe make an arrest when somebody knocked you off."

"Very thoughtful of you," Mara said.

"Very thoughtful of you to sic the Cloverdale cops onto us," Dogface said. "They thought it was hilarious when we showed our IDs."

"No charge for the entertainment," I said, "but why didn't we see you when my house burned down?"

"I'm sorry about that," Dogface said. "It looked like you were going to stay put for a while, so we checked in with the chief. Your house was burning when we got back, so we hung around to see what you'd do next."

"And trailed us to the Assisted Living Center?"

"You'd better be glad we did," Dogface said. "That's where that carload of hoods picked you up."

"Brill must have alerted them," I said. "My phone call would have told her the firebombs didn't kill us. They knew Dr. Sheldon was with us, so they'd know we had to take him home."

"We arranged a minor accident to distract them," Dogface said. "The weapons charges took them out of action."

"Thanks," I said. "Now you have the Fortier murder wrapped up."

"On the contrary." Dogface frowned. "We still don't know who killed her. What we do have is a new homicide that you say Brill Drisko committed, and she says you committed."

I tried to respond. "Brill told me she used the chloroform on Professor Fortier, and she said she injected the cocaine. I'll swear under oath to everything she told me."

Dogface threw me a disgusted glance. "Your sworn statement against hers? Her lawyer will take you apart on the witness stand."

"He'll do no such thing," Mara said, her chin raised again. She fished the voice recorder out of my coat pocket and handed it to Dogface with a look of triumph.

"Twenty-five minutes and it's still recording," she said. "I think you'll find everything Brill told him on there."

Dogface took it from her as if it were the Hope diamond. He pressed the "Off" button and then the "Play" button. Voices came through clearly:

Mara's whisper: Is this a fantasy, Press?
Mine: Not for me. It feels like enchantment, but it's as real as anything can get.
Hers: Then where does it take us?

I felt my face flushing. I knew I hadn't switched the recorder on. Certainly not at that intimate moment. A wave of frustration swept over me as I remembered how desperately I'd tried to reach the recorder while Brill was talking. So how ...?

Dogface clicked the "Off" button and said to Mara, "Are you telling me this thing was recording until you handed it to me?"

"Twenty-five minutes worth," Mara said. "Brill's confession comes later, and then you'll hear your own voice."

Dogface shook his head. "All right. Now let's go down to headquarters and get your written statements."

Mara gave me a proud glance enlightened by her secret smile. I had a lot of questions, but they'd have to wait till later.

Dogface arranged for Mara's car to be driven to the station. Then he and Sergeant Spencer piled us into the backseat of Dogface's personal car, a dark Chevrolet with a conspicuously bent front fender.

As we drove, my emotions plunged. If they'd been a bathysphere, they'd have set a record for new depths. My adrenaline highs from the fire and the encounter with Brill had drained me, my neck and the backs of my hands stung like a bad sunburn, and all I wanted to do was sleep and forget the whole thing. What I actually did was sink deeper into depression. I'd survived the fire and Brill's intended murder, but my house was destroyed, and I knew my full emotional reaction to that had not yet struck. I dreaded its arrival. Worst of all, Mara and I had learned the truth about Mitra Fortier's journal of fantasized romance, but we had no way to prove it.

Truth, The Daughter of Time, was still a missing person.

Our best efforts had not been good enough. Our reputations were ruined, and we were suspended from our jobs prior to being dismissed. Our actions in exposing Drisko would bring his company's failure, and that failure would bankrupt the college. We'd be remembered as the pair who cost the entire faculty their jobs.

I could have wished I were going to jail instead of Brill.

CHAPTER 42

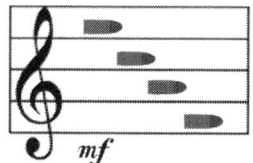

At the police station, officers separated Mara and me for paraffin tests, further questioning, and written statements. Through it all, my despair sank lower and lower.

With the official stuff done, Sergeant Spencer called his long-suffering wife, and Dogface brought us in for a final conference.

"You two don't look like people who just solved a murder," he said. "You look more like you're headed for the guillotine."

"We might as well be," I said. "We know the rumors about us are false, and we know why, but we can't prove it. Without proof, we've lost our jobs. Can we go now?"

Dogface scowled. "Not yet. Someone wants to talk to you."

He punched a few buttons on the phone console on his desk. Presently he said into the phone, "They're here," and pressed the speaker button on the console.

"Press and Mara?" It was the horned-toad voice of Freda Broyles. "Between you and the police, I haven't had a peaceful moment."

"I'm glad you're all right," Mara said. "We were afraid something had happened to you."

"It did," said the horned toad. "You and the police kept wanting me to break promises I'd made to Mitra. Detective Hahn was worst of all."

"He's truly terrible," Mara said. She smiled at Dogface, who blushed.

"He caught me taking those dresses out of Mitra's house," Freda continued. "Mitra had made me promise to take her journals if anything ever happened to her. But I couldn't find the journals, so taking her pretend dresses was the next best thing."

"She had the journals well hidden," Dogface said.

"He kept working me over with appeals to my conscience," Freda said. "And you two hit me in the same place. I finally had to choose between keeping my promise to the dead and preventing further harm to the living. Your suspensions decided me. So I tracked down Joe Cochran and gave him the same treatment you and Detective Hahn had given me."

I'd hate to have Freda give me the treatment. I could almost feel sorry for Joe Cochran.

"Joe argued for a while," Freda said, "but in the end he gave me the three journals he'd mouse-holed all these years."

Relief flooded through me. "That's great," I said. "Can we use them at our hearing?"

The horned toad laughed. "You can have the one I kept. President Cantwell has the other two. I ambushed him in the hospital and made him read the journals. He's much better, by the way. Before I left, he phoned Mrs. Dunwiddie, lifted your suspensions, and dictated a letter to faculty saying the stories about you two and Mitra were false."

"What about Dean-Dean?" I asked.

Freda chuckled. "He was out of pocket, but Mrs. Dunwiddie will give him the word. That'll add a little joy to her life for once."

"Thank you, Freda," I said. "You're a true jewel." An image flashed into my mind—the Renaissance emblem of a toad with a jewel embedded in its forehead. But I thought it best not to bring that into the discussion.

Mara also joined in thanking Freda.

Freda gave an embarrassed harrumph and said, "Well, that's over, and I've got work to do. Oh! President Cantwell said he had one other issue to take up with you, Press."

With that glad thought, she hung up.

Dogface handed Mara her keys. "You're free to go. I'm sorry about your house, Press. Let me know if I can help."

This was the man I'd feared was collaborating with organized crime. "Thanks," I said, "not just for the good wish but for everything."

We stood there a moment with neither of us knowing what to say next.

Mara broke the spell. "Come on, Cupcake, there's an all-night discount store where we can buy your essentials, and then we have to find you a place to stay. We can talk about your house tomorrow."

She led the way to her car, which the police had parked in a no-parking zone in front of the station.

"There's something I'd like to talk about tonight," I said as we drove away. "I'd like to know how my recorder got turned on. It was in my coat pocket inside my overcoat."

She gave me a reprise of that secret smile. "Gremlins," she said.

We drove on in silence. I should have felt relief that the last threat to my job and my freedom had been lifted, but my spirit took another plunge. My home of twenty years, the scene of my dearest memories, had been destroyed. I dreaded the administrative entanglements and all the heartaches that would bring me in the days to come. But at present, something worried me more.

What was the "one more issue" that President Cantwell wanted to take up with me?

CHAPTER 43

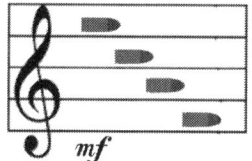

That night—two weeks ago now—we did visit the discount store and bought hat, gloves, and personal items. I spent the night in a motel, and Mara picked me up the next morning with news of a vacant apartment in the complex where she lived. I said that would start more rumors, but she waved the thought away.

"I've quit worrying about the Blatant Beast," she said. So much for Spenser's claim that the bite is incurable.

So I have a place to stay while I work through the aftermath of the fire. At the local Goodwill I found a replacement for the blue suit that was lost in the fire, and I bought another brown marker to keep my brown suit presentable. Emory Estes made me a reasonable deal on a replacement car that Manny Clampett says should last until Cindy is graduated and launched on a career.

Station KLYE trumpeted the news of Brill's arrest for the two murders. Appearing again out of her mushroom cloud with a bell ring, Francie LaBouche reported the impending failure of Drisko's company as a local tragedy while implying that Mara and I were responsible. Hidden in a subordinate clause came the news that we had been cleared of the false rumors against us. In a tone of regret, she reported the police department's investigation of Clyde Staggart.

Staggart is still missing. I presume Guido Stefano either got him out of the country or out of existence. Brill's recorded statement of intended flight got her held without bail.

In related matters, Dogface ... uh ... Detective Duggan Hahn ... is now acting Captain of Homicide. Sergeant Ron Spencer, having made amends to his long-suffering spouse, has been reassigned to Homicide.

In my appointment with Gordon Samstag, I expected a tongue-lashing for bankrupting the college. Mara insisted on going with me to share the reprimand. However, Samstag greeted us with regrets for loss of my house and congratulations on our winning out over impossible conditions.

"You found out about Dustin Industries without my help," he said, "so now you won't have to ask."

"I suppose I still should ask about your connections to Dustin," I said.

"None, past or present." Samstag tented his fingers. "Except that Jerry Vaughan asked about Dustin just before he crashed. His curiosity piqued mine. I traced Dustin's ownership to the Caymans. That warned me off."

His gaze moved from me to Mara and back to me. "So I stopped investigating and began selling the college's shares in Drisko's company as quickly as I could without alarming anyone. Further investigation might have produced 'inside information,' which would not have been legitimate."

"So that's why you told me to stop investigating," I said.

He smiled. "Exactly. I needed time to sell the last of the college shares."

"But I kept asking questions," I said. "How badly have I hurt the college?"

"Not at all." Samstag's smile spread into a grin. "I knew you weren't going to stop. So I dumped the rest of the college's stock the next day. That gave a cushion of several more days before the fur hit the fan. I don't expect any repercussions."

"Then the college isn't going bankrupt?" Mara asked. "We aren't all losing our jobs?"

"Hardly." Samstag stood, signaling the end of our interview. "The sales have established an enviable position of liquidity."

"How about your companies and that rocket failure?" I asked.

"The investigation blamed that on Drisko's quality control. From now on, we'll be more careful about our subcontracts."

Outside, Mara and I exchanged glances of relief.

Cindy brought Mark Weston home for the Valentine's Day holiday. He bunked in my apartment, and Cindy stayed with Mara. Mark is a solid young man, and Cindy could do a lot worse.

President Cantwell sent for me after his discharge from the hospital. He'd gone in on emergency, and a harried young ER doctor prescribed Augmentin for his pneumonia. But an older nurse noted that Cantwell had suffered a violent reaction to penicillin, and she knew that Augmentin contained a kindred drug, amoxicillin. She interceded, and the doctor gave him levaquin instead.

"Amoxicillin might have done me in," Cantwell said, "but that nurse knew her chemistry. We're going to tighten up the chemistry part of the nursing curriculum."

"By the way," he said as I departed, "I've told the architect to put a cross on the top of the fine arts building. We're going to proclaim our Christian heritage to the entire valley."

That was as close as he came to saying I'd been right several years ago about keeping chemistry in the curriculum and putting a cross on the fine arts building. Much to Dean-Dean's regret, the president plans to travel less and take a hands-on approach to campus affairs.

Dean-Dean's prestige has suffered since people learned about his students' response to answering the roll with how they felt. On a particular day, every student in every class answered, "I feel fed up with being asked how I feel." After the third day, Dean-Dean stopped calling the roll. I'm reasonably sure Arthur Medford's organizing skills were involved.

In other campus events, Freda Broyles' attitude has returned to normal—a cross between a horned toad and a porcupine. Malcolm Combes avoids me, apparently afraid I'll tell his secret of finding

Mitra's body. I won't, and I value his efforts to maintain academic standards.

Dathan Hormah is negotiating for a position with the inclusive seminary that gave Mara a full scholarship as a Wiccan. He'll be compatible there, though his Meribah Valley church will need a new pastor.

Our faculty colleagues treat Mara and me like nuclear weapons about to initiate Armageddon. The Blatant Beast still lives, though lately he seems to be on a leash.

Cynthia Starlington has not spoken to me since the fire. She's keeping company with a husky young math professor, who has begun wearing a colorful and expensive shirt. I hope it does not become a hair shirt.

In the campus grill, the female composition specialist told me that Hawthorne's Hester Prynne could not have been a cheerleader for the University of Alabama because the novel was published in 1850, and Alabama only began intercollegiate athletics in 1893. For such researches we spend years in graduate study.

The Cloverdale newspaper continues a controversy as to whether a local waitress actually served a man from Mars. The waitress holds her ground, though various letters to the editor argue she was mistaken. Mara reads these, looks at me, and shakes her head.

She and I have talked seriously about fantasy and the Imagination. We agree that for practical purposes the Renaissance version of Imagination vs. Reason is workable. As individuals, we humans never get anything entirely right, and thus we all live to some degree in fantasy worlds. Mitra's case was extreme, as was Steven Drisko's belief in his invincibility. But Mara now classifies the idea that she can do everything on her own as a fantasy, and I've concluded that I must have a broader purpose in life than just teaching history. We don't yet know where those conclusions will lead.

I have believed for some time that God uses events like the Synod of Whitby and the Peace of Wedmore to guide the great tides of history. But Mara's and my recent trials make me believe

He concerns Himself with waves as well as tides. Our own best efforts were not good enough to solve the complete complex of our problems. It took independent movings of conscience by Freda Broyles, Duggan Hahn, and Ron Spencer to develop the complete picture. It would be difficult to believe the Lord had no hand in those movings.

In our case, Truth did prove to be The Daughter of Time. But how generally does that principle apply? I keep remembering those documents of the McCarthy anticommunist hearings that are missing from the National Archives. How can Truth emerge if its basic documents are missing? But perhaps Time is not ready to give birth, or perhaps it is not yet God's time …

Limited by human understanding, we will never accurately perceive God's work in the world. But we see enough of it so that informed faith can assure us of the rest. "The Lord giveth and the Lord taketh away," and sometimes He taketh a way that we'd rather not travel. Mara thinks He is leading us both into a broader function in life. I'm inclined to agree.

I grieve the loss of my home. Yet that loss has freed me for a wider experience of life. I don't know what that will be, except that recently my internal orchestra shuts down for extended periods.

Mara and I continue to explore our growing friendship with increasing confidence. In church with her, influenced by the deep harmonies of hymns, I again feel a completeness I haven't known for years. She seems to share that feeling, and the woman who abhorred being touched now rests her shoulder against mine as we share the hymn book.

I have not asked her, though, why she needed to record my first words of love to her. I'm glad she did, of course, because that recorded Brill's confession. And I have not asked how Mara got through my buttoned-up overcoat to my suit-coat pocket to switch my recorder on without my knowing. That had best remain her secret.

Last fall I didn't know what I was going to do about Mara Thorn, but that is no longer the case.

I know exactly what I want to do if she will accept my proposal.

Made in the USA
San Bernardino, CA
29 October 2017